D0563922

Days of Grace

Days of Grace

Catherine Hall

VIKING

VIKING
Published by the Penguin Group
Penguin Group (USA) Inc., 375 Hudson Street,
New York, New York 10014, U.S.A.
Penguin Group (Canada), 90 Eglinton Avenue East, Suite 700,
Toronto, Ontario, Canada M4P 2Y3
(a division of Pearson Penguin Canada Inc.)
Penguin Books Ltd, 80 Strand, London WC2R 0RL, England
Penguin Ireland, 25 St. Stephen's Green, Dublin 2, Ireland
(a division of Penguin Books Ltd)
Penguin Books Australia Ltd, 250 Camberwell Road, Camberwell,
Victoria 3124, Australia
(a division of Pearson Australia Group Pty Ltd)
Penguin Books India Pvt Ltd, 11 Community Centre, Panchsheel Park,
New Delhi – 110 017, India
Penguin Group (NZ), 67 Apollo Drive, Rosedale, North Shore 0632,
New Zealand (a division of Pearson New Zealand Ltd)
Penguin Books (South Africa) (Pty) Ltd, 24 Sturdee Avenue,
Rosebank, Johannesburg 2196, South Africa

Penguin Books Ltd, Registered Offices:
80 Strand, London WC2R 0RL, England

First American edition
Published in 2010 by Viking Penguin,
a member of Penguin Group (USA) Inc.

1   2   3   4   5   6   7   8   9   10

Copyright © Catherine Hall, 2009

All rights reserved

Excerpt from "I've Got You Under My Skin" by Cole Porter. © 1936 (renewed) Chappell & Co., Inc. (ASCAP). All
rights reserved.

Publisher's Note
This is a work of fiction. Names, characters, places, and incidents either are the product of the author's imagination or
are used fictitiously, and any resemblance to actual persons, living or dead, business establishments, events, or locales
is entirely coincidental.

LIBRARY OF CONGRESS CATALOGING IN PUBLICATION DATA

Hall, Catherine, 1973–
Days of Grace : a novel / Catherine Hall.
p. cm.
ISBN 978-0-670-02176-5
1. World War, 1939–1945–Children–England–Fiction. 2. Teenage girls–Fiction. 3. Friendship in children–Fiction. 4.
Female friendship–Fiction. 5. Atonement–Fiction. 6. Kent (England)–Fiction. 7. Psychological fiction. I. Title.

PR6108.A46D39 2010
823'.92–dc22
2009050254

Printed in the United States of America

Without limiting the rights under copyright reserved above, no part of this publication may be reproduced, stored in or
introduced into a retrieval system, or transmitted, in any form or by any means (electronic, mechanical, photocopying,
recording or otherwise), without the prior written permission of both the copyright owner and the above publisher of
this book.

The scanning, uploading, and distribution of this book via the Internet or via any other means without the permission of
the publisher is illegal and punishable by law. Please purchase only authorized electronic editions and do not participate
in or encourage electronic piracy of copyrightable materials. Your support of the author's rights is appreciated.

For Anne-Marie

He who desires but acts not, breeds pestilence.

William Blake, *Proverbs of Hell*

It was August when I finally crossed the street. I slipped off a shoe and pressed my foot into the warmth of the doorstep, finding a space amongst the plastic bags and paper scraps that littered it. I sniffed at the air, swallowing the taste of roasted meat and smoke. At the end of the long weekend, the street was empty. Beer cans lay abandoned in the gutter and sacks of rubbish spilled out the remains of picnics. Birds hunched on branches, tucking their beaks into their chests. There was no-one to see me. I was safe. I untied my headscarf and wrapped it around my hand, then picked up a brick from the pile of rubble by the step. The dirty glass smashed easily. I reached through and lifted the latch.

The hallway was as I'd expected, smelling of old tobacco and gas. A stack of telephone directories filled a corner and a table was piled high with unclaimed post. The pattern on the linoleum was hidden under layers of dirt and the walls bore the marks of many tenants. Once-white paint, now a greasy yellow, flaked off the banisters. I knew without reaching for the switch that the bulb which dangled from the ceiling would give off no more than a dim glow. I walked across the hallway to the second door, as scratched and battered as everything else. It gave way to my push. The body was hunched on the bed, under a grubby sheet.

One

THE SICKNESS HAD STARTED IN MAY. IT CAME STEALTHILY at first, creeping up on me. Strange aches occurred, odd pains. At first I ignored them, convinced they were nothing, but as they grew stronger, I worried. Each night I fell asleep hoping that the dragging in my stomach would be gone when I woke. Soon it was the first thing I noticed each day.

It made me tired. I spent most of the time in my chair, wrapped in a blanket, staring out at the street. The window had nine panes of old, thick glass and I looked through it one pane at a time like a painter dividing up a landscape with his fingers, watching the comings and goings of Victory Road. The street had changed over the past few years and some of the houses had been smartened up. Window boxes appeared on ledges, red geraniums flowered and the stumps of railings grew back into tall spikes. Garden gates were hung and oiled, swinging open smoothly when the postman pushed them.

The house opposite mine was still shabby, a poor relation to the others in the row, blackened with dirt and stripped of everything that could be sold. Each window held just one piece of glass, giving the house a blank, indifferent appearance, and the flimsy front door had no knocker. The railings remained amputated and the garden had been smothered by concrete. Weeds straggled through the cracks. Tenants came and went, none staying longer than a few months.

It was June when I first noticed the girl. One morning, she was sitting at the downstairs window looking back at me. I ducked away, pretending to watch a group of children who were circling on bicycles like predatory animals. When I dared to look again, she hadn't moved.

I puzzled over what she was doing there. She was young, no more than eighteen, I thought, perhaps not even that. Girls her age had other things to do. I often saw them, prowling the streets in packs, strutting and swaggering like boys. I avoided them, afraid of attracting their attention. But this girl was different. She sat motionless, as if she were waiting for something, her thin shoulders poking out of a tight black vest. Despite her physical fragility, she had an air of determination about her. Her shoulders were squared and her face set, her little chin held high.

I was intrigued, and watched her for the rest of the day. She showed no sign of having noticed me but went on staring out of the window, straight ahead. At last, at dusk, she stood up. Her silhouette was a shock. A high, round belly stuck out from her body. It was jarring to see, grafted onto someone who was still a child herself. She yawned and stretched, then turned to draw the curtains, shutting me firmly out.

I watched the girl the next day, and the next day after that. All

4

through the summer I watched her at the window, staring into space as her belly grew, making the vest rise further and further up her torso. As the days passed, something odd began to happen. My stomach started to expand, as if in sympathy with hers. My skin stretched over a small potbelly, smooth and tight, as if I were young again. The rest of my body was shrinking. Skin hung loosely from my arms and thighs. It was as if I had a baby of my own trapped within, a malevolent little thing, a child who would never be born, staying inside until it had consumed all of me.

*

I didn't want any interference from doctors. I didn't want to draw things out any further than required. But as the summer wore on, I worried that I was losing my mind. I mislaid things. A stain developed on the bathroom floor from water that slopped over the sides of the tub when I forgot to turn off the taps. I found myself standing bewildered in rooms, unsure of how I had got there. I did not mind my physical disintegration but losing my capacity to think was something different altogether. One day in August I decided I couldn't put it off any longer. The time had come to seek medical attention.

I was on edge from the moment I left the house, knowing that I'd have to pass the prison. I hurried past it quickly, my head down, to the surgery. It was a cuckoo of a building, squeezed between two houses, squat and square and practical, with a blue sign outside listing the names of the doctors.

The doors slid open as if my arrival had been predicted. As I entered the smell of disinfectant caught in my throat, making me cough. I leaned against a pillar to catch my breath and looked about. It was a dismal place. Faded posters telling those who looked at them to change their ways were stuck haphazardly on walls that were blistered with peeling paint. A patch of damp crept down from the ceiling to the window as if it were trying to escape. Patients slumped on chairs around a table covered with magazines that were missing their covers. The only sound came from a small boy playing with a toy truck that had no wheels.

I went up to a counter with a sign on it that said *Reception*.

Like a hotel, I thought, and for a moment felt more hopeful, until I caught sight of the woman behind the desk, who was bending over some papers and muttering. I stood very still, waiting for her to notice me, looking at a vase of drooping carnations. The water was flecked with green scum.

Eventually she raised her head. 'Yes?' she said sharply.

'I think I should see a doctor,' I said.

'What's your name?'

I told her and she peered at a machine, stabbing at it with long, crimson fingernails.

'I can't find you. What time's your appointment?' Her voice was accusing.

Not like a hotel at all, I thought, sadly. I looked down at my feet, shifting my weight from one to the other.

'I haven't got one.'

She sighed, as if I had confirmed her suspicions. 'Then you can't see a doctor. You'll have to make one now and then come back. Who do you usually see?'

'I haven't been here before,' I admitted. 'This is my first visit.'

'You need to see your own doctor,' she said. 'You can't go to just any surgery. Where are you registered?'

Everything was a question. I was being cross-examined before I'd even entered the doctor's consulting room. I felt my heart begin to beat faster, speeding up to match the pace of her interrogation.

'Nowhere,' I muttered.

'What? I can't hear you.'

'I haven't got a doctor. I'm not registered anywhere.'

She looked at me sceptically. I forced a smile, trying to arrange my features into something that might suit her.

'All right,' she said, at last. 'We might be able to fit you in. You'll need to bring proof of address and identity. That means a utilities bill or a bank statement and a passport or a driving licence. And we'll need the name and address of your previous doctor so that we can get your notes and check your medical history.'

I didn't want her or anyone else to check my history, medical or otherwise. I didn't want them to know where I lived. I didn't want them to write things down about me for just anyone to see. I remembered the drill.

Be Careful What You Say. Like Everyone Else, You Will Hear Things That the Enemy Mustn't Know. Keep That Knowledge to Yourself – and Don't Give Away Any Clues. Keep Smiling.

'Thank you,' I said. 'I'll come back when I can prove who I am.'

She had gone back to her papers before the words had left my mouth.

*

The Holloway Road was choked with traffic fleeing the city. I stumbled the opposite way, my head spinning. The trip to the doctor's had unnerved me. There was someone I wanted to see. I made my way past the Indian restaurants and the off-licences, flat-fronted pubs and bookmakers, the flooring shops with giant rolls of carpet stacked on the pavement. I avoided the enormous hall of the Seventh Day Adventists, offering salvation for sinners. My own salvation was up the little side street. I walked along it, wondering why I'd left it so long to go back.

The minute I pushed open the door and heard the jangle of the bell, I felt better. I stood for a moment, drinking in the shop's familiar smell, soothed by its particular, contented silence.

'Can I help you?'

It wasn't the voice I'd been expecting. I turned to see a young woman sitting behind the desk. She was smiling brightly, waiting for me to answer. I tried to hide my surprise.

'Isn't Stephen here?'

'Not today. He takes Wednesdays off.'

'Oh,' I said.

'Had you arranged to see him? I can call him if you like.'

I kept my voice even. 'It doesn't matter. I was just passing by, that's all. I'll have a look around while I'm here.'

She nodded. 'If you need any help, just ask.'

I went into the next room and stood in front of one of the shelves. I ran my hands over soft leather bindings, feeling the raised lettering with my fingertips like Braille. Fat novels stood next to slim volumes of poetry, rubbing shoulders with dictionaries and encyclopaedia sets, atlases and cookery books, their covers spotted and stained. I scanned their titles, looking for ones that I recognized. I couldn't afford to take a gamble. I wanted a proper story, with characters to care about and hope for, something to take me away from myself.

I was out of sorts after my trip to the surgery. I wanted to talk to Stephen. My disappointment made me realize how lonely I'd become. I took down old favourites and flicked through them, reading pages at random, but none of them was what I wanted. It was a while before I saw it, a slim book with a faded dust jacket, not the sort of thing that I was looking for at all, not a novel, strictly non-fiction, a textbook or a manual. My hands shook as I pulled it off the shelf. I turned to the list of chapters, looking for answers. This was the one, I decided. It would tell me all I needed to know. There would be no doctors, no examinations, no evidence for anyone to find. My disease would stay a secret, my own last secret.

I took the book to the girl and counted out coins.

'Would you like to leave Stephen a message?' she said. 'Shall I tell him you were here?'

'No,' I said. 'Don't worry. It wasn't important.'

*

I made coffee, strong and hot, carried it to the sitting room and put it on the table next to my chair. I wrapped the blanket around myself and settled a cushion behind my head. I found the chapter and started to read.

WHAT ARE THE SYMPTOMS? said the first line, in capital letters.

Loss of appetite, vague indigestion, nausea, swelling in the abdomen, abnormal bleeding.

None of that was news but the next question was intriguing.

WHAT DOES IT MEAN FOR YOU?

The answer was surprisingly simple.

Your body is made up of cells and they repair and reproduce by dividing themselves. But sometimes the cells are abnormal and get out of control. They carry on splitting and they cluster together into a lump, which invades and destroys the tissue around it. If left untreated it will spread to other parts of your body and do the same again.

There it was, written down in black and white, confirmation of how my life would end. It was almost a relief to have it spelled out. I read on.

By the time it is detected, it may have been growing for many years.

This was no surprise. I knew exactly when I had started to go bad.

However, treatment is available. Many patients fight the disease and win.

I didn't want to fight it. I'd lived long enough. I closed my eyes. 'I'm coming,' I whispered. 'I'm coming to join you, my love.'

Two

If I had been given the choice, I would have taken my chances and stayed. I didn't want to go. I didn't want to leave her and I said so. But it made no difference. I was going; Ma said I must. We sat at the table eating bread and dripping. I liked bread and dripping but I wasn't hungry. I stared at the floor as she said it again.

'Nora love, there's going to be a war. I want you to be safe. It won't be forever. When it's all over you'll come back and it'll be as if you were never away.'

Two woodlice were hurrying towards one of the table legs. I fixed my eyes on them instead of Ma.

'It'll do you good to live in the country. You'll have lots of fresh air and space.'

The woodlice had almost got to the table, little grey shapes running one after the other. I didn't care about fresh air and space. I wanted us to stick together, like them.

'I don't want to go,' I said. I pushed my plate away and looked up at her. Ma's face was my favourite thing to look at in the world, the first and last thing I saw each day, but she wasn't pretty now. She had two dark patches under her eyes like smudges of coal dust and she was frowning. It was early still, but the room was made dim by the paper we had stuck up over the windows the week before. I had cut it into squares with the scissors that Ma used for bacon, leaving smears of grease along the edges. If I went she would be left in the dark. The thought of her sitting alone at the table every night made my stomach twist and churn.

'Please don't make me go,' I said. 'You won't have anyone left.'

'You can't stay here,' she said. 'You mustn't worry. I'll be all right.'

'I won't go.'

'You're going, and that's that. God's already taken your father from me. I'm not about to lose you too.'

The anger in her voice made me angry too and I stamped on the woodlice, crushing them under my shoe. If I was to be sent away from her, I thought, why should they be allowed to stay? But as soon as I had done it I was sorry.

'What if the bombs come, Ma, like they say they will? What if one of them hits our house? You'll be killed.' I pictured myself standing by a coffin and my eyes began to prickle with tears.

'I'm not going to die,' she said. 'Come here.'

I ran to her and she held me, stroking my hair like she had when I was a little girl. We stayed together like that until the room was dark, then we prayed to the Virgin, kneeling side by side at the foot of our bed.

'Look after Nora,' Ma said, in a small, cracked voice. 'Keep her safe for me. Help her to be good.'

She held me all through the night and in the morning the back of my nightdress was damp from her tears.

The next day was the first of September. It should have been my first day at my new school. I woke feeling sick. I lay in bed, listening to the whistle of the kettle, waiting for Ma to come and tell me that it had all been a bad dream, that there was no war and that I could stay. But when she came it was to tell me to hurry.

I put my hands on my stomach. 'I've got a pain, Ma. It hurts, here.'

She patted my shoulder. 'Nora love, you've got to go. Get dressed now. I've made tea.'

I knew she didn't believe in my stomach ache. Slowly, I put on the uniform that she had sat up late so many nights to stitch and went downstairs to the kitchen. As we walked through the streets to the schoolyard, I was angry and afraid. When Ma held out her hand, I shook my head. I wanted to stamp my foot and tell her that my stomach really did hurt. But I knew it wouldn't make any difference. I had never seen Ma so determined, so I said nothing.

When we got there it was crowded but strangely quiet. Some of the little ones were crying, clinging to their mothers, and a few of the bigger boys ran about, pretending to shoot at each other like soldiers. But most of us were silent and still, waiting to see what was going to happen. I knew that nothing I said or did would change anything. I couldn't stop the war. I couldn't even make Ma change her mind about sending me away. I didn't know where I was going, where I would sleep that night or where I would wake up in the morning. All I knew was that Ma wouldn't be there with me. I swallowed hard, trying to force back the panic that was rising in my throat. When a whistle screeched and a teacher clapped her hands to make us listen, I thought I was going to be sick. A hush fell over the schoolyard.

'Say goodbye to your mothers and line up in pairs,' the teacher shouted. 'Quickly, now. We've no time to lose.'

Suddenly everything was movement and noise.

I tried one last time. 'I want to stay here and be killed with you.'

Ma shook her head sadly. 'Don't say things like that. It's not right.'

She pressed something into my hand. It was the little picture of the Virgin and Child that hung from a hook on the wall next to our bed. I saw it every night before I went to sleep. I liked how they were together, the two of them, just like me and Ma.

She put her arms around me and held me tight, pressing her cheek against mine.

'Remember, Nora, I'll always be with you,' she said quietly. 'We'll always be together.'

I closed my eyes and breathed in her smell, carbolic soap and sweat, filling my nose with it to take with me to wherever I'd end up. The next thing I knew, she was gone and I was holding the hand of a boy who was smaller than me, aged five or maybe six. Two lines of snot trickled towards his mouth, making me feel even sicker. I couldn't bear to look at him. I stared instead at the label that hung from a piece of string around my neck.

Nora Lynch, it said, in tidy teachers' handwriting. *Aged 12 years.*

It reminded me of the words on Pa's gravestone. *James Lynch. Died 1929, aged 25 years.* It made leaving Ma even worse and I hated her for making me go. I wouldn't turn my head to look at her as we marched out of the schoolyard in a crocodile. We shuffled like prisoners, our heads down, staring at the ground, and even the birds were quiet as we went.

*

As the train jerked out of the station, the boy sitting next to me began to whimper. One of the older girls tried to put her arm around his shoulders but he pushed her away.

'You're not my mother,' he shouted. 'Get off me.'

Hearing him say *mother* did for us and soon we were all in tears. I pressed myself into the corner and stared through the dirty window, wishing that I was back at home, curled up in bed with Ma. It was the first time she hadn't been around to put things right. I looked down at the palm of my right hand, marked with a silvery scar from when I had lifted the kettle off the fire without a cloth. Ma had picked me up and carried me to the back yard, where she held my hand in hers under the tap until our fingers were red with cold. I touched the patch in my eyebrow where no hair had grown since the day I had tripped on the doorstep and hit my head. That time Ma had taken me to the doctor. I remembered his sour breath as he leaned close to examine me.

'She'll live,' he had said. 'She'll live.'

If anything happened to me now she wouldn't be around to make it better. I would have new scars that she wouldn't know anything about. I pressed my face against the window like she had pressed her cheek against mine in the schoolyard, trying to pretend that she was with me.

One by one, the others fell asleep. My eyes were heavy but I was determined to stay awake. I wanted to know where I was going. As the train pulled further away from London and from Ma, I leaned back in the leather seat and stared out of the window at fields that stretched on endlessly, further than I could see, a hundred shades of green. The train passed through empty stations, each like the one before it; a platform with a bench, a white fence and flowers planted in tubs, all so different to the crowds and soot at Waterloo that it was hard to believe we were in the same country.

After a while I felt the pain in my stomach, worse than before, stabbing at my insides. The potted meat in the sandwich that Ma had given me was beginning to smell, making me gulp. I got to my feet, suddenly wanting to be alone and out of sight. I remembered that when we had boarded the train there had been a rush for the lavatory. I would hide myself away in there.

I picked my way past the sleeping bodies and over gas masks and suitcases, then crept along the corridor, holding my stomach as I went, swallowing back the sour taste of sick. Eventually, I arrived at a small door marked W.C. When I opened it, the smell made my stomach heave and I stood at the threshold, trying to decide if I could bear to go in. I made up my mind when a group of boys came charging along the corridor. Pinching my nose with my fingers, I slipped inside, locked the door, pulled down my old school knickers and sat on the lavatory. I slumped on the seat, trying to lift up my feet away from the sticky floor and keep my balance as the train rocked from side to side.

I was trapped in the lavatory with nowhere else to go. Leaving Ma had been the end of everything good. Since then, every minute had brought something new and worse, as if it were a test of how much I could stand. But the next thing to happen was the worst of all. The train lurched suddenly and I threw out my hands to steady myself against the walls, losing hold of my knickers, which fell to my knees. I glanced down at them and what I saw made me blink in horror. There was a mark on them, a strange smear against the grey cotton. It looked like rust, or blood.

I turned hot and then cold. My heart was beating so hard I felt as if I would choke on it. When I dared to look again, my thighs were trembling. It was still there, a brownish smudge, evidence of something that I knew at once was very bad. Slowly, I brought my hand down from the wall and touched my thigh. I rested it there, frightened of moving it further, then, as if they belonged to someone else, I watched my fingers creep between my legs and then I felt them touch that part of myself that I had never seen, never mentioned and touched only when I was washing, as quickly as I could.

I brought my hand back up to my face and touched my fingers to my nose. An odd smell, of iron and darkness, filled my nostrils. It was like an animal, or meat that had been left out somewhere warm. I lowered my hand and made myself look at it. My fingertips had blood on them, not red like the sort that spilled from a scraped knee or a cut finger, but a dark, dirty brown, something shameful. I was bleeding between my legs.

I shivered with fear as I realized what it meant. God was punishing me. I had hated Ma for sending me away. I had stamped on the woodlice, refused to hold her hand on the way to the schoolyard and not looked back when I left.

'Honour your mother and father,' the Sunday School teacher always said. It was one of the Ten Commandments. I didn't have a father but I had Ma. I hadn't honoured her. I had despised her instead. I had said I would rather die than leave her behind, but now that I was gone it was happening all the same.

The only hope I had, I decided, was to pray. I would confess my sins and ask for forgiveness like I did in the little booth each week before Mass. Perhaps God would listen to me then. I closed my eyes.

'Bless me, Father, for I have sinned.'

I told him all of it, from the woodlice onwards, leaving nothing out, and just as I came to the end of it, the train stopped moving. For a moment, everything was peaceful and still. I opened my eyes and looked down at my knickers, hoping for a miracle, but it was no good. The blood was still there. My confession hadn't changed anything. I began to cry, hot tears that dropped onto my thighs as if they were trying to wash them clean.

A knock came at the door, and then a woman's voice.

'Is anyone in there? Open up, please. We've arrived. Everybody must get off the train. Come along.'

I had no more choice about it than I'd had about anything else that day. I pulled my knickers up and wiped my fingers on my skirt, stepped out of the stinking lavatory and went back to the compartment. It was empty apart from my gasmask and the pillowcase that held my things. I picked them up, made my way along the corridor to the end of the carriage and climbed down the steps to the platform.

*

We were taken to a place that smelled of animals, and was divided by wooden fences into pens. I sat on the ground in the dust, feeling numb, watching the teachers try to calm the little ones. Women dressed in hats and suits like the ladies that Ma cleaned for were giving out glasses of lemonade and cups of tea. I had never seen a lady make a cup of tea. It was as if everything I knew to be true had changed in the time that it had taken to leave London. I drew my knees up to my chest and rested my head on them, closing my eyes and wishing that Ma was there to tell me what to do. I stayed like that for a while, shutting everything out, drifting in and out of sleep, until I heard a girl's voice, high-pitched and clear.

'Mummy, look! Look at that girl, there, in the corner. Don't you think she looks like me?'

All I wanted was to keep my eyes closed and pretend I was back with Ma, but the voice went on calling.

'Please, Mummy. Can't we have her? We could be friends, I know we could. Please.'

I tried to melt into the fencepost that I was leaning against, to make myself invisible, but her voice grew closer and louder until at last I could feel her standing in front of me and I had no choice but to open my eyes.

I didn't think I looked like her at all. She was a girl out of a picture book. Her eyes were blue and her cheeks pink, as if someone had coloured them in with a pencil, and her pale hair hung to her shoulders. She wore a flowered dress and brown leather sandals that had just been polished. Mine were still damp from the lavatory. I tried to tuck them underneath me.

'Hello,' she said. She was smiling. Her teeth were very white.

I stared at the ground, feeling dirty and shy.

'My name's Grace. What's yours?'

'Nora,' I said.

'Nora.' It sounded different when she said it, as if it could even be pretty. 'Nora what?'

'Nora Lynch,' I said, still looking at the ground.

'How old are you?'

I wasn't used to questions. 'Twelve.'

'When will you be thirteen?'

'In a month. October the fifth.'

The girl let out a little shriek. 'My birthday's October the tenth. We're almost exactly the same age. Please come to stay. You must! Please say you will.'

I raised my head and we looked at each other. She smiled at me again, a wide smile as if she thought me coming to stay was something thrilling. I couldn't help but smile back.

The lady who was standing next to her spoke, her voice soft and low. 'Hello Nora,' she said. 'I'm Mrs Rivers, Grace's mother.'

Everything about her was nice to look at. She wore a pale blue coat like the Virgin Mary in the picture that Ma had given me and her eyes were kind.

'Would you like to come and stay with us for a while?' Mrs Rivers asked. 'We're to take in an evacuee.'

Grace grinned at me again. 'Of course she will!' she said. She picked up my pillowcase in one hand and my gasmask in the other and there it was, decided, just like that.

*

I don't know how long the journey took, that first day at the very start of it all. I had never been in a motor car and I sat in shock, intoxicated by the smell of the leather seats and Mrs Rivers' perfume. I stared out of the window as we glided through the countryside, which they said was called Kent. It stretched out all around us, more different to London than I could ever have imagined. The city was straight lines, corners and edges. Each street had a name, a beginning and an end. The countryside was different. Grasses and flowers spilled over fences and ditches and grew up along the middle of the road, jostling for space, all mixed up together, making it impossible to know where anything started or stopped. The roads twisted and curved through tunnels made by trees, a dark world in which everything was cool and green.

Even the village seemed to have grown up out of the earth. Houses built of reddish brick nestled low, their roofs close to the ground as if they were reaching to touch it. Each one stood apart from its neighbour in a garden that stretched between the front door and the road, filled with flowers, more colours than I had ever seen together. In the middle of the village was a patch of grass with a stream running through it and a pond with ducks. Beyond the water, stretching up above the houses, was a church spire. Mrs Rivers turned the steering wheel towards it and we began to bump along a track so narrow that if I had reached out through the window I could have picked flowers from the hedgerows that grew on either side.

I didn't reach out to touch the flowers. I kept my hands clenched in my lap. The church spire had reminded me of my punishment from God. I would go into Mrs Rivers' house bleeding because of my wickedness. My skin began to itch. As we drew closer to the church, I started to sweat. I knew that soon we would come to a stop and I would have to get out of the motor car. My stomach twisted with fear. If the blood had soaked through my skirt it would be there for everyone to see.

Sure enough, when we got to the church, Mrs Rivers stopped the motor car.

'We're here!' said Grace, pointing to a house that stood next to the churchyard.

It wasn't like the other houses in the village. It stood alone behind tall iron gates with no neighbours. Like the church, it was built of stone the colour of winter sun, cool and pale, and separated from the rest of the world by railings. In the churchyard I saw row after row of tombstones, hunks of rock carved into crosses and angels. Each one meant a body, I thought to myself, one dead body in the ground. As I looked at them, wondering what it would be like to be buried forever under the earth, I heard a ghostly noise. I listened hard, trying to make out what it was. Gradually, the noise became louder and clearer and finally I realized that it was people singing, something grave and slow.

Grace giggled. 'It's Evensong,' she said. 'Father takes it every day at six o'clock.'

I was puzzled.

'My husband is the rector of the village,' Mrs Rivers said.

I still didn't know what she meant and my face must have given me away. 'The vicar. The priest, if you like. We live in the rectory, the house next to the church. This is your new home.'

I didn't see how it could be true. Priests didn't marry, I was sure of it. They were beyond temptation and the sins of the flesh. A priest who was married would be no different to any other man. I was confused, not knowing what to believe. I shivered. If Mr Rivers really were a priest, I was in trouble. I would have to make my confession to him. I would have to go into the little booth and tell him about my wickedness towards Ma, about the cruel things I had thought and, worst of all, about the bleeding. I would be disgraced. My head began to spin and suddenly all I could see was darkness.

*

The first thing I noticed when I woke was the softness of the sheets. I was used to rough ones that always felt damp no matter how long we left them to dry on the line. These sheets, as smooth as Ma's cheeks, were tucked in tightly around a narrow bed. I had never slept on my own. I stretched out my arms to the sides of the bed, wedging my hands between the mattress and the sheet and looked about.

I was in a pretty room with striped paper on its walls. Flowered curtains, pink and white, hung at the windows. A fireplace held a stack of kindling ready to light and above it was a mirror in a golden frame. Next to the bed was a little table with an alarm clock. On the other side of the table was another bed with a pink coverlet pulled up over it.

I tried to cast my mind back to what had happened. As I lay there, trying to think, I realized that, rather than being dressed in my old cotton nightdress, I was wearing a pair of striped pyjamas. I didn't own any pyjamas. Somebody had taken me out of my school uniform and put them on me. Whoever it was would have seen me without my clothes. Whoever it was had seen the blood.

It must have been Mrs Rivers, I thought, Mrs Rivers, who had stood at the station in her pale blue coat, Mrs Rivers, whose hands in their soft leather gloves had controlled the motor car with the lightest touch, Mrs Rivers, who smelled of lemons and cleanliness. My cheeks burned and I curled up into a ball, hiding myself under the blankets.

After a while I began to feel as if someone was watching me. I drew back the corner of the blanket and looked out. Perched on someone's knee like a tiny child was a ragdoll. It was dirty and worn and missing one of its eyes. The other eye seemed to be staring at me nastily, as if it knew everything. I shrank back under the bedclothes but after a minute I heard somebody cough. I looked out again to see Mrs Rivers.

'Oh, you're awake!' she said. 'I'm so glad. I was beginning to worry about you.'

I couldn't bring myself to look directly at her.

'Are you feeling better?'

I nodded.

'Do you remember what happened?'

There was no way of escaping her kindness. I shook my head.

'You fainted. One of the churchwardens came out of Evensong to carry you up here. It's Grace's room. We thought it would be nice for you to share.'

I looked about for Grace. Mrs Rivers smiled.

'I told her to leave you in peace for a while. You must be very tired.'

I looked at Mrs Rivers' hands, holding the doll around its middle. They weren't like Ma's, red raw from scrubbing floors. Mrs Rivers' skin was smooth and pale and she wore a shiny ring on her wedding finger. My cheeks grew hot at the thought of her hands touching me.

'Have you ever fainted before?' she said.

'No, Miss,' I said.

'Do you know why it happened?'

I lay still with my eyes closed, hoping that if I kept quiet she might give up and go away, but it didn't work. I felt a hand on my forehead, smoothing back my hair like Ma would have done.

'I didn't mean to do it,' I blurted out. 'I didn't, I swear.'

Mrs Rivers went on stroking. 'When did the bleeding start?' she said.

I kept my eyes closed. 'Today, Miss. On the train. But I didn't meant to be bad to Ma. I just didn't want her to send me away. I didn't mean to be wicked. And now I'm being punished for it.'

Her hand stopped. 'What do you mean?' she said. 'Who's punishing you?'

'God, Miss. He's making me bleed until I'm sorry.'

Mrs Rivers sighed. 'Look at me, Nora,' she said.

She waited until I turned my face to her and then she said, 'Didn't your mother ever tell you about the curse?'

When I was smaller Ma had told stories at night, stories from Ireland about gypsies and their curses on the people who crossed them. But I suspected that Mrs Rivers meant something different.

'No,' I whispered, feeling small.

What Mrs Rivers told me then was terrible and I stared at her in horror as she said it. It was as strange a story as the ones that Ma told me at bedtime but it wasn't a story, she said, it was the truth. It was a curse that would never be lifted, no matter what I did. It happened to all girls. It even happened to Mrs Rivers. It must have happened to Ma, I thought, but she had never said a word about it.

I wondered how many other secrets she had kept, what else she hadn't told me. When Mrs Rivers left me to sleep, turning out the light as she went, I lay awake for a long time thinking about it, feeling hard and cold.

Three

I FELT BETTER ONCE I'D MADE MY DIAGNOSIS. I WOULD meet my fate in due course. In the meantime, I went to the library and took out a book, something more uplifting than the one I'd found in the bookshop, a guide to the beginnings of life rather than to its end. On its cover was a picture of a woman smiling at a baby.

Each morning I made coffee on the stove, filling the bottom half of the pot with water, patting down the coffee grounds and screwing on the top. I drank it in my chair, taking small sips as I read both books, preparing for both eventualities.

I always knew when the girl was at the window. I felt it in my bones. The hairs on the back of my neck would rise and I would lift my head from my book to see her sitting there, straight-backed, her belly getting bigger by the day.

My own small Menace grew too, swelling out my abdomen. As

the summer dragged on, neither of us moved much. Whilst I sipped my coffee, the girl drank what looked like milk from a beer glass, pint after pint of it throughout the day. I wondered where she got it. There was no milk float anymore and I never saw her leave the house to go to the cornershop. No-one came to visit her, no friends, no midwife, no father of the child. She seemed as alone in the world as me.

I was cowardly, never daring to cross the road and knock on the door. There was something about the way she held herself that discouraged it. I knew all about hiding away from the world, but as her belly grew, her solitude worried me more and more. I wondered whose time would come first. As I compared the size of the girl's belly with the pictures in the manual, I thought it would be her. I guessed that the baby would be born by October. I decided to keep a close eye on her, to be ready to help if she needed me.

*

In the end, D-Day came earlier than I'd thought. It was the August bank holiday, humid and hot. Windows opened along the street as the temperature rose and people blinked as they came out of their houses, scrabbling in handbags and pockets for sunglasses. Parents shepherded excited children into cars, piling folding chairs and hampers of food into the back.

I stayed still, watching and waiting. At noon her curtains were still closed and I felt the first pangs of anxiety. I tried to keep calm, telling myself that she was probably resting, as the book had said she should towards the end. But as the afternoon turned into evening, and the street filled up with cars again, dusty from the day's excursions, I began to worry. I had been at the window all day. I would have noticed a taxi or an ambulance. I would have seen her leave. If the girl was giving birth, she was doing it alone. I imagined her, too proud to ask for help from anyone, twisting with pain on the bed and I knew that I had to go to her.

As I crossed the street, my panic grew. I hadn't thought of how to get into the house. The book hadn't included that in its instructions. There was no point in ringing the bell. I had seen enough deliverymen stand outside, their fingers uselessly pressing, waiting for a reply. I had seen them calling in vain, trying to attract attention. It wasn't the sort of place to encourage casual visitors. But nor did it have the complicated alarms that had appeared on some of the other, smartened houses in the row, and I knew from a lifetime of living on Victory Road that there were ways and means of breaking in. They were reported in the newspaper every week. The upper half of the door held two thin panes of glass and there was just one hole for a key. It was possible.

As I walked up the path I tussled with myself, asking why I was doing something that was bound to lead to trouble. There would be consequences, I knew. But by the time I reached the doorstep, I had decided that I had nothing to lose. I was going to die, after all. At least this time I would be doing something good.

I untied my headscarf and wrapped it around my hand, then picked up a brick from the pile of rubble by the step. The dirty glass smashed easily. I reached through and lifted the latch.

*

I feared the worst when I saw the body on the bed, but as I moved closer the grubby sheets twitched. Despite the room's terrible stuffiness, the girl was shivering. She lay on her side, gasping loudly, showing no sign of having noticed an intruder. As my eyes became used to the dim light, I edged my way around the bed. I reached out towards her, thought better of it, moved away, then reached again.

'Hello,' I said.

'Mum?'

The hope in her voice made me shiver. I knew I wasn't the person she wanted. When she saw me, she screamed.

'I'm Nora,' I said quickly. 'I thought you might need help.'

She peered at me.

'I know you,' she said. 'You're that old woman from across the road. You've been watching me.'

It had never occurred to me that I might have seemed strange to her.

'I'm sorry,' I stammered. 'I wanted to make sure that you were all right. I mean, with the baby.'

'I'm fine.'

'But you can't do this alone.'

Her voice was fierce. 'Why not?'

'Please let me help.'

'Why? Are you a nurse?'

'No.'

'What do you know about it, then? Have you got children?'

I swallowed. 'No, but I've read a book,' I said. 'I think I could help.'

I knew I didn't sound convincing. I wasn't even sure that it was true. Part of me wanted to creep away, back over the road and into my house, to not become involved, but the next minute the girl began to pant so hard that it sounded as if she were trying to blow out some kind of blockage from her lungs. She grabbed my arm, her fingers pressing hard into my flesh.

'Help me!' she screamed. 'Please.'

She held onto me until the contraction had passed and then collapsed back against the thin pillow, breathing hard. I could think of nothing to say and so I looked about the room. It had once been part of a fine house, I thought, for a fine family, but there was nothing fine about it now. A drawing room had been chopped in two, divided clumsily with plasterboard, leaving space for little more than the chair that I had seen from my window and the narrow bed. Damp edged across the walls, making the paper lift and peel. The faded carpet was worn, the movements of previous tenants marked by tracks between the bed and the makeshift kitchen that stood against one of the walls. The beer glass that I had seen her drink from stood on the draining board, next to the sink.

'Shall I get you some milk?' I asked.

'It's gone off,' she said. 'The electricity ran out.'

I went over to the refrigerator, opened it, gagged and quickly closed the door again.

'What did you say your name was?' the girl said.

'Nora.'

'I'm Rose.'

I went back over to the bed. She had a sweet face, small and pointed, with freckles scattered across her cheeks and nose, making her look even younger than I had thought. But her forehead was creased into a frown and she held herself tense. She was wearing the same black vest that I had seen her in all summer. The lower half of her body was covered by the sheet, for which I was thankful.

She looked as if she was about to say something else but just then a tremor passed through her body and she grabbed hold of my arm again. I was beginning to think that I should find someone to help, someone who really knew what to do. I hadn't meant it to happen like this, for it to go this far.

'Shall I call an ambulance?' I said. 'I think you should go to hospital. There's a telephone box on the corner. It wouldn't take me very long.'

'Please don't leave me!' she whispered. 'I'm scared. Don't go.'

And so I stayed. As the evening became night, more contractions came and she clung to me. I found myself singing old songs to her and stroking her hair, which soon became dark with sweat. I found a candle and stuck it to a saucer. It burned hesitantly at first, then stronger, throwing shadows against the wall. The shadows danced as draughts crept under the door and made the candle flicker.

Early in the morning, she began to make a different sort of sound, desperate and low.

'The baby's coming,' she said. 'I can feel it.'

I felt myself flush as she kicked off the dirty sheet. Apart from her vest she wore nothing. She lay on her back, clenching her fists, her monstrous belly rising high above her. I made myself look between her legs and saw a dark circle begin to expand, wider with every push that she gave. Her flesh was stretched so far that it looked as if it would tear if it went any further, but as it kept on stretching I realized that the circle was the top of the baby's head. It began to protrude out of her, revealing eyes, a nose and finally, a chin. When a pair of shoulders appeared, I took hold of them, half catching and half pulling until suddenly it was there in my hands, a small, slippery thing, covered in a layer of something white and streaked with blood.

In that instant, something that had been clenched tight inside me for as long as I could remember was released. I stood, holding the child, tears pouring down my cheeks.

'Look, Rose, it's a little girl,' I croaked.

I laid the baby in her arms. Our eyes met and she smiled, then looked at her daughter with such tenderness that I had to turn away.

*

I followed the book's instructions to the letter, cutting the umbilical cord, wrapping the child in a towel, making a newspaper parcel of the strange, bloody afterbirth and taking it to the rubbish bin outside. Rose and the baby slept, their chests rising and falling peacefully. Despite my tiredness, I couldn't sleep. I paced about, thinking.

In an effort to clear my head, I opened the curtains a little. As I watched, the sun began to rise, turning the sky a delicate shade of pink, the colour of the baby's skin. It made the street look almost beautiful, fresh with the promise of a crisp September. As dawn became morning, golden light shone through the window, warming my bones. People began to leave their houses to go to work, pleasure spreading over their faces as they paused to sniff the air. It would be a good day, I decided, a fine first day for Rose's child.

I turned my head to look at them, still sleeping. The morning light made the room look even worse than it had done the night before, revealing stains on the ceiling and balls of dust at the edges of the carpet. The bed sagged under the slight weight of its occupants. Its sheets had seemed grubby enough in the candlelight but now I saw that they were streaked with dirt. The pile of the chair that I was sitting on was stuck together in hard little clumps where something had spilled on it. This bedsit was no place for a baby, I thought.

Music began to thud through the wall but Rose slept on. It was the baby who woke her, mewing like a kitten.

'Good morning,' I said.

For a moment she looked bewildered, then she smiled. 'It's you!'

'She's hungry,' I said. 'You should feed her.'

'I don't know how.'

The book had explained it but the daylight made me awkward. Eventually, the baby solved the problem herself, groping with her mouth and suckling greedily. I looked out of the window at my house, wishing that I were alone in the kitchen like any other morning, making coffee with no-one else to think about. But then I heard Rose murmur something to the child.

'How could she have wanted to get rid of you? You're perfect.'

Her words had an immediate effect on me.

'You and the child must come and stay with me,' I blurted out.

I didn't know why I had said it but I was suddenly convinced it was the answer.

She looked astonished. 'It's very kind of you,' she said, 'but I'm really okay here. Anyway, I can't afford anything better than this.'

'I don't want your money,' I said quickly. 'But I have a house. I'm the only one who lives in it and it's too big for me. This room is too small for you and the baby. I could give you your own room, much nicer than this one.'

'But you don't even know me,' she said. 'Why are you doing this? Why did you come here last night?'

If I had an inkling of the reasons for my rashness, I had no intention of telling her; at least, not yet.

'I felt sorry for you. I know what it's like to be on your own.'

I saw her wonder whether or not to believe me.

'You can't suddenly invite me to move in. We've only just met.'

'We've been watching each other for weeks.'

'That's the other thing. You could be anyone. It's a crazy idea.'

'It's not crazy,' I said. 'And neither am I. I'm lonely, that's all.'

It was true. The illness had robbed me of the few friends I had left. I had pushed them away, not wanting them to know what was wrong. This girl and her growing belly had been the only thing to interest me. She had jolted me out of my solitude.

'I'd be helping you, but you'd be helping me too. We could keep each other company. It would be much better for the baby. Look at this place.'

She glanced at the room, wrinkling her nose as if she were noticing for the first time how squalid it was.

'It's hardly suitable for a child,' I said. 'Is that music always so loud?'

32

She nodded.

'The baby won't be able to sleep through music like that. My house is quiet and so am I.' I tried my best to sound convincing. 'Please come, for the child's sake. Just try it out. If you don't like it, you can always leave.'

She leaned back against the dirty wall, weighing up the offer. I watched anxiously, waiting for her to answer. At last, she nodded.

'All right,' she said. 'Thank you. We'll come, for a while anyway. Let's see if it works out.'

I felt a rush of happiness. 'That's wonderful.'

'I want to give you something in return,' she said.

I wondered what it could possibly be. 'Thank you, but it's really not necessary.'

She smiled. 'Please. I want you to name the baby. Choose a name you really like, one that means something to you.'

I didn't hesitate for a second. I smiled back at her. 'Grace. Let's call her Grace.'

Four

When I woke, the hands of the alarm clock pointed to half past ten. I scrambled out of bed, threw on my uniform and hurried out of the room. I found myself in a hallway with five doors facing a staircase with a polished wooden banister curving out of sight. I stood at the top of it for a moment, gathering my courage, then began to creep down the stairs, staying close to the wall.

The only pretty thing in our Bethnal Green rooms was a white china pitcher painted with pink flowers. It had been a wedding present, Ma said, and the one thing she couldn't bear to sell when Pa died. In this house, which I remembered from the previous day was not called a house but a rectory, everything was beautiful. I looked about in wonder. The sun was shining through a window halfway down the stairs, throwing light onto a painting of a woman holding a baby. The painting was old and the woman looked sad. She seemed to be staring at something outside the picture, something far away that she would never be able to reach because she was trapped in her painted world. She made me think of Ma and I was suddenly sad as well. I caught sight of Mrs Rivers' Virgin Mary coat, hanging in a row of other coats by a door, and I ran down the stairs. If I could just touch it, I thought, I would feel better. But as I reached towards it, a chiming noise rang out like a warning. I jumped in shock. A second chime rang out and I looked around to see where it had come from. Behind me was a tall grandfather clock. I stood, trembling, wondering what to do. I could make a bolt for it, I supposed, run out of the door and back to London and Ma. But I knew that I wouldn't get far. The only other thing to do was to stay and wait to be found by someone who would decide what happened to me next. I was still standing by the coats when Grace burst through a door to my right. She grinned at me like she had at the station.

'You're ready!' she said. 'That's lucky. They sent me to get you. We're to go to the church as soon as we can. There's going to be an announcement on the wireless. Come on.'

She took my hand and led me through a kitchen, out of a door and across a lawn to a gate in the railings, then we were in the graveyard. We wove between the headstones and jumped over graves, hurried along by the urgent ringing of the bells. Just as we got to the porch at the front of the church they stopped. Grace smiled again.

'Just in time,' she said.

Outside it was a sunny day, busy with the sound of the bells and the birds, but inside the church everything was silent and still. Our run from the rectory had made me hot but now I shivered in the cool air, which smelled of polish and damp. As my eyes adjusted to the light, I saw that this church wasn't like the one at home. It had no figures of the saints, no golden candlesticks, no paintings. The flower arrangements on the window-ledges were dropping their petals and the carpet in the aisle was faded and frayed. But the church was full, packed with people sitting quietly, waiting. The only space was next to Mrs Rivers, who was sitting alone up near the altar, wearing a red suit and a hat with a feather in it. Grace and I walked up the aisle towards her, side by side, keeping step. Mingled with the polish and the damp was another smell, one that I recognized from the train, the smell of fear. As I took my seat next to Grace I began to be frightened too and I shivered again, wondering what would happen next.

Suddenly the congregation stood. A tall man came past us, his hands clasped in front of him, wearing a long black gown that went right to the floor. Over it he wore a white smock that, like the church, had seen better days, splashed with mud up the back and dotted with moth-holes along the hem.

'That's Father,' Grace whispered.

So there he was, that strange thing, the married priest, Mrs Rivers' husband, standing in front of us, almost close enough to touch. The back of his neck was scrubbed and red. He held his head very still as he spoke and his voice was solemn, as if he were saying something important. I wasn't really listening to what he had to say. I was looking at a man who was bending over something on a table next to Reverend Rivers, a polished wooden box that sounded almost as if it were alive, one minute hissing and crackling, the next letting out an angry hum.

'It's a wireless set,' Grace said. 'Mr Chamberlain's about to tell us if there's going to be a war. Everybody's frightened because the fathers will have to go and fight the Germans.'

I didn't know who Mr Chamberlain was but I wanted to hear what he had to say, to know what was going to happen to me, if I was to stay in this strange place or if I would be allowed to go home to Ma. I screwed up my eyes as tight as I could and prayed for the news to be good.

The voice that came from the wireless sounded tired and sad. It was Mr Chamberlain, I supposed. I opened my eyes and leaned forward to listen.

I am speaking to you from the Cabinet Room at Number Ten Downing Street. This morning, the British Ambassador in Berlin handed the German government a final note, stating that unless the British government heard from them by eleven o'clock that they were prepared at once to withdraw their troops from Poland, a state of war would exist between us. I have to tell you now that no such undertaking has been received, and that consequently this country is at war with Germany . . .

So there it was, the thing that Ma and I had hoped and prayed wouldn't happen, the thing that would keep me from her.

. . . The situation in which no word given by Germany's ruler could be trusted and no people or country could feel itself safe has become intolerable. Now we have resolved to finish it . . .

I wondered how long that would take.

. . . May God bless you all. May he defend the right, for it is evil things that we shall be fighting against – brute force, bad faith, injustice, oppression and persecution; and against them I am certain that the right will prevail.

For a moment nobody said a word, then a baby started to cry and people began to turn to each other and whisper. Reverend Rivers, who had sat in the pew opposite us to listen to the broadcast, got to his feet. His expression was grave.

'Let us pray,' he said.

Like everyone else, I dropped to my knees. Reverend Rivers prayed for England. He prayed for the village. He prayed for the King and he prayed for the men who would fight for us. I said *Amen* when he had finished but I wasn't thinking of the King and the soldiers. I could only think of Ma. I wondered if she were in church like us, but on her own, with nobody to turn to. She would be safe there, at least; not even the Germans would dare to bomb a house of God. But she wouldn't be able to stay there forever. There would come a time when she would have to go back home. I imagined bombs falling like deadly raindrops, soaking the London streets with blood.

I wanted Ma to be with me in this church instead, holding my hand, the two of us looking after each other like we always had. Tears spilled down over my cheeks and onto my hands as I prayed. I made myself as small as I could, tucking in my elbows, keeping my head down and my hands pressed tightly together under my chin. I tried to cry quietly so that nobody would notice, but it was no good. Grace knew. I could feel her watching me. She pressed her shoulder against mine and whispered in my ear.

'I'm sorry about the war. But I'm not sorry you'll be staying. I'm glad.'

Reverend Rivers cut the service short after that. We sung one hymn, quietly and quickly, then he walked down the aisle and stood in the porch to say goodbye to the congregation, which followed him without speaking. By the time we got to the porch, after everyone else had gone, Reverend Rivers was already turning to come back inside, as if he wanted to get away from the sunshine and back into the gloom of the church. I could see why. It seemed too bright for a first day at war.

Mrs Rivers was the first to speak. 'This is Nora,' she said.

Reverend Rivers looked blank.

She sighed. 'Our evacuee. She arrived last night while you were taking Evensong. I told you about her over supper. Don't you remember?'

'I chose her!' Grace said. 'Her birthday's just before mine. We're almost exactly the same age. Don't you think we look like each other?'

An odd look passed across Reverend Rivers' face, then he stretched out his arm and put his hand on my head. 'Welcome, Nora. God bless you.'

His voice was like Mr Chamberlain's, solemn and low. I couldn't think of anything to say. I stood very still, feeling awkward, waiting for him to take his hand away.

'I must see to lunch,' said Mrs Rivers. 'Come along, girls. You can help.'

*

Mrs Rivers sent us to a room that had tall windows looking out onto the garden and curtains that hung all the way to the floor. In the middle of it was a long table made of dark, polished wood. On the table was a bowl of flowers that looked as if they were made of the same material as the curtains, something velvet and fine. The room was filled with their scent. I stood in the doorway, puzzled at what the room was for.

'What's the matter?' Grace said.

I knew somehow not to tell her that I was used to a table that we covered with sheets of newspaper because we didn't have a cloth, and that it wobbled because the woodlice were eating their way through its legs.

'Nothing,' I said. 'Only, I've never seen a room like this before.'

'What do you mean? A room like what?'

'One that's like a kitchen but with just a table and some chairs and nothing else in it.'

'It's a dining room,' she said. 'Haven't you ever seen a dining room?'

'A dining room?'

'It's for eating in.'

I was astonished at the idea of a room that was only for eating in.

It was bigger than our kitchen and front room put together. To hide my surprise, I went over to the table and bent to sniff the flowers. I closed my eyes and breathed in deeply, filling my nose with their smell.

'What are you doing?' Grace asked, putting a pile of knives and forks on the table with a clatter.

I opened my eyes quickly and stood up. 'It's these flowers. They're the nicest thing I've ever smelled.'

She frowned. 'Don't you have roses in London? They're just from the garden. Mummy picks them. She's like you, she thinks they smell nice.'

'Roses.' I said the word slowly, testing it out on my lips.

'Say it like me. Roses.'

'Roses.' But I couldn't say it like she did, no matter how hard I tried. I began to stammer, ashamed that I couldn't get my mouth around the word.

She said it again. 'Roses.'

It was the latest thing to catch me out in this strange place, the countryside, where all the rules were different. If I couldn't even speak like the people who lived there, I thought, I didn't stand a chance. I bit my lip, trying to hold back tears. I didn't want her to see me cry again. I wanted to tell her that I wasn't like this. I never cried at home. The past two days had somehow made me different and I didn't like it.

Grace touched my shoulder. 'Nora? I'm sorry. I didn't mean to be hurtful. I thought it was funny, that's all.'

I sniffed. 'Funny?'

She smiled. '*Row*-sis,' she said, in my voice, rolling her eyes at me. '*Row*-sis.'

She did look funny as she said it and I couldn't help but giggle. She giggled too and I felt a small spark of hope.

'Come on,' she said. 'We'd better get on with it. We'll be in trouble if the table isn't laid in time.'

It took us a while to do it. Each time that I put a knife or a fork in the wrong place, Grace would say '*Row*-sis' and it would set us off again. By the time we were finished my cheeks were sore from laughing.

*

I discovered other things that day. The best was roast beef. As lunchtime grew close, a thick, savoury smell drifted through the rectory, making my mouth water and my spirits lift. Ma and I ate plain food that was white or grey; bread and dripping, boiled potatoes and stew. The food that Mrs Rivers set down on the rectory table was bright like stained glass in a church window. The slices of meat that came away from Reverend Rivers' carving knife were as pink as a blush. Mrs Rivers put two pieces on my plate, next to orange carrots, dark green spinach and roast potatoes the colour of gold, then she poured on gravy that settled in pools around it all. I shifted forward in my chair.

'Let us give thanks,' said Reverend Rivers. Mrs Rivers and Grace put their hands together and bowed their heads. I copied them, hoping that he would be quick.

'For what we are about to receive, may the Lord make us truly thankful.'

As I mumbled *Amen*, I stole a glance at Reverend Rivers from behind my hands. He had taken off the smock but was still wearing the long gown. It had little buttons all the way up the front of it to his throat, small buttons like the ones on a nightdress. I had never imagined that I might sit at a table with a priest. Reverend Rivers didn't look like any man I had ever known. He was so thin that he looked as if he would snap in two if he bent to pick something up. His face was pale and his eyes were hidden behind thick spectacles.

His hands, still clasped together from saying grace, were very white against the black cuffs of his gown, not a man's hands at all, but the soft, clean hands of a woman who didn't go out to work.

But I was more concerned with what was on my plate than with Reverend Rivers. The smell of the food rose up to my nose, thick and strong. I picked up my knife and fork and cut through one of the pieces of meat. I stabbed at it with my fork, added a potato and dipped it into the gravy.

I wanted to keep the taste of that first mouthful forever, holding the meat and potato on my tongue as the hot gravy ran down my throat. Swallowing seemed like a shame. But the mouthfuls that followed were just as good. I put iron-tasting spinach next to buttery carrots and softened the saltiness of the potatoes with gravy. I cut a slice of beef into little pieces and piled them all onto my fork, then filled my mouth as full as I could with meat, liking the resistance that it gave as I chewed.

When I looked up from my plate, I realized that I had eaten much faster than anyone else. Half of Reverend Rivers' food was still untouched and Grace had picked out her meat but left her vegetables to one side. Mrs Rivers had eaten hardly anything. I had soaked up the last bit of gravy with half a roast potato.

'You have an appetite, child,' said Reverend Rivers.

Food was just what I ate when Ma put it in front of me, nothing more than a way to fill my stomach. I had never been lost in it like this. But I knew I couldn't explain that to Reverend Rivers, who didn't look as if he would ever be carried away by anything. I suddenly remembered that gluttony was a sin and I stared down at my plate, concentrating on the blue and white flowers twisting around the rim.

'I expect you were awfully hungry,' said Mrs Rivers. 'You didn't have any breakfast and you missed supper last night.'

What had just happened had nothing to do with hunger. It was something else, I wasn't sure what, a feeling of being woken up by things that were different and new. But I didn't know how to explain any of that to Mrs Rivers and I wanted to please her, so I said 'No, Miss.'

My voice sounded strange, like when I had talked about the roses. It seemed out of place in the rectory, with its polished furniture and curtains that went all the way down to the floor. Grace had made it better by making me laugh but now, sitting at the table with my guardian angel, Mrs Rivers, and her husband the priest, it mattered again.

Mrs Rivers gave me a look that reminded me of the way that Ma was sometimes when she kissed me goodnight. 'Don't worry, you'll soon get used to being here. Make yourself at home. You're part of the family now.'

'How long will she stay?' said Grace. 'Must she really go back when the war's finished?'

'Don't be silly,' said Mrs Rivers. 'Nobody knows how long this terrible war is going to last. Nora will stay with us for as long as it is safer for her to be here than in London. After that she'll go home, of course.'

'Will she come to school with me? She could share my desk. We could be in the same dormitory.'

Mrs Rivers looked as if she were about to say something that she knew Grace wouldn't like. 'I'm afraid you won't be going back to school until the war's over. Your father and I have decided that it wouldn't be safe. It's better that you stay here with us.'

Grace flushed and pushed her plate away from her. 'But I have to go. All my friends are there.'

'That's enough,' said Mrs Rivers. 'I'm sure that most of your school friends will be staying at home like you. And anyway, you won't be alone. Nora's here. She'll be your friend.'

I liked the thought of being Grace's friend. She wasn't like any girl I had known before. Everything about her was bright, from her tartan skirt to the sparkle in her eyes. Her skin seemed to glow, as if it were lit up like the painting in the hallway, and her hair was like the roses, velvet and fine. There was something about her that was exciting, something about the way she seemed to say what she thought as soon as it came into her head. I wanted to be her friend. I wanted her to like me.

'Please let me go,' said Grace, looking at Reverend Rivers, who was frowning down at his plate. 'Father,' she said, more loudly.

He looked up and peered at her through his spectacles. 'What?'

'Mummy says I'm not allowed to go back to school.'

He put down his knife and fork and clasped his hands together as if he were about to start praying again.

'Grace,' he said. 'We're at war. Your school is on the coast. That will be the first place to be invaded. We cannot let you go. You'll stay here until the war is over.'

But she wouldn't give in. 'How will we ever learn anything?' she said. 'You're always telling me how I don't know enough.'

Reverend Rivers nodded. 'I've thought of that. You're too old to go to the school in the village, so I have decided to teach you myself. Every morning you and Nora will come to my study for lessons.'

Grace looked horrified but Reverend Rivers carried on speaking. 'Nora, do you like to learn?'

I liked going to school but I wasn't sure I would like lessons from Reverend Rivers. He was strange. I would be too frightened to answer his questions. But I knew I mustn't tell him so.

'Yes, Father,' I said.

'You can't call him that,' Grace snapped. 'He's not your father.'

It wasn't what I'd meant. I had said it because he was a priest. My father had been Pa. Father was a word for the church.

Reverend Rivers looked at me thoughtfully. 'Where is your home?' he asked.

'London, Father.' I bit my lip.

'Yes, but which part of the city?'

'Bethnal Green.'

'And is your church in Bethnal Green?'

'Yes, Father.'

'And what is its name?'

'Our Lady of the Assumption.'

He nodded, as if I had answered something that he had been puzzling over. 'So you are a Roman Catholic.'

I felt as if there was some sort of danger behind his questions but I didn't know what it was. I nodded, to stop myself calling him Father again.

'What's Roman Catholic?' asked Grace.

'It's another sort of church,' said Reverend Rivers. 'But Nora says she likes to learn. She'll soon get used to it.'

*

After lunch I helped Mrs Rivers with the dishes. Even that was different to the way we did it at home, heating water on the fire and taking care not to burn our fingers when we first dipped the dishes into it. At the rectory hot water came straight out of the tap, splashing down into the sink. Mrs Rivers took one plate at a time, slid it into the water and rubbed it clean, then laid it on the draining board. I stood next to her, holding each piece of china very carefully as I dried it with a cloth and put it on the table. It was thin enough to make me nervous. Grace dashed about noisily, stacking pans and throwing cutlery into drawers.

I kept quiet, watching Mrs Rivers. I was close enough to smell her lemon scent. She seemed out of place at the kitchen sink, blowing away the strands of hair that fell into her eyes as she bent over it. As the pile of things to be washed grew smaller and the stack on the draining board rose, a layer of yellowish grease formed on the surface of the water. The sight of her long, fine fingers dipping into it seemed somehow wrong. I remembered how they had felt on my forehead the night before. I liked Mrs Rivers. I moved closer to her.

'Miss,' I said. 'Miss, I could finish the dishes for you.'

Mrs Rivers was staring out of the window and didn't seem to have heard me.

'Miss,' I said again, and tugged at her sleeve. She looked down at me and for a moment it was as if she didn't know who I was. Then she recovered herself.

'What did you say, dear?'

Now that I had her attention I felt foolish. I couldn't tell her that I thought her hands were too good for the grease. I mumbled that I could finish the dishes if she liked. She smiled.

'You're a good girl, Nora,' she said, taking the tea towel from me and drying her hands on it. 'Your mother would be proud of you.'

I blushed at the idea that Mrs Rivers might think I was good. I didn't think Ma would be proud of me, not after the way I had been with her the day before. Mrs Rivers took my hands in hers. I could feel the grease from the dishes on them like a second skin.

'We'll finish these together and then I shall help you write to your mother,' she said. 'You must tell her that you're safe. She'll be worried about you.'

*

And so, when all the pretty china had been put away in the dresser and each pan hung on its hook, Mrs Rivers took off her apron and went to find a pencil. I ran upstairs to fetch the postcard that the teacher had given me and then we sat at the kitchen table to write to Ma. Grace was full of suggestions.

'Say you've found a sister,' she said.

'Hush, Grace,' said Mrs Rivers. 'Don't be tiresome. Nora can decide what to write for herself.'

Grace put her elbows on the table, propped up her chin with her hands and rolled her eyes at me. I stared down at the small piece of card. I couldn't have written about any of it, even if Mrs Rivers and Grace hadn't been there. The things I wanted to tell Ma would have filled a book but I didn't have any of the words. I wanted to tell her that I was sorry for how I'd been with her. I wanted to say that all I wanted was to lie in bed with her curled around me like always, feeling safe. I wanted her to know about the bleeding. But at the same time as wanting to tell her those things, I wanted to punish her by keeping them to myself. I put my arm around the card and bent my head close to it. I told her I was staying at a rectory and that the weather was good. It was the truth, but not all of it and I may just as well have written nothing. When I had finished, I laid down my pencil and pushed the postcard away. Mrs Rivers picked it up.

'There,' she said. 'Your mother will be pleased to know you're safe. Grace will take you to the village to post it.'

*

On our way to the village we went through a garden behind the rectory that was filled with plants set out neatly in rows. The straight lines reminded me of the streets at home. Butterflies flitted about them, little wisps of colour dancing in the still air of the afternoon. I couldn't see what it was about the plants that attracted them. They weren't bright like the ones in the front gardens I'd seen the day before, but solid and practical looking, creeping close to the ground.

'What are they?' I asked Grace.

'What do you mean?'

'What sort of plants are they? Why are there so many of them? Why haven't they got any flowers?'

Grace stared at me like she had when I sniffed at the roses, as if she couldn't believe I didn't know.

'They're vegetables,' she said. 'You know, things like carrots. Or potatoes. We had some of the carrots for lunch.'

I hadn't ever thought of where vegetables came from. Ma and I bought them from the barrow on the corner of our street. My mouth began to water at the memory of lunch and although I was still full from it, my stomach rumbled.

'Will you show me?' I said.

She giggled. 'If you like.'

She led me into a long tunnel of plants that wound themselves up canes towards the sky. Sunlight rippled through the leaves, throwing shadows on her face. She felt amongst the foliage.

'They're almost finished,' she said. 'It's the end of the season.'

She felt a little further. 'Here you are!'

She held out something green, the size and shape of a finger.

'What is it?'

She drew her thumbnail down its side, then flattened it out.

'There you are. Peas.'

I took one and put it in my mouth. It tasted of sunshine and sweetness. I was amazed.

'Wait until October,' she said. 'We'll go bramble picking so Mummy can make a pie.'

She set off again, making her way to the end of the tunnel, and then we climbed over a fence into a field. It was like being transported into the view that I had seen from the train. Fields were all about us, spreading for miles, like a quilt made out of patchwork, crisscrossed with hedges. A flock of sheep grazed on a hill in the distance, moving slowly about it like clouds. The sun was still high in the sky and I felt it on my face as we walked along, the grass tickling my feet through my sandals. Birds twittered like they had done that morning, little bursts of happy song.

'It's beautiful!' I said.

'I'll show you all of it,' said Grace. 'We're going to have fun.'

*

By the time we had been to the village to post the card in the letterbox, the weather had changed. Clouds gathered in the sky as we came back along the track and by the time we reached the churchyard, it had started to rain. My uniform became sodden and heavy with water. As we stood dripping in the kitchen I heard the sound of a piano. I had never heard a piano being played without someone singing next to it but now there was no voice, just notes, hundreds of them, coming so quickly that I almost expected them to trip up over one another. I was too shy to ask where the music was coming from. I had asked too many questions that day. But as if she knew what I was thinking, Grace said, 'It's Mummy. She does it every day. She plays for hours and hours, the same things over and over.'

I found it hard to believe that music like this came from Mrs Rivers' calm, cool hands.

'Can we see her?' I asked.

'We'll have to be quiet. She doesn't like to be disturbed.'

I followed Grace to another new door and waited as she turned the doorknob and put her finger to her lips. We stood in the doorway watching Mrs Rivers. Her eyes were closed and she swayed as her hands moved like scurrying animals over the keys. That was where they belonged, I thought, not in a sink filled with greasy water. On the piano they were quick and alive. Mrs Rivers looked as if she were somewhere else, somewhere she would much rather be.

'That's why I wanted to stay at school,' Grace whispered. '
'Mummy and Father don't talk much. She's either digging in the garden or playing the piano, like now. He's in church or his study. It's as if they don't even notice I'm here.'

She grinned at me suddenly, and it was as if the sun had come out from behind a cloud.

'But now *you're* here. If I've got you none of it matters.'

Five

AS I GOT READY FOR ROSE'S ARRIVAL, I FELT BETTER THAN I had done in months, full of hope and purpose. It would be a new start. I hummed as I cleaned the house, starting at the top as my mother had taught me. I could almost hear her giving me instructions.

Don't take the dirt up with you, Nora; always bring it down.

There was plenty of dirt to collect. I hadn't cleaned since my illness had begun. Dust had settled like a layer of grey snow on the skirting boards, blunting the edges of furniture and gathering in balls under beds. Spiders hung shrivelled in corners. I'd always liked cleaning, putting things in order. I went into rooms that had been closed up for months, where the air was warm and still as if the last of the summer heat was hiding there, avoiding the autumn. I threw open the windows, letting in the breeze.

I had missed being busy. In the top floor bedroom, I took a rag and wiped away the dust, watching it curl across the cloth in thick crests. I wrestled open the tin of beeswax and spread it over the chest of drawers and the little rosewood bookshelf, working it into the grain. I brought up a bottle of vinegar and cleaned the window with a newspaper, then put sheets and blankets on the bed and smoothed them down neatly. I swept the floor and shook the rug out of the window.

When I had finished, I stood for a while, looking out over the rooftops and down into gardens, little summer spaces where families cooked food on barbecues at weekends, drinking bottles of beer and sunbathing on plastic chairs, listening to music on the radio. Children splashed in colourful paddling pools, shrieking and laughing as they flicked water at each other.

My own garden was tangled and overgrown. Like the house, it had had no-one but me in it for a very long time. We could clear it out, I thought. The baby could play in it. I could plant flowers again to brighten it up. I wondered if there were any left that I could pick to put in Rose's room.

*

I walked about, peering into tangled bushes and borders. The consequences of my neglect were evident. The garden was wild and the grass had gone to seed. Convolvulus had spread everywhere, choking whatever dared stand in its way. The only things of beauty were the statues, the Three Graces, bought at a house clearance in Suffolk on a whim. Ivy wound around their alabaster ankles as if it were trying to pull them down into the underworld and algae rose up their thighs like a rash, but they were tougher than they looked. They had withstood the weather for decades and rejected the many advances of vandals. They had heard my confessions, their blank faces never passing judgement. I had wept at their feet, their stone skin soaking up my tears.

'We're going to have company,' I told them. 'Another Grace.'

The beauties went on staring silently into the distance as I made my way around the garden, trying to find something suitable. No flowers seemed to have survived the summer, so I turned back towards the house. But as I picked my way along what was left of the path, a bird began to sing and I looked up to see it. Peering towards the trees, I noticed a rambling rose growing up a trellis. There was one red flower left and it was within reach.

A rose for a Rose, I thought, and smiled.

I reached up, fitted my fingers between the thorns and snapped it off. I carried it back to the house in triumph, holding it up in front of me like a bridal bouquet.

※

Next, I put together afternoon tea. I'd gone shopping that morning, walking the extra distance to the Casablanca Convenience Stores. I discovered it many years ago, attracted by the name. The film was the closest I ever got to Africa, but stepping inside was enough to spark my imagination. The music on the battered radio was from another world and the mix of smells, of coffee and spices, tomatoes and meat, made my senses quiver. The vegetables arranged in boxes on the pavement outside were an education.

The supermarket close to the house had long queues and bored assistants. In the Casablanca Convenience Stores I was often the only customer. There was no need for name badges when the staff never changed. The same man had been running it for more than twenty years. He smiled when I came through the door and I smiled back, pleased to be shopping for an occasion.

I wandered around the shop, picking up a loaf of soft white

bread, a slab of butter and a box of Darjeeling teabags. I went outside to get some tomatoes. They were juicy and plump, still linked
together on the vine and smelling of summer. As I was looking at
them, the shopkeeper came up behind me.

'They're good today,' he said.

He ran expert fingers over the tomatoes, squeezing them and
putting them to his nose to sniff. He picked a couple out.

'These are the best.'

I was eager to tell him about Rose. 'I'll need a few more than
usual,' I said. 'I've got a visitor. I'm making afternoon tea.'

'Ah,' he said. 'Then you should take some cakes as well.'

He took me to the bakery counter. Little pastries were laid out
neatly in rows.

'Taste this,' he said, handing me one, dusted with sugar and
topped with nuts.

It wasn't like the cake I remembered at afternoon tea, solid and
often rather heavy. This was light, almost dissolving on my tongue.
There was no rule about what sort of cake to serve, I decided. It
didn't have to be traditional.

He put the cakes into a little box that he tied up with string and
put with the rest of my things into a plastic bag.

*

When I got home, I put the box of teabags next to the stove and filled
the kettle, ready for when she arrived. I poured milk into a jug and
arranged the cakes on a plate. I buttered the end of the loaf and
sliced it as thinly as I could without tearing it, six times. I cut off the
crusts and put pieces of tomato between the slices, sprinkling salt
and pepper over them.

This is real life, I thought. This is what people do.

It was a long time since I'd had a visitor. I hoped I'd get it right.

I put the tea-things on a tray. The crockery was chipped and stained and my old bone-handled cake forks, unearthed especially for the occasion, were covered with smears. I began to polish them with a soft cloth, rubbing them clean.

Be careful, I told myself. Don't let your guard down. Don't give anything away.

When the doorbell rang, I made my way along the passage, smoothing my hair with my hands. I stood very still for a moment, gathering my nerves, then took a deep breath and opened the door. Rose stood on the step, a bulging holdall hanging from her shoulder and two shopping bags at her feet. She was wearing a cheap-looking pair of trousers and her usual black vest. The trousers were too short for her and flapped about her ankles. Her feet were bare, slipped into plastic sandals. She was clutching the baby, who was asleep, wrapped up in what looked like an old sweater.

I smiled. 'Hello again.'

'Hello,' she said shyly. 'Are you sure about this?'

I wasn't, but she didn't need to know it. 'Of course,' I said. 'Come in.'

*

Although she had only come from across the street, it was as if she were from another world. Surrounded by my old furniture, she looked younger than ever. She perched on the edge of her seat like a restless bird, ready to fly off at the slightest suggestion of danger. I watched her look about the room, taking in her surroundings, forming an impression.

'Would you like something to drink?' I said. 'A cup of tea, perhaps?'

She answered quickly. 'Okay.'

I hurried to the kitchen and lit the gas. While the water was coming to the boil, I kept myself busy, taking napkins from the drawer and folding them neatly, adding them to the tray. When the water was ready, I poured some into the teapot, swirling it about to warm it up. The little ritual calmed me. I dropped in the teabags and filled the teapot to the top, then picked up the tray and carried it through to the sitting room.

Rose was feeding the baby, looking down at her with soft eyes. The teaspoons clattered in their saucers as I came through the door and she flinched.

'I'm sorry,' she said, sounding flustered. 'She was crying. I think she was hungry.'

'That's all right. I didn't mean to startle you. I'll pour the tea. You can drink it when you're ready.'

I listened to the sound of the baby snuffling as she suckled. When she had finished feeding, Rose reached awkwardly for her tea. I watched her try not to spill it as she lifted the cup over Grace's head. Her nervousness made me warm to her.

'Would you like me to hold her so you can eat?' I said. 'You must be hungry.'

'Are you sure you don't mind?'

'I'd like it very much.'

I held out my arms and she lowered the baby down into them. She fitted easily into the crook of my arm, light enough for me to hold without effort as she nestled against me. I laid my hand on her head, feeling her wispy hair and the perfect shape of her skull, marvelling at how small it was. But the next minute I felt a stab of pain so sharp that it made me want to fling her to the floor. I was suddenly revolted by the little mass of flesh in my arms, jealous of how much time she had left to live. For a moment, I wanted to destroy her.

The clock chimed and I remembered where I was. Just as quickly as it had come over me, the feeling disappeared, leaving me shaking and horrified.

'Have some sandwiches,' I said quickly, hoping that Rose hadn't noticed. 'I made them for you.'

She piled her plate up high, then began to push the food into her mouth, hardly pausing to chew and washing it down with gulps of tea. I remembered how thin she'd been without the camouflage of her clothes. I sat back in my chair, not wanting to interrupt, cradling the baby and feeling ashamed.

When Rose had finished the last of the cakes, she looked up at me and grinned.

'Thank you,' she said. 'I was starving. That was great.'

I began to feel more cheerful again. The tea had been a success. 'Would you like to see your room?' I said.

Her shyness had gone. 'Yes please,' she said eagerly, holding out her arms.

I passed her the baby.

'Will you be able to manage?' I asked. 'It's at the top of the house. There are lots of stairs.'

She nodded. 'I'll be fine. She weighs hardly anything.'

I led the way upstairs, steadying myself against the banisters. Now I had cleaned it, I liked my house again. I liked its carefully hung pictures and furniture chosen over the years. I resolved not to neglect it, to make it a home, a place for Rose and her child. For some reason, her opinion mattered to me. I wanted her to like it too. I wanted her to stay.

The effort of climbing made my heart hammer in my chest, and when we got to the top of the stairs, I took hold of the doorknob and stood for a second, recovering my breath. Then I pushed open the door, stepping back to let Rose pass.

The room was warm from the evening sun, which made the

polished furniture glow. Rose's bed looked inviting, covered with a flowered counterpane and I had made another bed for the baby from a drawer, fitting a pillow into it as a mattress. I'd found a crystal vase for the last rose of summer and I was pleased that I'd bothered. The rose was the finishing touch, I thought, something alive and new.

But when I turned towards Rose she didn't look as I had hoped she might. Her face was pale and her lips pressed tightly together. As I watched, two fat tears slid out of the corners of her eyes. A moment later, others followed, rolling down her cheeks and onto the baby, whom she clutched to her chest like a doll.

I took hold of her arm and led her to the bed. I sat next to her, waiting. Her voice, when she could finally speak, was small.

'I'm sorry, Nora,' she said, wiping her face with her sleeve.

I patted her arm.

'It's the rose. Mum used to put one next to my bed when I came home from school for the holidays.'

Her voice broke. Timidly, I put my arm around her shoulders.

'Shh,' I whispered. 'Shh.'

We stayed like that until the last of the sunlight had gone and the room was dark.

*

Later, I settled into the window seat in my bedroom, overlooking the garden. It was midnight, always my favourite time, when the world is quiet for a while, the day has passed and there is space before the next begins. The window was open and the cool night air carried in smells of the garden. I picked up the silver case from the nightstand, turning it over in my hands, tracing the delicate engravings with my fingertips and feeling along the curves of the initials. I pushed in the small catch with my thumb and the case sprung open to reveal cigarettes nestled under a piece of fraying elastic. Carefully, I pulled one out and passed it under my nose as if it were a cigar. I tapped it on the windowsill, then lit it. As the smoke drifted into the room I inhaled it deeply, my eyes closed, and she was there, as always, summoned by the smell. Cigarettes were one of the things that she developed a passion for, one of the things that I hated then but became faithful to later, seeking out her brand in small shops in back streets. Over the years, I developed the habit of burning a single one each night, like incense at an altar, to remember her.

That night I wanted more than memories. I wanted advice.

'Grace,' I whispered. 'Are you there? Are you listening? Something's wrong. I can see it in everything she does. I don't know what to say to her. I don't know what to do. Should I help? I'm frightened of interfering. You know what happened the last time I did it. Tell me what to do, please tell me.'

But there was no reply. I was entirely alone, surrounded by the night. The garden was as still and dark as ever, the only movement coming from the trees as they shifted in the wind, the only sound the rustle of leaves. I wondered if I would last long enough to see them fall.

Six

The war would be over by Christmas, they said, but it wasn't. By Christmas it had hardly begun. Grace and I helped Mrs Rivers hang blackout curtains at every window in the rectory, passing her pins and holding up the heavy cloth until our arms ached. We waited, listening to the wireless every night for news. They gave it a special name, the Phoney War. We looked up the word in Reverend Rivers' dictionary.

Fake, it said, *a sham*.

I did not know then that things are often not what they seem. There were dark places in the countryside with only the birds to see what happened in them. The rectory had carpets to sweep bad news under. There was space for secrets. The war wasn't the only phoney thing that autumn, but I didn't notice. I was wonderfully happy, happier than I had ever thought possible. Each morning I woke up knowing that by the time I went to bed again I would have learned something new. At night I dreamed, strange and astonishing dreams of things and places I had never known existed. It was as if I had been born a second time, into a life that was so thrilling that sometimes I found it hard to breathe.

I gobbled down my lessons as greedily as my first Sunday lunch. From the moment I walked into Reverend Rivers' study, I was bewitched. It wasn't like the rest of the rectory, polished and perfect. I had never seen so many books in one place, squeezed onto shelves and piled up on the floor in great wobbling stacks that looked as if they might fall over at any moment. The room smelled of paper, a thick, satisfying smell that mingled with the scent of tobacco from Reverend Rivers' pipe. I felt as if anything was possible in this room, as if I could take all the words in the books and make them into whatever I wanted. I stood and stared at them, spelling out their titles, trying to guess what they might be about. Reverend Rivers must be very clever, I thought. I wondered what it was like to know so much. I felt a strange excitement flicker inside me at the thought that one day I might know some of it too.

'You may touch them.'

I jumped, suddenly shy at the sound of Reverend Rivers' voice, but after a moment my curiosity got the better of me and I moved closer to the shelves, running my hands over the leather bindings as if I could absorb the information held inside them through my fingertips.

'So you like books?' Reverend Rivers asked.

I nodded, my attention still focused on the volumes in front of me.

'Then we shall enjoy our lessons.'

Grace let out a snort. I was shocked. No-one I knew would ever have dared to make a sound like that in lessons. It would mean a ruler against the back of your knees, or worse. Reverend Rivers sighed.

'I don't know how they managed to teach you anything at that school of yours, Grace. You're a savage. Still, we will try to make the best of it. Sit down, both of you, and we'll begin.'

Grace and I sat at Reverend Rivers' desk, whilst he paced about the room and asked us questions. I did my best, ashamed of how little I knew. Grace knew lots of the answers but gave them automatically, in a bored voice.

'There appear to have been some gaps in your education, Nora,' Reverend Rivers said finally.

I hung my head. He was right. The questions he had asked were beyond me.

'You can't be blamed for that. You have a logical mind. You can think. That is what's important. It's a good start.'

*

The study quickly became the room in which I felt most at home, soothed by the smell and excited by the books. Like me, Reverend Rivers seemed to be more at ease there. Outside, he was distant, as if his thoughts were somewhere else. He didn't speak much. He spent most of his time in the church or walking in the graveyard with his arms behind his back, looking like a tall ghost in his black gown, which I learned was called a cassock. Sometimes he came to the sitting room at night to listen to the wireless, hunched in the big leather armchair and looking into the fire. But when he taught us he was suddenly alive. When he showed us countries on the globe or explained a mathematical problem his eyes were bright and his voice strong, like it was when he read out his sermons on Sundays. Our lessons were nothing like the ones at school had been. We never recited multiplication tables or spelled out words on a blackboard.

Instead he took down books from the shelves and read to us. We looked up words in the big blue dictionary that he kept on his desk and checked our facts in the *Encyclopaedia Britannica*, which was heavy and important and filled a whole shelf. The more I learned, the more I wanted to know. I came to understand that there were possibilities that I had never thought about because I hadn't known the words to think them. Reverend Rivers lent me books that I devoured in bed by candlelight, staying awake for hours after Grace had gone to sleep.

Grace didn't feel like I did about lessons. She found them dull. She always took the seat that faced the window so that she could stare out at the garden whilst Reverend Rivers talked. It was the only time I ever saw her be still. She was subdued, all her usual energy drained away. She never picked up a book outside the schoolroom. I wondered if that was the reason for the strangeness between them. When he asked questions he looked at me for the answers, not her. He didn't ask if she wanted to borrow any books. When he looked at her handwriting he sighed. I felt bad for stealing his attention but also for the way that, when the clock in the hallway struck one o'clock, she would begin to shuffle and shift in her chair. It made me sorry to see Reverend Rivers realize that she was waiting to be dismissed. His eyes would lose their sparkle, the curious blankness would come down over his face and he would give a nod. Grace would hurry out of the room as fast as she could and I would follow her, feeling divided and uncomfortable.

But my regret never lasted long. It went as soon as we opened the door at the back of the rectory and stepped out into the garden. The afternoons were ours. Just as I loved being in the study, Grace loved being outside. It was where she belonged. The minute she left the house she seemed to grow taller.

'Come on, Nora!' she would shout, and we would run through

the meadows, throwing back our heads to feel the sunshine on our faces, laughing out loud and whooping with pleasure. She knew every inch of the fields and woods around the village, every path and every hidden place, and she shared them all with me. It was our own private kingdom, where we ruled and there was no-one to tell us what to do.

Reverend Rivers spent the mornings teaching me how to think about the world but in the afternoons Grace and I lived it. He taught me how to use my imagination; she liked to do things with her hands. She showed me the rabbit warrens on the side of the hill, the badger setts in the woods and the stinking secret place where the farmers left dead sheep to rot into skeletons. She taught me to build dens by balancing branches against a tree-trunk and weaving grasses amongst them to make walls. We dammed streams, piling up rocks in the water to make it cascade down.

She wasn't like the girls I knew in London. We had all been rather timid, always told to be good. There wasn't much trouble to be found in our cramped backyards and our mothers didn't let us out onto the streets. I had liked my friends because we were the same. I liked Grace because she was everything I wasn't. When I was with her I felt as if I could do anything. Nothing scared her. She looked like an angel but she liked to do things that were bad. She took me scrumping in other people's orchards, shinning easily up the trees and throwing apples down to me. We would race back to the woods and sit in one of our hideouts, cramming our mouths with sweet fruit until our stomachs ached.

In my very first week in Kent, when it was still warm enough to seem like summer, Grace taught me to swim. She took me through the woods to a pool that she called the Forgotten Lake because nobody knew about it but her. It was her favourite place in the world, she said, and I could see why. The water was a deep green, the colour of ivy, and very still, apart from a few small ripples on the surface from the wind. It was perfectly secret and silent and as soon as we were there, it was as if the rest of the world didn't exist.

As I stood on the bank, wondering how deep it was, Grace began to pull off her clothes. Soon she was at the edge of the water, dressed only in her knickers. I looked away. I had never seen another girl without her clothes on. Ma had always taught me to be modest. Even when she washed in the tub in front of the fire, she was careful what she revealed. And at any rate, she was my mother. Seeing her didn't make my cheeks grow hot and my heart beat fast.

'What's the matter?' Grace said. 'Come on. I can't show you how to swim if you don't get in.'

'I'm cold,' I said.

'Don't be silly! The water's had all summer to warm up. Look at me. I'm not cold, I promise.'

'Someone might see us,' I said, knowing that she wouldn't accept the excuse. She laughed.

'Don't worry about that! Nobody ever comes here. I told you, I'm the only one who knows about it. There's no-one to see you but me.'

I didn't know how to tell her that she was enough to make me ashamed. Six months before it would have been all right. I had looked just like her, skinny and simple like a boy. I didn't like the way I'd changed since then. I wanted us to be the same. She had chosen me at the railway station because of it. I didn't want her to see that under my clothes I was different.

'I'll cover my eyes if you like,' she said. 'But hurry up! It's no fun standing here on my own.'

I knew there was no way out of it. As she put her hands over her eyes, I took off my blouse, my skirt, my socks and my sandals, until I was standing like her in only my knickers. I folded my arms over my chest.

'All right,' I said. 'I'm ready.'

She took her hands away from her eyes. 'Come on!' she shouted and I followed her into the pool, deeper and deeper until the water was up to my armpits. It was achingly cold.

'Isn't it wonderful?' Grace said.

I nodded, pressing my teeth together to stop them chattering.

That afternoon she was patient, teaching me to swim, explaining how I should kick my legs at the same time as I pushed forward with my arms. She held me up in the water and didn't mind when I panicked and splashed.

'Don't worry,' she said, 'I won't let you drown.'

The feeling of her hands under my ribs as she helped me keep afloat was as good as having Ma's arms around me in bed. We swam every day after that until the trees began to drop their leaves into the water. I soon came to understand why Grace loved it. When I was at the lake, floating on my back and feeling the sun on my face, I felt perfectly peaceful and happy, as if nothing else in the world mattered. It was hard to believe that there was a war going on at all.

One day when we were at the lake, I heard someone cough. I looked around quickly, treading water. A man was standing next to a tree, a tall man whose arms hung loosely at his sides. He didn't seem to have noticed me. He was looking into the distance, at something or somebody else. I swam over to Grace, who was floating on her back with her eyes closed. I touched her arm.

'What's wrong?' she said, opening her eyes.

'There's a man over there, in the trees. He looks strange.'

'Where?'

I pointed to where the man was standing.

'There he is,' I said. 'Can you see him?'

But Grace was waving in his direction and smiling. 'Don't worry,' she said. 'It's only William,' and she began to swim towards him.

I followed her, my arms and legs heavy. Before I had seen him, I had been enjoying the feeling of the water against my skin. Now I felt naked and ashamed. The water felt much colder than before and I shivered at the thought of him seeing me through my underclothes. But Grace stopped swimming when the water was still deep enough to cover her chest.

'William!' she called. 'Come and say hello to Nora.'

He didn't move.

'Come on!' she said. 'There's no need to worry. She won't bite. She's our evacuee.'

As he came closer I saw that he was not quite a man, but older than a boy. He moved as if it cost him a great deal of effort and when he got to the water's edge he stood like I had done that first time, awkwardly, as if he didn't know what to do next. I looked at him closely, trying to puzzle out what it was that made him odd. It was partly to do with his clothes. His trousers flapped above his ankles and he wore an old tweed jacket that was too small for him. His wrists poked out of the cuffs, thin next to his stubby hands. The rest of him looked strange as well. His hair stuck up in clumps as if it had been chopped with something blunt, but his face was as smooth as if a barber had shaved it that morning. His skin was dark from the sun and his lips looked like a girl's, soft and full. He was chewing the bottom one, staring at the ground.

'I haven't seen you for ages,' said Grace. 'Where have you been?'

He looked up. 'I've been hiding from the bombs, Miss.'

His voice was deep and cracked, as if he didn't use it very often.

'But there aren't any. That's why they're calling it the Phoney War.'

He smiled, looking shy but at the same time proud.

'That's because of me. I've been hiding so the Germans don't know where to drop them.'

'But the Germans aren't looking for you.'

He looked at the ground again and muttered something.

'What?' said Grace.

He shook his head.

'Come on, William!' she said. 'Tell us.'

'Got to be careful. That's what they said on the wireless.'

'Where have you been hiding?'

He shook his head again. 'I'm not telling, Miss. Walls have ears. That's the other thing they said.'

Grace giggled, and suddenly skimmed the water with her hand so that it splashed in his direction. It glinted in the sunlight as it flew through the air and hit him.

Now she's done it, I thought, but I was wrong. He laughed and lifted his hands to catch the drops.

'Nora's from London,' said Grace. 'I chose her to come and live with us. Don't you think she looks like me?'

'Hello,' I said.

William didn't reply. He was rubbing water into his hands and wrists as if it were something precious.

'Well, I think she does,' Grace said, and dived underwater. I couldn't think of anything to say so I dived too, swimming until my lungs felt as if they were about to burst. When I came up for air, he was gone.

We often saw him after that, in the woods where he trapped rabbits, by the lake or standing on the little hump-backed bridge on the outskirts of the village. He was always alone and would stand still for hours on end, looking into the water.

'He doesn't ever swim,' Grace said. 'He just likes to look at it. He won't say why.'

I understood how he felt about water. At the lake, I liked the depth that went on forever, the cold sensation that rose up my body as I waded further in and the way that, if I stayed there long enough, my fingers swelled and turned white. I spent hours in the rectory bathroom, feeling a secret thrill each time I turned the hot water tap, fighting the temptation to fill the bath to the brim, past the line that Reverend Rivers had painted five inches from the bottom. He called it the Plimsoll Line and gave us a lesson on ships. We were saving water for the war effort, he said, and we must be sure never to fill the bath above it. Once a week I lay back and stared at the wobbly black line, promising myself that one day, when the war was over, I would find the biggest bath I could, fill it to the brim and stay there for as long as I wanted, never letting the water go cold.

*

For months there were no bombs and no invasion. The fright of the first day in church was replaced by a dull worry that one day something might happen. Nobody knew what it might be or when. The only thing to do was to wait. The long summer became autumn in a matter of days and then, almost before the leaves had time to drop from the trees, it was winter. When lessons were over we passed the time reading books or playing cards. In the evenings we sat with Mrs Rivers, listening to the sighs and whistles of the fire. She knitted, clicking her needles as surely and quickly as she played her piano. Reverend Rivers stayed in his study, smoking his pipe, the smell of it drifting under the door of the sitting room. When we were by the fire with the curtains pulled tight and the gas-lamps lit, it seemed impossible that anything could ever change. Even when the wind howled outside or rain threw itself against the windows, the rectory was solid. On those nights I curled myself into an armchair, hugging a cushion to my chest and reading a book, feeling perfectly content.

It was on one of those nights that Reverend Rivers came into the sitting room. It was strange to see him out of his study and we looked up at him, wondering why he was there. He made his way to the fireplace and stood in front of it, looking ill at ease.

After a moment he cleared his throat and began to speak. 'I have something to tell you,' he said, and his voice wasn't sure and clear like it was in the pulpit on Sundays or when he was explaining algebra in the schoolroom, but stumbling and low.

Mrs Rivers, Grace and I waited, saying nothing.

He coughed. 'What I mean to say is—' He stopped again. I stared at him, trying to work out what was making him so uncomfortable.

'Ah, what I mean to say is that I have received a letter from the authorities. As you know, most of the evacuees have gone back to their homes in London.'

I put down my book and sat up very straight.

'It seems that the situation is by no means as serious as originally feared.'

A prickling sensation began to creep up my spine.

Reverend Rivers hesitated, as if he wasn't sure what to say next. He seemed to be choosing his words very carefully. 'So the question is – ah – the question is whether Nora should go back home too.'

I felt as if a window had blown open and wind was rushing all around me. Grace leapt up and ran over to me. Her face was pale. She squeezed herself next to me in the armchair and wrapped her arm around my shoulder.

'She can't go.' Her voice was fierce. 'She belongs here with us.'

I looked over at Mrs Rivers, who had put down her knitting and was staring at Reverend Rivers as if she hadn't understood what he had said. I looked at Reverend Rivers. His expression was sorrowful but there was something else in it too, something that I couldn't puzzle out. He was pressing his lips together as if he were trying to stop himself from saying something. When he spoke again, he seemed to be struggling to keep his voice even.

'Grace!' he said. 'I am not suggesting that I want Nora to leave. But we have been asked a question and we must give an answer.'

'Then the answer is no. She mustn't leave us.'

As soon as she said it I knew she was right. I knew it in every part of me, right to my bones. But Reverend Rivers looked grave and I knew there was something else he had to say. Grace's words hung in the air as he spoke.

'There are other considerations,' he said slowly. 'Nora might want to go back home. She may not want to stay here. It is a long time since she saw her mother, nearly four months. The decision has to be hers.'

I felt stupid and lost, like when I didn't know an answer in the schoolroom. I imagined sitting on the train, leaving behind the hundred shades of green and the Forgotten Lake. In London there were no rivers to swim in, no apples to steal from trees and no books to take me to places where anything might happen. Hot tears welled up in my eyes at the thought of losing it all, and when Grace squeezed my hand they began to roll down my cheeks.

But there was another reason for my tears. Reverend Rivers' words had made me remember Ma. In my excitement at being in this new world, full of distractions and diversions, I had stopped thinking about her. I had forgotten her just as I had forgotten my friends. It was as if London had never existed.

I could feel Grace's fingers, tangled up with mine, and our pulses, beating together. I couldn't bring myself to speak.

'Please don't leave me,' Grace said in a small voice. 'You're supposed to be my sister, remember?'

A strange noise came from where Mrs Rivers was sitting. I looked over at her. She was pressing a handkerchief to her eyes. I couldn't bear the thought of upsetting her. I loved Ma but she had let me go. She had wanted me to leave. Grace and her mother wanted me to stay.

'Please,' I said. 'I want to stay here with you.'

Grace let out a yelp of happiness and squeezed my hand so tightly that I thought my fingers would break.

Reverend Rivers looked at me for the first time since he had come into the room. His lips twitched. 'Very well,' he said. 'I shall write to the authorities and to your mother.'

*

Ma wrote back, not to Reverend Rivers but to me. Her handwriting was as I remembered it from shopping lists, small and crooked, slipping and sliding off the faint ruled lines.

Dear Nora,

I hope that you are in good helth and that your feet are not too cold in bed without me there to rub them worm. I am sending some socks that I knited for you to make sure that you don't catch a chill. I am sure that it is colder in the Countryside than here. Reverend Rivers wrote me a letter and he said that you were no truble to him. He said that he was happy to keep you in Kent and so was his wife. He said that you wanted to stay. The Fox boys came back. They wanted to come home. They didn't like it in the Countryside. They said that they were always kept hungry and the lady didn't treat them well. It was ever so nice to see them. If you are ever unhappy you must write to tell me. As soon as I have the money for a ticket I will come to visit.

Remember that I will always be with you.

Your loving Mother

Reverend Rivers was strict about spelling, making us write out corrections fifty times. I was ashamed of Ma's mistakes, wondering what Reverend Rivers would think if he saw her letter. That night I cried myself to sleep, my hand resting on the letter under my pillow. It seemed to me that the distance between us was becoming much further than just a train ride.

Seven

THE DAY AFTER ROSE'S ARRIVAL I WOKE EARLIER THAN
usual, unnerved by the knowledge that someone else was in the
house. It had been many years since I had shared it and I was beginning to understand the consequences of my invitation. She would
come to know the daily details of my life. She would become familiar
with the little routines and rituals that filled my days.

My solitude had been hard-won, requiring constant protection. I
had allowed Rose into it and now there would be an entanglement.
We would not be able to confine our conversation to the present;
that much was evident from her tears when I had showed her her
room. There would be questions. The past would intrude, both hers
and my own.

I needed to think. I took my coat from the cupboard and knotted
my headscarf under my chin, then slipped out of the house. It was a

sunny day, just on the turn between summer and autumn and the blue skies made me feel better. My feet fell into their usual rhythms, taking me along old routes. My mind cleared and, although it hadn't been my original intention, I made my way to the Holloway Road.

The trestle tables outside the shop were piled high with second-hand books, their covers easy and familiar. I thought of the first time I'd gone there, remembering how long I had stood outside, gathering the courage to go in. It had been a sanctuary, a place where I learned to be different, where I became somebody new.

When I saw the tall figure putting books on the shelves, I felt a spark of mischief. I crept up behind him as quietly as I could and tapped him on the shoulder.

He jumped and spun around. A slow smile spread across his face. 'Nora!'

Gripping my shoulders with his long fingers, he bent to kiss me on the cheek. I breathed in the smell of his aftershave. Standing back, he looked me up and down.

'Hello Stephen,' I said.

'Where've you been?' he said. 'I've missed you.'

I shrugged. 'I've been busy. You know.'

'Have you got time for coffee?'

I nodded eagerly.

'You can tell me what you've been doing all summer. Give me your coat. I'll hang it up.'

As he disappeared into the back of the shop with it, I pushed a finger into the compost of a pot plant. It was nice and damp, well watered. He had always been good at keeping things alive. Sunshine poured in through the front window and the room seemed to hum, as if the books were calling to me, telling me that things would be all right. I felt curiously alert, exhilarated by the possibilities on the shelves.

Stephen came back, carrying two mugs, his glasses misting up with the steam. We sat at the little table in front of the fireplace.

'I've got some biscuits if you're hungry.'

'That's new,' I said. 'You never had biscuits before.'

'It's Lucy,' he said. 'She brings them in. She's got a sweet tooth.'

'Lucy?'

'Your replacement. Or should I say, the new girl. You're irreplaceable, of course.'

'And you're charming,' I said, enjoying it as much as always. 'I think I've met her.'

He looked surprised. 'When?'

'A few weeks ago,' I said, trying to sound off-hand. I didn't want to tell him about the time I'd come to find a shoulder to cry on. He didn't need to know. 'I dropped in but you were out. It was a Wednesday. She said that's your day off.'

'She never mentioned it.'

'I didn't say who I was.'

He shook his head. 'You're such a dark horse. You should have told her to tell me. I've been worried about you. I wish you'd get a phone. At least then I could call you.'

I raised an eyebrow.

'I know, I know. You don't like to be disturbed. You can look after yourself. But I haven't seen you since your party.'

I smiled, remembering the people spilling out onto the street, laughing and chattering. There had been music and even some dancing, right there on the pavement. I'd worn my best dress and high-heeled shoes. Stephen had made a speech and they had raised their glasses in my honour.

To Nora and her bookshop! I had been flattered.

You knew a lot of people, I thought. Why did you push them all away?

'So what's made you so busy that you don't have time to see us? I thought the whole point of being retired was that you could go around paying visits.'

I didn't know what to say. When I had first been tired, I hadn't been able to tell him why. It was partly the shame of it. I hadn't wanted to talk about things like that, to mention those parts of my body. But it was pride as well. I didn't want his pity. I had taken him on years before, taught him how to run the shop, passed on the tricks of the trade. I had enjoyed it, had been pleased that there would be someone who could be trusted to do things the right way, the way that I'd been taught. But when I sold him the shop it was a terrible wrench. I had looked after it, shaped it, watched it grow. It was like giving away a child. Stephen had understood, keeping me on two days a week, an arrangement that suited us both. When I had finally realized I couldn't do it any more, I hadn't been able to admit that I was ill. I had blamed it on old age and he had believed me.

I didn't want to tell him about Rose, either. I could picture his face as I told him I'd taken in someone I didn't know, someone with a baby. He'd think that I'd gone mad.

'Oh, this and that,' I said. 'I've had a lot to sort out.'

He knew me well enough not to pursue it.

'Well, at least you'll have had plenty of time to read.'

I realized I hadn't read anything but the manuals for weeks. In the same way that I had stayed away from the bookshop I'd stopped reading, as if I were shutting myself off from the world completely. I looked at the shelves, at the names of writers who had kept close counsel with me, sitting through candle-lit dinners and sharing my bed at night. I had spent charmed hours with them. I had been drunk in their company. I wanted to be drunk again. I was tired of facts. I had been reading about the implications of my illness for long enough. I wanted to lose myself, to dive into a story that made me hold my breath as if I were swimming underwater, my body weightless, swept along by a current of words.

'Actually, I haven't been reading that much,' I said. 'Can you think of anything you'd recommend?'

He frowned, tapping his upper lip with his finger. Then he grinned.

'I've got some boxes that have just come in, from someone who's moving abroad. I bought them as a job lot, so I've no idea what's in them. But we could have a look through.'

I remembered the finds we had made over the years, the thrill of coming across something unexpected. I smiled back at him. 'That's a wonderful idea.'

He brought out four cardboard boxes from the back room and put them down in front of me. We began to sort through them. I was happy, relishing the job, something more than household chores. We worked for half an hour and when all the books were sorted, we sat back and looked at the piles that we'd made.

'Why don't you take a couple?' he said. 'Close your eyes and pick them out. Leave it to luck.'

I remembered Stephen's love of taking a chance.

'All right,' I said. 'Why not?'

He spread out some books on the table.

'Close your eyes.'

He took hold of my shoulders and steered me in the right direction. My fingers brushed against cloth bindings and flimsy paperbacks.

'Go on,' he said. 'Just pick.'

I pointed at random. 'This one . . . and this . . .'

'Now you can look.'

In his right hand he held a novel by Thomas Hardy that I hadn't read since I was a girl. In his left was Mary Shelley's

Frankenstein. I was pleased. I had always felt an odd sympathy for the monster.

Stephen looked slightly crestfallen. 'You've read them before, haven't you?' he said.

'It doesn't matter. There'll be bits I don't remember.'

He saw me to the door.

'Come again,' he said. 'Soon. Don't stay away.'

I nodded.

'Mind how you go,' he said, waving as I set off down the street.

*

I felt cheered by my visit to Stephen. I made my way along the pavement, pleasantly invisible, light and free, of no interest to the shoppers who struggled past, laden with bags. But before long, Rose and the baby crept into my thoughts. Children were everywhere, being pushed along in prams or strapped to their mothers' chests in strange contraptions. I imagined Rose waking up to find me gone. I hadn't thought to leave a note. I began to feel guilty.

As I walked past the chemist's I saw a display in the window, cardboard cut-outs of laughing children. I decided to buy Rose some things to make up for my sudden disappearance.

When I went inside, there was the usual shuffling as the shop assistants jostled to avoid serving me, slipping one by one into the back room where they prepared the prescriptions. I pretended not to notice and went up to the counter. The girl behind it seemed preoccupied, rearranging the boxes of medicine, brisk in her neat white uniform. I knew that she was perfectly aware of my presence.

I cleared my throat. The girl looked up. She was frowning.

'I'm sorry,' she said, not meeting my eyes, 'I can't sell you any more painkillers. It's too soon. You bought some last week.'

It was true. I knew all the chemist's shops on the Holloway Road, flitting between them to get enough pills. This one sold the best and strongest medicine, in plain white packets with instructions in a script I couldn't read. I guessed at the dose, taking the pills until the pain went away. I was never sure if I'd left enough time between my visits to the shop. Usually, I began to tremble at the prospect of a refusal as soon as I went in the door. But this time I held my head high, buoyed up by my morning with Stephen.

'I don't want medicine,' I said. 'I'm here to buy things for a child. A baby.'

'A baby?'

'Yes. A small one, just born.'

For the first time in all the months that I had been going there, she smiled.

'A grandchild! Is it a boy or a girl?'

I seemed to have become respectable. I decided not to contradict her.

'A little girl. She was born two days ago.'

'Has she got a name?'

I was eager with my reply. 'Yes. She's called Grace.'

The girl nodded approvingly. 'That's a lovely name.'

'I chose it myself,' I said.

It was as if I had given her some sort of password. She came out from behind the counter and led me to a part of the shop I'd never seen before, a whole wall crammed with packets and bottles, cartons and jars, everything pink or blue or white. I didn't know what Rose needed. I had no idea what was in the holdall she'd brought with her. I wondered how prepared she'd been. She might have had all these things already. But then I thought of the shabby little room I'd found her in and I doubted it. I bought everything the girl suggested and she packed it all up into bags. By the time I left we were almost friends. She even held the door open for me as I went.

*

When I got back to the house, Rose was in the kitchen. I unpacked my bags and laid out what I had bought.

'This is for you,' I said. 'I mean, for the baby.'

Rose touched the packages one by one, looking dazed.

'But Nora,' she said, 'you didn't have to buy anything for us.'

'I wanted to,' I muttered, embarrassed. 'I wanted to help. She needs those things. And who else is there to look after you?'

*

That night I couldn't sleep. Memories tumbled over each other, almost faster than I could think them, jostling for attention, clawing me back from my new preoccupations as if they were jealous of the baby and Rose. I tossed and turned, and then the night sweats came, terrible sweats that smelled of disease and decay. The sheets grew damp. In the early hours of the morning, I decided to take a bath.

I didn't switch on the light in the corridor. I'd made my way along it in the dark often enough. When I felt tiles against the soles of my feet I knew I'd reached the bathroom. I closed the door behind me and leaned against it, relieved. As part of my preparations for Rose, I had polished and scoured, pouring bleach over every surface, scrubbing between the tiles with a toothbrush, ruthless with the germs. Now I inhaled its icy cleanliness, liking the smell.

I took a towel from the airing cupboard and put it on the heater to warm. I turned the hot tap as far as it would go and went over to the window-ledge, where my cold cream and talcum powder stood next to Rose's collection of bottles and tubes. I flipped open the tops of some of them, squeezing out small smears onto the back of my hand. I sniffed at unfamiliar scents.

It was a long time since I had let myself open the box but the new scents made me think of it and once the thought was there, I couldn't help it. I went back over to the cupboard, felt under the piles of linen and took out the old blue tin. I traced its battered edges with my fingers then lifted the lid, releasing a sweet, dusty smell. I handled the contents carefully, like relics, running my fingers over the lipstick and the matching powder compact in its golden case. Although I knew it had dried up years before, I took the stopper from the bottle of scent and touched it to my throat.

I switched off the light so as not to see myself as I pulled my nightdress over my head and stepped into the bath, wincing at the heat. I lowered my body down slowly. I sat for a moment, feeling the steam rise up around me, then lay back in the darkness.

The radio was in its usual place on the stool next to the tub. I switched it on. A woman spoke, her voice soothing and low, reciting the familiar list.

There are warnings of gales in Tyne, Dogger, German Bight, Humber, Thames, Dover, Wight, Portland, Plymouth, Biscay, Fitzroy, Sole, Irish Sea, Shannon and Rockall. The general synopsis at 0100: Low Malin 992 expected Northern Ireland 996 by 0100 tomorrow. Low 200 miles west of Fitzroy 1008 expected Thames 996 by same time.

Everything about it was right, the words and the way that she said them, like a poem or a song. The music came afterwards, a waltz for the end of an evening. I brought my hands to my face, spreading my fingers, feeling my skin stretched tight over my jaw. I moved them down, tracing the tendons in my neck, two knotty ropes tied to my collarbone, attached to shoulders that fitted easily under my palms. I touched my chest, flattened like pillows after a sleepless night. My belly, in contrast, was a hard, high mound. I rested my hands on it, feeling a pulse beat clear and strong. I held on tight, as if it were a lifebuoy bobbing about on the sea.

Stormy waters ahead, I thought, wondering if I would manage to stay afloat.

*

On my way back to the bedroom, I bumped into Rose, who was standing at the top of the stairs in the dark. I felt myself flush, as if I'd been caught doing something I shouldn't. Rose was awkward too.

'I couldn't sleep,' she stammered. 'I was going to get a glass of water.'

She looked like a little girl in her pyjamas. I felt a sudden rush of tenderness towards her.

'I can't sleep either,' I said. 'Come on, I'll make us something to drink.'

When we got to the kitchen, Rose stood by the table, looking ill at ease.

'Sit down,' I said, 'I'll do it.'

She sank down onto one of the chairs and I brought a blanket, tucking it around her. I pulled the old bolster across the bottom of the door to keep out draughts, then poured milk into a pan and stood at the stove, stirring it with a wooden spoon. The faint hiss of the gas was the only sound in the room. When the milk began to pucker, I poured it into two mugs and carried them over to the table.

'Drink it whilst it's hot,' I said, pushing one of the mugs towards her. 'Go on. It'll help you sleep.'

She picked it up and took a sip. Her hands were gripping the mug so hard that her knuckles were white. She looked miserable, her shoulders hunched and the colour drained from her face.

'Rose,' I said. 'Why are you so unhappy? What's wrong?'

'I'm sorry,' she said. 'Mum used to make me hot milk when I couldn't sleep.'

'Where is she?' I asked.

Rose shrugged. 'At home, I suppose.'

'Does she know about Grace?'

Rose shook her head. Her voice was fierce. 'She didn't want me to have her. She wanted me to get rid of her. She said that having a baby would ruin my life.'

I shifted uncomfortably in my chair.

'She told me I was making a fool of myself,' Rose went on bitterly. 'And that he'd taken advantage.'

I looked at her in horror. 'You don't mean that the baby's father—?'

'No!' she said. 'It wasn't like that. I was in love with him.' Her eyes were dark with anger. 'I thought he loved me too.'

She wouldn't say anything more about it. After those first furious words, she drank her milk quickly and went to bed, saying that she was tired. I stayed at the table for a long time afterwards, thinking.

Eight

Almost as soon as I had decided to stay in Kent, the war began in earnest and everything changed. Mrs Rivers stopped baking on Saturdays, and Sunday lunches were no longer feasts. Food was counted up and measured out into rations not big enough to cover the pattern on our plates. I dreamed of the end of winter and the arrival of summer, when Grace and I would climb trees again and swim in the Forgotten Lake but it didn't happen like that. By the time it was warm enough to stop wearing pullovers we had a new Prime Minister who said the Germans were getting closer. We followed their movements on Reverend Rivers' globe. France wasn't far from England. Like the Germans, evacuees were on the move but this time they weren't coming to Kent. They were leaving the apple orchards and the sea behind and heading north.

Grace and I kept quiet, hoping that no-one would think of sending me away but I soon began to understand that we didn't need to worry. What we did mattered very little. Reverend and Mrs Rivers were so wrapped up in their own unhappiness that they hardly noticed us. When I had first arrived at the rectory, I had been so captivated by my new world that I hadn't noticed the peculiar tension that hovered between them, but now I saw that something wasn't right. I was beginning to see how words left unsaid often meant more than ones spoken out loud. Solemn voices on the wireless at night told us to keep our eyes and ears open for things that were suspicious or kept hidden.

Things are not always what they seem, they said. *Look beyond what you see.*

But it was difficult to see through closed doors. Mrs Rivers continued to spend most of her time at the piano, practising scales for hours on end, and Reverend Rivers shut himself up in his study. The sound of her piano and the smell of his pipe smoke would drift under the doors of their rooms and hover uneasily in the hallway, as if even those disconnected parts of themselves couldn't bear to be together. I didn't know how married people were with one another. I couldn't remember Pa at home in Bethnal Green. I only knew Ma and me, who sat in one room together and slept in one bed at night. If being married was like this, I thought, I couldn't understand why people did it.

Saturdays were the worst, when we had no lessons because that was the day when Reverend Rivers wrote his sermon. As soon as breakfast was over he would hurry to his study and stay there until late at night, not even coming out to eat. Mrs Rivers would go to the drawing room and start her scales, stabbing her way up and down the keyboard. Grace and I would wash the dishes as quickly as we could and then slip out of the house to our new hiding place. We no longer dared go to the lake. The birds that I had watched from its banks the summer before had been replaced by fighter planes that swooped and dived, so low that they seemed close enough to reach out and touch. The newspapers called it Spitfire Summer after them and they were always there, roaring as they chased the German aeroplanes across the sky, their machine guns rattling in frantic bursts. Swarms of enemy bombers flew over like deadly black beetles, with fighter planes as escorts. The Spitfires danced among them, trying to shoot them down. We watched their sharp wings cut across the clouds, slicing through them, twisting like courting birds, and we tried to work out how they stayed up in the sky. Birds flapped their wings; we could understand them. The Spitfires were a raging, noisy mystery.

One Saturday at the beginning of July, Grace said that she wanted to show me something. As she led me through the graveyard to the back of the church, I began to feel uneasy, as if all the sadness of the people who had lost someone was hovering in the air. It was Reverend Rivers' territory, and I felt him there too, almost expecting him to come out from behind one of the gravestones.

'Where are we going?' I said.

Grace put her finger to her lips, bent down and began to rummage in a pile of flowerpots. After a moment she brought out a key. She turned to me and smiled.

'Here it is! I knew I'd find it.'

'I don't think we're supposed to play in church,' I said uncertainly. 'God wouldn't like it.'

'It's not for the church,' she said. 'And we're not playing. We're keeping safe from the Spitfires. We're finding sanctuary, like in the Bible. You should know, you're the one who likes reading and God.'

'Well then, where's it for?'

She led me to a little hut that was built onto the side of the church. 'Here.'

I was nervous. 'We'll be in trouble if anyone finds us.'

'But they won't, not if we only come here on Saturdays. Father's always busy with his sermons then and the only other people who come are the ladies to do the flowers on Fridays. We'll be perfectly safe, I promise. It'll be our special place.'

She put the key in the lock, turned it and pushed open the door. I followed her inside. It smelled like the church; of dead flowers, damp and old wax. Vases that I recognized from Sunday services stood on a shelf that ran along the back wall. The floor was covered with leaves and twigs. In the corner were buckets, a dustpan and a brush.

'We can clean it up,' Grace said. 'We'll make it nice. It'll be a house all of our own.'

From then on, every Saturday, as soon as Reverend and Mrs Rivers had shut themselves up in their rooms, we would slip out of the rectory, through the vegetable patch, into the graveyard and around the back of the church to the hut. We swept out the leaves and brushed away the cobwebs, using upturned buckets as chairs as we played at being ladies from the village drinking tea.

'Home sweet home!' Grace would say in a high, refined voice, holding out her little finger as she pretended to drink from a vase, and I would giggle. I loved the way she could mimic anyone she wanted, from the grumpy woman in the village shop to her own father when he read out his sermons in church. I knew it wasn't proper to laugh at a priest but she made it so funny I couldn't help myself.

As the summer went on, there were so many dogfights between the aeroplanes that we grew used to them and stopped being frightened. When we heard the sound of aircraft engines approaching we brought out our buckets and sat in the doorway with our hands held to our ears, waiting to catch the first glimpse of them. They were beautiful as they wheeled and turned, the sunlight reflecting off their silver wings. The vapour trails that came after them made patterns in the sky. But one day they came too close and we were frightened all over again. We heard them before we saw them, a low humming noise becoming louder by the minute and then they were suddenly there, two planes chasing each other. It was impossible to tell who was after whom. The roar of the engines filled our ears as we hunched on our buckets, frozen at the noise, then the machine guns started, clattering like a thousand hailstones smashing against a roof. Spent ammunition bounced off the gravestones, then there was an almighty crash and Grace screamed as one of the planes swooped over our heads, so close that it seemed about to fly straight into the church. I looked up and saw the pilot in his leather helmet and goggles, his eyes wide and staring straight at us.

'Run!' shouted Grace and we sprinted as fast as we could, over the graves, through the gate, across the rows of cabbages and peas and into the rectory through the back door. We leaned against the wall, gasping for breath.

'We were lucky,' I said. 'I thought that was it. I thought—'

Grace shot me a peculiar, warning look and I stopped talking. She was frowning, her head tilted to one side, listening to something. Two voices became clearer until we could make out every word. Reverend and Mrs Rivers were arguing. I had never heard either of them raise their voice before but now they were practically shouting.

'I cannot understand why you find it so hard to allow me any comfort,' said Mrs Rivers. 'You know perfectly well that playing my piano is the only way I can forget.'

'But I have specifically asked you not to play on Saturdays. It's distracting. I need to concentrate on my sermon,' said Reverend Rivers. 'Tomorrow the congregation will expect me to attempt to make sense out of these attacks. I have to give them some sort of reassurance.'

'Reassurance!' Mrs Rivers sounded bitter. 'It's all very well your reassuring everyone else in the village. What about me?'

'I have a duty to the parish. Terrible things are happening. Men will be called away to fight and some of them will be killed.'

'I wish they'd drop a bomb on this house. And on the church,' said Mrs Rivers. 'At least that would put a stop to all of this.'

'Evelyn! That's a wicked thing to say. I refuse to believe that you mean it.'

'I do mean it,' Mrs Rivers said in a flat voice. 'You know I do.'

I looked at Grace. She had gone very pale. I decided that it was better to be outside with the bombers than in the rectory listening to this. She let me pull her to the door and through the graveyard back to the hut. We walked slowly, not caring any more about attacks. Once we were inside, we sat on the buckets. Grace was trembling.

'Are you all right?' I said carefully.

Her voice was bleak. 'I can't decide what's worse, them not talking to each other, or shouting like that. It's horrible.'

'But what was it about?'

'I don't know. She's been sad for as long as I can remember. And sometimes she gets so angry, like she was just now.'

Her shoulders began to heave. I put my arm around her and held her as she cried, feeling her tears soak into the thin material of my blouse.

We stayed in the hut until evening, when we were too hungry to wait there any longer. It was a warm night and the air was so calm and still that it was hard to believe what had happened that afternoon. A haze of heat hung over the fields and my nose twitched at the smell of freshly mown grass. The only sound from the skies was the call of a cuckoo, somewhere far away. Nothing bad could happen on an evening like this, I thought. And sure enough, when we walked into the kitchen, Mrs Rivers was waiting for us, smiling as if nothing had happened and buttering bread for our supper. Her eyes were red but she had put powder on her face and combed her hair. I thought of the pamphlet that had come in the post from the new Prime Minister, Mr Churchill.

Be Careful What You Say! Like Everyone Else, You Will Hear Things That The Enemy Mustn't Know. Keep That Knowledge to Yourself – And Don't Give Away Any Clues. Keep Smiling. There's a Lot of Worry and Grief in the World – And You Can Lessen it by Being Good-Tempered and Considerate.

So I didn't ask anything about Mrs Rivers wanting the rectory to be bombed. And I didn't tell Grace what I saw later on that evening. Reverend Rivers didn't come to supper. After we had eaten, Grace went to take a bath and I helped Mrs Rivers with the dishes. When we had finished, she picked up her sewing and I pretended to be engrossed in *Rebecca*, which Grace and I were taking turns to read, keeping it out of Reverend Rivers' sight. We had stolen it from a box of books donated for the village fête. Neither of us had read anything like it before. It was the only book I'd ever seen Grace pick up outside our lessons. She said she was in love with Maxim de Winter, the hero.

I knew that Mrs Rivers wouldn't notice what I was reading. She was distracted, making a few stitches at a time, then going back to unpick what she had done and starting all over again. Suddenly she caught her breath. I looked over at her. She had pricked her finger. Tears were swimming in her eyes.

'Excuse me, Nora,' she muttered, and hurried out of the room. I waited for a moment and then slipped out after her, following as she stumbled across the garden to the graveyard, her arms wrapped around her body as if she were trying to hold herself together. I ducked behind the hut, where I stayed, watching her closely. She stopped and looked down at one of the graves. Her legs seemed to give way underneath her and she fell to the ground.

I wondered what it meant, if Mrs Rivers' unhappiness was because of a lost romance that she had to keep hidden for always, if the rectory held secrets like the great house in *Rebecca*. When at last she left, picking her way unsteadily back through the graveyard, I went over to the grave. I was disappointed with what I found. The cross was bare, without an inscription, just rough grey stone, as bleak as Mrs Rivers' face.

*

When September came I thought Ma might come to visit for my birthday but the Blitz began, trapping her in London. Nearly three years would pass before she came to Kent. By then I was sixteen.

Many things changed while I was waiting for her to come. Every day the wireless brought news and it was usually bad. For fifty-seven nights I listened to hear where the latest Blitz attacks had been, anxiously praying that Ma would be all right. When Germany invaded Russia, I borrowed books from Reverend Rivers to find out what Russia was like; thick, heavy books that described a very different sort of countryside to Kent. We spent less time in the fields and woods and more in the vegetable patch, digging for victory as we were told to, planting row after row of cauliflowers. One week there was a special collection for rosehips, and we gathered buckets of them from the hedgerows, taking them to the sour-faced woman in the village shop who paid us threepence a pound.

There was never enough of anything and, as if our bodies were doing it to spite us and the ration books, we were both growing taller, filling out. Neither of us fitted into our clothes and finding shoes became impossible, so most of the time we went about in gumboots. Mrs Rivers helped us cut down her old dresses but Grace had no patience for sewing and my stitches were messy and loose. Our hems drooped and our seams fell apart as we dug in the garden.

Books were the only things that weren't in short supply. Reverend Rivers continued with our lessons and I liked them even more than before. I had lost some of my shyness, becoming quick to answer his questions and daring to come up with some of my own, as if I were building myself up out of the things that I read. Grace and I didn't see much of the other girls in the village. She had never known them especially well because she had always gone away to school. Besides, there was a peculiar distance between the rectory and the people who came to the church every Sunday. We even sat in a different part of it, in the pews near the altar. But I didn't mind. When I wasn't with Grace, I was reading, finding new friends on the pages.

Sometimes it was a relief to be alone. After Spitfire Summer, I had started to feel things, strange things that made me afraid. I didn't tell Grace everything any more. I didn't want her to know about the dreams I had, troubling dreams that jolted me awake at night. I would make out Grace's shape under the bedclothes, rising and falling as she breathed, imagining myself drawing back the blanket, then the sheet, lifting her nightdress so that I could see her body's new curves. I wanted to touch her skin. I wanted to press myself close to her, winding around her like the creeper that covered the front wall of the rectory.

I knew that if I told her I would ruin everything. I followed the rules. I was careful what I said. But the rules didn't say I couldn't think about her. I thought about her all the time.

*

The morning of Ma's visit, I woke early. I tiptoed out of bed and pushed aside the blackout. Light was just beginning to creep over the treetops. It would be a sunny day, like when I had arrived at the rectory. She would come on the train like I had. I tried to picture Ma, sitting in the corner of a compartment, looking out at the same fields I'd looked at, the hundred shades of green.

Taking care not to wake Grace, I slipped back into bed and reached into the drawer of the little table that stood between us. I took out the picture of the Virgin and Child that Ma had given me in the playground. I looked at it whenever I wanted to remember her. I lay on my stomach and traced the Virgin's face with my finger, wondering if under her veil her hair was long and dark like Ma's. Grace yawned in her sleep and shifted. I kissed the Virgin's forehead.

'I'll see you soon,' I whispered, and put the picture back in the drawer.

*

I wanted to look nice for her, to make her proud. I wanted her to see how much Grace and I looked like each other. We were both tall now, taller than Mrs Rivers. The only difference between us was our hair. Grace's was pale blonde like winter sunshine. I was dark like Ma. But apart from that we were each other's mirror image. It made William laugh and clown around, pretending to mistake one of us for the other. The army hadn't wanted to take him and so he had joined the Home Guard. He spent hours patrolling the orchards around the village, looking for Germans and practising his shots. He taught us how to use his air rifle, using apples as targets. They exploded in a dramatic, satisfying way, filling the air with the smell of fruit. But the day of Ma's visit wasn't the time for shooting apples. Grace and I wanted to look like ladies.

She was almost as excited as I was. After breakfast, she made me close my eyes, then put something cool and smooth into my hands. It was her soap ration. Grace had started to care about being clean. It wasn't like when I had first arrived in Kent, when she had never minded if she ripped her clothes climbing trees or got dirty running through the fields. Now she spent hours in the bathroom every morning, rubbing soap into her skin inch by inch and rinsing it off with jugs of water. Her ration was precious and I was touched.

'Thank you,' I whispered.

'There's something else for when you've washed,' she said. 'Go on, hurry up.'

*

Her idea was like all of her plans, thrilling but slightly dangerous. She wouldn't listen to my doubts.

'Come on, Nora,' she said, taking my hand and pulling me after her. 'It's only a bedroom.'

I found it difficult to imagine a man sleeping there. Everything about it was like Mrs Rivers. The wallpaper was the colour of primroses, flowered curtains hung over the blackout and the bed was covered with a pink counterpane made of a shiny material. I couldn't picture Reverend Rivers sleeping under it. I couldn't picture him and Mrs Rivers sharing such a small space, but this was the bed they slept in together every night, the proof. The thought of it made my cheeks grow hot and I turned away so that Grace wouldn't see. When I turned back to her she was sitting on a stool at a dressing table that had three mirrors, like the paintings in church at home; a main one in the middle and two smaller ones at its sides. On the table were a silver hairbrush, a jar of face cream and a tray that held a tangle of hairgrips and the string of pearls that Mrs Rivers wore on Sundays. Grace was holding a bottle filled with something golden.

'Look at Mummy's scent,' she said. 'It's lovely. Come and smell it.'

She shifted along the stool and I sat down next to her.

'Let's put some on,' she said.

I was beginning to feel uneasy. 'I don't think we should. You know it's rationed.'

'She won't mind. And we won't use very much of it. Your mother's coming all the way from London to see you. You want to smell nice for her, don't you? I bet you anything she'll be wearing scent.'

I didn't think Ma had ever worn scent. I'd never seen a bottle like this in our house.

'I'll put some on your throat and your wrists,' said Grace. 'That's what Mummy does. You can put some on me too. Come on, hold up your hair.'

I lifted my hair and she squeezed the little pink bulb at the neck of the bottle. I felt a cool mist against my skin and smelled lemons.

'Now you put some on me.'

She held out her wrists and I squeezed the bulb. She rubbed them together then brought them to her throat.

'Did you know that scent smells different on every person?' she said.

I shook my head.

'It's true.'

'I believe you.' I breathed in, feeling giddy.

'Smell it on me,' she said.

'I can smell it already.'

'You need to smell it on my skin. Here.' She pointed to her throat.

I didn't move.

'Go on, silly!'

I pressed the tip of my nose to the hollow at the base of her throat, closed my eyes and inhaled. I smelled the same fresh scent that was in the air but under it, Grace's own smell, heady and unsettling.

*

The combined smell of Mrs Rivers and Grace stayed in my nose as I waited for Ma, standing on tiptoe to catch a glimpse of the bus. I gave myself a little shake. Ma was coming. As soon as I saw her, sitting on the back seat, peering out of the window, I felt as if my heart would burst with happiness.

'Ma!' I shouted, waving at her. I ran to the door of the bus and there she was, standing in front of me, my mother, whom I had wished for so many times as I laid in bed at night, my mother, who didn't keep secrets and never shut herself away from me, my mother, who couldn't play the piano and didn't wear scent. My mother. Ma.

We stood and looked at one another. She seemed smaller than when I had left her in the schoolyard. Then she had bent to kiss me goodbye. Now it was me who had to bend to kiss her. We held onto each other tightly and I breathed in a smell that I had forgotten, her smell: carbolic soap and sweat. When we finally let go, Ma took hold of both my hands.

'Oh, Nora,' she said quietly.

When Reverend Rivers had asked me if I wanted to stay in Kent or go back to London I had still been angry with Ma for sending me away. I had fallen in love with the world of the rectory, a place where everything seemed possible. And so I had chosen my new family, the Rivers, over Ma. I had told myself that they wanted me and that she had not. Now I was ashamed. I smiled, a small unhappy smile.

'Come and see where I live,' I said, and turned towards the rectory.

As we came close to it my stomach began to heave with anticipation. I rang the doorbell as if I were a visitor, suddenly shy. Footsteps sounded in the hallway and then Mrs Rivers was in front of us.

I watched them look each other up and down.

Mrs Rivers was the first to speak. 'Mrs Lynch. I'm Evelyn Rivers. How do you do?'

'Thank you for looking after Nora,' Ma said.

'We're very fond of her. She's a credit to you.'

I looked at my feet, wondering where Grace was. The next

minute she appeared behind Mrs Rivers, smiling at Ma. I felt like everything was all right again.

'Hello,' she said.

I wondered if Ma found her voice lovely like I did. I said a little prayer in my head.

Please God, let them see each other like I do.

*

Reverend Rivers came out of his study to join us for afternoon tea. Mrs Rivers had been saving up our rations and it was like the first Sunday all over again. There were egg and tomato sandwiches with the crusts cut off, arranged on one of the plates with blue flowers around the rim. She had made scones and there was even jam to go on them, made with raspberries that we had picked from the garden. Best of all was the cake, two layers of sponge, dusted with sugar like morning frost.

I saw Ma's eyes grow wide as she walked into the dining room. I wanted to be alone with her, to tell her that I had thought the same; that I had found it hard to believe that there could be a whole room just to eat in. I wanted to warn her that there would be strange silences as we ate and that Mrs Rivers always pushed her food around her plate without eating very much of it. I wanted to tell her that Reverend Rivers came alive when he was teaching us and that Mrs Rivers could play the piano so beautifully that it made me cry. I wanted to tell Grace things too. I wanted to take her hand and run out of the back door, through the fields to the Forgotten Lake where I would tell her that in London my mother wasn't timid and quiet like a mouse, that in London she could stand up to anyone. Instead, I was trapped in the dining room, perched on a chair, not knowing what to say.

Ma's skin looked as if a layer of dust had settled over it. Her forehead was crossed with lines that I hadn't seen before and she had a new habit of pressing her lips together as if she were biting them. Her hair wasn't the shiny black that I remembered, but smudged with grey, and dusty like her skin. She answered Mrs Rivers' questions so quietly that it was difficult to catch her words. Her voice seemed out of place in the rectory, next to the polished furniture and fine china, and I began to feel uneasy. The feeling grew as I saw Ma looking at me with puzzlement in her eyes and I realized that just as her voice sounded strange to me, the way that I spoke now was odd to her. I remembered how Grace had giggled at the way I said roses. Since then I had tried to copy her, to make my voice like hers. As the afternoon wore on, I heard myself speak with Ma's ears. I became lost in my sentences, caught up in the sound of what I was saying, knowing that Ma was trying to understand how I had become a stranger.

It was during an especially long pause that Ma reached for the shopping basket that she had brought with her.

'Nora love, I made you a birthday present. But you've grown. I don't know—'

She passed me a package wrapped in newspaper. I stared dumbly at the headlines, trying to put off the moment when I would have to open it, knowing that it would be something that would not fit into the rectory world.

'Go on, open it!' said Grace.

I picked apart the knotted string and lifted back the folds of newspaper. My present was a cardigan knitted out of greyish wool, a cardigan made for a child. It was something I would have worn when I was still Ma's little girl, when she was everything to me. I understood then that things would never go back to how they had been before the war. I tried not to look disappointed but I could see from Ma's face that I hadn't managed it. There was another pause and then Mrs Rivers was kind.

'What a pretty cardigan!' she said.

'I'll unravel it,' muttered Ma. 'I'll make it into socks.'

It was too late to pretend that things were all right. I hung my head in shame, wanting the visit to be over. When at last it was, I walked with Ma down the front path through the garden, carrying her basket with the cardigan stuffed back into it. I felt it bump against my leg like my gasmask when I had walked out of the school-yard and away from her. I wanted it to hit me hard, to leave a bruise as a punishment.

When the bus came, Ma turned to me. She lifted her hands to my face and held it for a moment, a strange, fierce look in her eyes.

'You'll always be my girl, Nora,' she said. 'And I'll always be your Ma.'

She pressed her lips to my forehead, then took her bags from me and climbed up the steps.

Nine

AFTER OUR LATE-NIGHT TALK IN THE KITCHEN, I AVOIDED
discussions that could turn into more than an exchange of facts,
talking instead about practical things. Rose did the same. The child
was our main topic of conversation, our diversion from the compli-
cations of the past. She was our excuse for early nights, and we both
withdrew to the safety of our rooms as soon as supper was over. We
circled about each other like this for almost two weeks, separate and
pleasantly polite. I knew all about keeping secrets, but I was curious.
I wanted to know what had happened to Rose to make her hide
herself away. If we were talking about her, I thought, then at least we
would not be talking about me. One morning, as we were having
breakfast, I came out with it.

'Rose, who is Grace's father?'

She sighed, as if she'd been expecting the question.

'He's an academic. I met him in my first week at college.' A flush stole across her cheeks. 'Well, I didn't exactly meet him. I went to one of his lectures.'

I remembered girls from the university near the shop, coming with their reading lists, chattering loudly, their bags stuffed full of papers. I found it difficult to imagine Rose in that world. She was too quiet, too withdrawn.

'What was it about?'

'History. The Second World War.'

I shivered involuntarily.

'I hadn't expected lecturers to be like him. He wasn't much older than us. And he was so excited about what he was saying. He didn't even use any notes. I went to all his lectures after that. I took in a tape recorder, one of those small ones like journalists use, and I'd play it back at night in bed. It was like he was there with me. One day I went up and asked him a question. We got talking and he gave me the name of some books he thought I should read. I spent all week in the library so I'd have finished them by the next time I saw him. He seemed impressed that I'd bothered. We went for coffee. I couldn't believe that someone like him was interested in anything I had to say. For the first time since I'd got there, I felt like I belonged.'

I knew what was coming. I recognized the plot.

'We had a drink a few days later, in a pub by the river. It was still warm enough to sit outside. There weren't very many people about. We drank beer and talked until closing time. I remember looking at the water while he went to the bar and thinking it was all perfect. I was so happy. We stayed until it was dark.'

There were no surprises to her story. She had begun to sleep with him, secretly of course. He had a wife, another academic.

'I went to one of her lectures,' Rose said. 'I didn't really listen to what she said. I wanted to see what she looked like.'

The flush in her cheeks darkened.

'I didn't feel guilty at all. I just wanted her to be gone so I could have him. But she turned up one day at his study. I was frightened by how calm she was. It was worse than if she'd shouted and screamed.'

'"Don't think you're the first girl I've found here," she said. "And I'm sure you won't be the last."'

'She told me to get out and I went as fast as I could. There were only a few days of term to go so I packed my things and got the train home. I couldn't think what else to do. I wasn't looking forward to the holidays. It was the first Christmas without Dad.'

She stopped abruptly, as if she hadn't meant to say it.

'What do you mean?'

Rose shook her head. 'I don't want to talk about it. I can't.' Her voice was bitter. 'I just wanted to hide myself away in my room but I couldn't. I had to be with Mum. She kept inviting people round. They wanted to know all about university. I couldn't tell them I hadn't made any friends because I was only interested in my lecturer and that he was married and I'd slept with him anyway. I kept hearing Mum talking about me, being proud. I couldn't stand it.'

She was speaking quickly now, as if she wanted to get the story over with.

'I felt sick all through the holidays. I couldn't eat. Then on Christmas Eve we were watching television and suddenly I knew what was the matter. It was a nativity play, and when I saw the baby in the manger I just knew. We were supposed to be going to my aunt's for dinner but I told Mum I was feeling awful. I must have looked pretty bad because she believed me. As soon as she left I went to find a chemist's. It took hours to find one that was open. There was nobody in there except me. I picked up the first test I saw. The shop assistant said *Happy Christmas* but I couldn't say anything back. I just ran out.

'I didn't want to do the test at home, so I went to the pub on the corner of our street. I couldn't think of anywhere else to go. I went to the toilet at the back. It was horrible. My feet kept sticking to the floor. Someone started banging on the door while I was waiting for it to work but I couldn't say anything to her, not even that I'd be out in a minute. I counted up the cigarette ends on the floor while I was waiting for the second line. I went cold all over when it showed up. I read the leaflet again to be sure but I knew it was right. I couldn't move. I just sat there, staring at it, until someone else knocked on the door and I realized I'd been in there for ages.'

The baby stirred in her sleep.

'Do you think she can hear me?' Rose said, worried.

'No,' I said gently. 'Go on.'

She dropped her voice. 'We always have a special breakfast on Christmas Day. Dad and I used to bring it up to Mum in bed. I was trying to pretend everything was all right. I'd even made her a stocking like he used to, just a few little things, but when she was opening her presents, all I could think about was the baby and what I was going to do.

'As soon as she'd opened the last one she asked me what was wrong. I knew I wouldn't get away with lying. She went mad when I told her. I've never seen her so angry. She asked me all sorts of questions. She wanted to know everything.

'She made me tell her who the father was. She went on and on about it. She wanted to phone the university and report him. I told her I'd started it. I said it was my fault. She said she didn't understand how I could have been so stupid. I knew she was right.

'"Well, at least it's not too late to get an abortion," she said. "The clinics will be open after Boxing Day. We'll phone them first thing in the morning."

'I knew it didn't make sense to keep the baby. I knew I could get rid of it over the holidays and go back to college without anyone finding out. Nobody would know except me and Mum. But I didn't want to go back. I thought of what his wife had said, about him having lots of girls. I felt stupid. I didn't want to see him again.

'I told her I wouldn't have an abortion. She said I'd regret it for the rest of my life and I'd ruin my chances of ever doing anything interesting. Then she said something really awful.

'"If you go through with this you'll go nowhere. Your whole education will go to waste. You'll end up like I did."

'I'd always thought I'd had a happy childhood. It was suddenly as if all that had been a lie. I ran up to my bedroom. She tried to come in. I heard her knocking at the door but I wouldn't talk to her. I left that night after she'd gone to bed. I took all the money I could find. I hung around the bus station all night. It was freezing. There weren't any buses because it was Christmas so I had to wait until morning. I caught the first one to London. I couldn't think of anywhere else to go. I found a job in a bar and stayed there until I started to show, then they kicked me out. They didn't want a pregnant barmaid. I'd been sharing a flat above the bar with the other girls who worked there but when I got the sack I had to move out. I didn't want to live with anyone after that. I wanted to be on my own. That's how I ended up in the bedsit.'

'Have you spoken to your mother since then?' I asked.

A stubborn look passed over her face, and she hugged the baby close to her. I noticed her nails, bitten to the quick.

'No,' she said. 'I don't want her to know where I am. She'd only take over, like she always does. And I can't forgive her. I never will.'

'And Grace's father?'

'I don't want to see him again.' She shook her head. 'You know, it's funny; I used to think about him a lot when I was sitting at the window. But now I can't even remember what he looks like. I remember lots of things about him but I can't remember his face. I don't know why. It's strange.'

I didn't think it was at all strange. I understood it very well. My memories of Grace never added up to how she really was. As the years passed, it was almost as if I had imagined her. My memory was never any match for the truth of her, and she was always impossible to pin down, dancing just out of my reach, exactly as she did when she was alive.

Ten

It was so very nearly all right. If it weren't for what happened next, I would have counted the war as the happiest time of my life. But once it all began, one thing led to another until it wasn't all right at all.

I brooded over Ma's visit for a long time, trying to puzzle out why it had gone so wrong. I had been ashamed of her and ashamed of myself for feeling it and now something between us was broken. She would always be Ma but she wasn't the one who meant the most to me any more. I had hoped that the things I had started to feel for Grace would go away but they didn't. After Ma's visit they grew stronger, leaving no space in my mind for anything else. No matter how hard I tried, I couldn't get rid of them. They were like the weeds that grew in Mrs Rivers' vegetable patch, which came back however many times you pulled them out because the roots were still there under the surface, ready to sprout all over again.

I thought of how I had come to the rectory, frightened and bleeding, and of how Mrs Rivers had comforted me by saying I was no different to other girls. If I could find someone who felt like me I would feel better, I thought, and I began to search, reading as many books as I could, late into the night, moving my eyes quickly over the pages until the words became a blur.

Shakespeare came the closest of anyone to describing it. I was bewitched by his plays, worlds made up of words, the opposite to the silent rectory, full of things that were left unsaid. Reverend Rivers had been shocked to find that I didn't know who Shakespeare was. One morning he had taken down a heavy, important-looking book from the shelf and put it on the desk between us.

'Can either of you tell me what this is?' he asked.

Grace shrugged. Annoyance flickered in his eyes and he turned to me. 'Nora?' he said, sounding hopeful.

I hated to disappoint him. I wondered if it was something religious.

'The Bible?' I guessed. It was about the right size, I thought.

He frowned. 'Let me give you some clues. These are the collected works of a playwright who lived from 1564 to 1616. He was from Stratford-upon-Avon. His plays include *Hamlet*, *Julius Caesar* and *Macbeth*.' He said the titles in the same way that he announced the readings in church, as if they were significant.

I shook my head.

'Do you mean to say you've never heard of William Shakespeare?'

'No,' I whispered. 'They didn't teach us that at school.'

For a moment, he looked as if he didn't believe me. Then a gleam came into his eye, a spark that I had seen before, when he was particularly excited about teaching us something new.

'Well then, Nora, you're in luck. You have some of the

greatest writing in the English language here, just waiting for you to discover it.'

Grace was staring out of the window, looking bored.

'The history plays would be the most appropriate to start with, I suppose. They have so much to say about war. But I prefer the tragedies. We'll begin with *King Lear*.'

Grace let out a groan.

'What's the matter?' he said.

'I don't like Shakespeare,' she muttered.

'You're impossible! If you're not careful, I'll stop teaching you altogether. You'll end up knowing nothing.'

She tossed her head. 'I mean, I don't like Shakespeare when it's all about battles and kings. It's dull. Can't we read something with a love story? What about *Romeo and Juliet*? Nora would like it better, I know she would.'

'No,' he said firmly. 'Nora will start with *King Lear*.'

They glared at each other for a moment. Reverend Rivers looked away first. Grace rolled her eyes at me and shrugged.

We read the play out loud. After each speech Reverend Rivers made us stop and talk about what was happening and what the characters meant by what they said. I was surprised that he liked this play, filled with wildness and extremes. I looked at him with new interest as he paced about the room, waving his arms in the air as he spoke.

'Listen to the language!' he said. 'Ask yourselves why Shakespeare has chosen these particular words. Try to imagine what would be happening on stage.'

Grace had the part of Cordelia. She read her lines in a flat, disinterested voice, not seeming to care whether or not they made sense. I could see Reverend Rivers struggling to keep calm. Eventually, he lost his temper.

'Grace!' he snapped. 'Will you at least *try* to make an effort? You'll find it much more interesting if you put some feeling into it. Listen to Nora. She's managing, and it's the first time she's read any Shakespeare at all.'

'It doesn't mean anything,' she said.

'What?'

'It's not real. I don't care what happens to any of them. They may as well die. What difference does it make?'

'Why must you insist on being so flippant?' he shouted. 'You're such a disappointment to me, Grace, you really are.'

She looked as him as if he had struck her, then pushed back her chair and ran out of the room. Reverend Rivers leaned against the fireplace with his head in his hands. I stood up to go after her, unsure of why he was so angry.

'Can I borrow it?' I asked timidly.

He looked at me as if he didn't know who I was.

'Borrow what?' he said.

'The Shakespeare. I'll be careful with it, I promise.'

He let out a deep sigh, then nodded. I picked up the heavy book and left quickly, anxious to avoid any more trouble.

I read all of Shakespeare's plays. From his lovers' speeches, I learned that I wasn't alone. The words were there. But they weren't words that girls said about girls. And I felt something more, something like King Lear's madness on the Heath, something violent and wild. I was afraid that one day I would be lost, not able to keep myself from touching her. I felt like a monster, like Caliban in love with Miranda, and I knew that no good could ever come of it.

*

Things were made worse by our new way of spending the afternoons. We had brought an end to our childish tea parties in the hut.

'I've had an idea,' said Grace one day.

'What is it?' I asked, feeling nervous. Grace's ideas were becoming more dangerous. The more reckless the plan, the more appealing she found it and I always followed because doing something forbidden kept us together in our little band of two. I would have done anything she suggested, and somehow she knew it.

She smiled. 'It's a good one. Kneel down, close your eyes and hold up your hands as if you're taking communion.'

The last time she had told me to close my eyes and hold out my hands, she had dropped a dead mouse into them, laughing at me when I screamed. I frowned at her.

'This time it's something good, I promise. It's nothing dead.'

I knew that there was no point in trying to resist. I got down on my knees, closed my eyes and held out my hands.

'For what you are about to receive,' said Grace, imitating the solemn voice that Reverend Rivers used in church, 'may the Lord make you truly thankful.'

'Amen,' I said, as if I really were at the altar rail. Something heavy dropped into my hands.

'You can open your eyes,' said Grace.

I looked down. 'What is it?'

Grace grinned. 'It's a key, silly.'

I gave her a little push. 'I mean, where's it for, what does it unlock?'

'It's for the vestry in church.'

'But why should we want to go into the vestry?'

Grace's grin grew wider. 'Because that's where Father keeps the communion wine.'

I was shocked. 'But Grace – we can't!'

I liked the church. Being in it was like being in a place where time had stopped. The air was musty, as if it had been there forever and the thick walls muffled the screams of the Spitfires. The stained glass in the windows was the only truly bright thing that I had seen since the war had begun, glowing yellow, red and blue for the Virgin's cloak as she knelt at the foot of the cross.

There was another reason why I liked the church but I was ashamed of it. I liked it because once I was inside I could drop my guard. I didn't have to watch what I said because the words were written down for me. Everything we needed to say was in the Book of Common Prayer, which I held up in front of me all the way through the service. When I knelt next to Grace, the scratchy wool of the prayer cushion pricking at my knees, my first prayer was always that Reverend Rivers would talk for a long time so that I could keep close to her. As Reverend Rivers prayed for the King, for England and her Allies, for the men from the village who had gone to fight and for strength to come to the rest of us, I stole glances at Grace. I let my shoulder rest against hers, feeling the warmth of her body next to mine.

Taking communion was almost as good. I liked the ceremony of it, walking slow steps up the aisle and waiting in line to approach the wooden altar rail that divided us from Reverend Rivers and the stooping churchwarden who stood at his side. When he was behind the rail, Reverend Rivers was like someone from another world, not our teacher, nor the Saturday hermit in the study. His robes and his words made him something else. For those short minutes when I knelt next to Grace at the rail I wasn't in Kent or in the church. I was somewhere intoxicating.

The body of our Lord Jesus Christ, which was given for thee, preserve thy body and soul unto everlasting life. Take and eat this in remembrance that Christ died for thee, and feed on him in thy heart by faith with thanksgiving.

The bread was dry, as if it really were from a body preserved for hundreds of years. I liked the way it melted slowly on my tongue.

The blood of our Lord Jesus Christ, which was shed for thee, preserve thy body and soul unto everlasting life. Drink this in remembrance that Christ's blood was shed for thee, and be thankful.

The wine was a taste of danger, dark and sour. Drinking it outside church would have consequences, I knew, and I guessed that they would be bad.

'We can't,' I said again.

'Girls from the village get tight, sometimes, when they go to dances with the GIs,' Grace said dreamily. 'I heard two of them talking about it one day after church. They said it was like floating. They said we could all die tomorrow so they might as well enjoy themselves.'

'But it's holy wine. It's the blood of Christ.'

'No, it's not. It isn't holy until it's been blessed. Before then, it's just wine. It isn't anything special. And even when it's been blessed it's not really his blood. It's still just wine.'

I was beginning to feel flustered and hot. I knew that she was wrong, that it did become blood the moment it was blessed. But I knew as well that she was determined to drink it. I tried again, my last attempt.

'What if your father finds out? We'd be in so much trouble. He'd send me away.'

She shook her head. 'Why should he find out?' she said bitterly. 'He never notices what I do. You know that. All he cares about is his parishioners and his sermons and choosing the right hymns. He cares for his pipe more than he cares for me. He likes you because you're clever and you like his lessons, but he doesn't pay you any attention outside the schoolroom. It's as if he doesn't even see us.'

I wasn't sure she was right. There were times when I had looked up from my plate at supper and noticed him looking at me oddly, as if he were trying to puzzle something out. But I didn't want to tell her that. Her feelings were hurt enough.

'He's bound to notice that the wine's gone,' I said.

'No, he won't. I've thought of a way round it. There are lots of bottles in there. They keep them in a cupboard and the key's hidden behind one of the big Bibles. I saw Father put it there. All we have to do is take one bottle at a time and only drink some of it, then we'll fill it up with water and put it back. They won't notice, and even if they did, they wouldn't guess it was us.'

She looked at me with mischief in her eyes. 'Anyway. It's like the girl said. A bomb might hit us or the church and then it wouldn't matter anyway.'

Whenever Grace said things like that I worried in case God was listening. She was careless about him in a way that I could never be. It was one of the things that put me in awe of her.

'Shall we, then?' she said. 'Do say yes, Nora. I've planned it all. We'll go to the vestry and get a bottle to take to the lake. We can hide in the grass. No-one will see us.'

I could never refuse her and this time was no different. Her excitement was infectious. Besides, there was something else. I had heard about girls getting tight at dances. Things happened. Perhaps I would find out if I had any reason to hope.

'Oh all right,' I said finally. 'Let's do it.'

*

We sat in the long grass, tussling over who should take the first drink, suddenly nervous. Eventually, Grace put it to her lips, tipping back her head as she drank. She shuddered as she swallowed the first mouthful and shook her head, blinking.

'Golly,' she said. 'It's awfully strong.'

She passed me the bottle. I looked at it doubtfully.

'Go on,' she said. 'It's not so bad.'

She sat back on her heels and pressed her hands together as if she were praying. She began to speak once again in the voice of her father at the altar.

'The blood of our Lord Jesus Christ, which was shed for thee, preserve thy body and soul unto everlasting life. Drink this in remembrance that Christ's blood was shed for thee, and be thankful.'

I looked out over the lake. The air was perfectly still, undisturbed by wind. I could smell the wild garlic that grew at the water's edge, at once both sweet and sour. Everything was lazy and slow, a perfect afternoon. I took the bottle and copied Grace, tipping back my head to swallow.

Minutes passed. We watched a heron fly over the lake, skimming the water with its feet as it looked for fish.

'Can you feel anything?' asked Grace.

I thought about it, wriggling my toes to see how they felt. 'No,' I admitted.

'Neither can I. Let's have some more.'

This time I held the wine in my mouth for a moment before I swallowed it, rolling it over my tongue. It was sweeter without the metal taste of the chalice and I liked the burning sensation that it made as it went down my throat. As the afternoon went on and we drank more and more, I began to feel absurdly happy. My arms and legs were comfortable and loose. Drinking wine was like being in church, where the rest of the world didn't matter, an easy, sunny church without a roof where you could lie back on a bed of cow parsley and laugh until your stomach ached. Everything was brighter. I felt as if the sun and the wine were heating me up and that if they carried on I might burst into flames.

I was tired of saying one thing and meaning another, of always thinking before I spoke. We had been like sisters. We had shared everything. My longing for Grace was the first secret I had kept from her. Knowing that I had managed to keep it had allowed me to wonder and to hope. If I could do it, so could she. I had let myself dream that she might feel like me, hiding it like I did, saying nothing. I wanted something to happen. I wanted to provoke some kind of reaction. I took a deep breath, closed my eyes and began to sing a hymn.

> *Amazing Grace! How sweet the sound*
> *That saved a wretch like me.*
> *I once was lost, but now am found*
> *Was blind but now I see.*

My voice mingled with the buzzing of a thousand small creatures in the grass.

> *Twas Grace that taught my heart to fear,*
> *And Grace my fears relieved;*
> *How precious did that Grace appear,*
> *The hour I first believed.*

Singing made my heartbeat slow down but my body stayed as tightly wound as the grandfather clock in the rectory hallway. Grace said nothing. I didn't dare open my eyes to see if she understood. All I could do was to carry on singing, listening to my voice, shrill and out of place in the peace of the forest. It was a long hymn and I was trapped in it, having to finish it, feeling more stupid with every line.

Just as I was coming to the sixth verse, I felt a sharp pain just above my elbow, as if someone had stabbed me with a needle. I screamed and opened my eyes to see Grace looking at me, grinning, her cheeks flushed from the wine. The pain in my arm made me forget my embarrassment.

'Why are you smiling?' I snapped. 'I've been bitten. Look.'

'It was a wasp,' she said. 'It was crawling over you for ages, all the time you were singing.'

'But why didn't you get rid of it? Why did you let it sting me?'

'I was listening to you sing. You were perfectly still so I thought it would fly off and you'd be all right. I didn't think it would sting you.'

My eyes filled with tears. 'Well it did. It hurts. It hurts a lot.'

Grace had stopped smiling. 'Don't cry, Nora,' she whispered.

'I can't help it. It hurts.'

As she leaned towards me I could smell the wine on her breath, a ripe, almost rotten smell that seemed somehow to suit her. I began to tremble with hope as she came closer. My cheeks were hot. I closed my eyes again, unable to stand the anticipation, waiting to feel her lips on mine.

But they never came. Instead, she took hold of my arm and I opened my eyes to see her peering at the sting, a small sharp peak amongst the gooseflesh that had broken out all over me. As she brushed her finger over it I caught my breath.

'I could suck it out,' she said.

I almost choked. 'What?'

'I could suck out the sting. It's like a little arrow that the wasp pricks you with. It stays in you and that's what hurts. If you suck it out it doesn't hurt any more. Mummy did it once to me, when I was small. Do you want me to try?'

Without the wine, I might have said no. As it was, I nodded quickly, not trusting myself to speak.

She lowered her face to my arm. My heart began to hammer and as she pressed her lips to my skin, a warm feeling spread through my body. When she touched the tip of her tongue to the spot where I had been stung, I felt a pulse between my legs. The world was made of

Grace and me, the sensation of her lips pulling on my skin and the sound of my breathing, which was getting harder and faster the longer she sucked. I was so absorbed in it that I didn't notice William until he was standing right beside us.

'Hello,' he said. 'What are you girls doing?'

I sat up immediately, blushing. Grace rolled onto her side and pulled something from her tongue.

'Hello,' she said. 'Nora got stung by a wasp so I was sucking out the sting. Look!'

She held out her finger towards us. On the end of it was something that looked like a small length of white thread, which she flicked into the water. She was as calm as if she had been found knitting socks for the troops. My cheeks were still blazing. I looked down at my arm. On it was a red mark where Grace's lips had been, like the marks that the farmers painted on sheep to show who owned them.

Grace smiled at William. 'What have you been doing?' she asked.

He lifted his rifle. 'I've been setting up targets in the wood there. I'm practising for when the Germans land.'

'But you're a good shot already, aren't you?'

He looked flattered. 'I'm not bad.'

'I liked it when you showed us how to shoot apples,' Grace said, giving him one of her best smiles. 'We'll have to get some more practice. Will you help us?'

I was baffled by the way that Grace was acting. She had never shown so much interest in William. Just a minute before she had been sucking my skin and now she was asking him to sit next to her, patting his arm and smiling up at him. I began to feel uneasy and then, as she lay back on the crushed cow parsley with her arms crossed behind her head, rather desperate. I wasn't sure what was happening but I wanted it to stop.

'Let's go and do some shooting now,' I said. My voice sounded loud and falsely cheerful. 'Why don't you show us your new targets?'

'I'm feeling lazy,' said Grace. 'Let's save the targets for tomorrow.'

She was beautiful against the white flowers, her hair almost as pale as they were. The wine had stained her lips red. I wanted to throw myself on top of her and kiss her until my lips were the same colour as hers. I could see from the way that William was staring that he wanted to do the same and I was filled with a sudden fury that made me want to roar out loud, to scream that I had loved her first. I wanted to beat at William's chest with my fists and shout that if he touched her I would kill him. I wanted to slap her flushed cheeks and tell her to stop what she was doing, that it wasn't fair.

But I did none of those things. A small voice in my head held me back.

Be Careful What You Say, it whispered. *Don't Give Away Any Clues. Keep Smiling.*

I scrambled to my feet and snatched up William's kitbag and rifle, then I swung them up onto my shoulder and ran into the wood, on and on until I came to the clearing where he liked to set up his targets. Two lopsided scarecrows were bound to trees with rope, like prisoners waiting to be executed. Their bodies were made of scraps of sacking, stitched together roughly and stuffed with straw. One of them wore an old pair of trousers tied around its middle with string and the other had a sheet, draped like a dress. Somehow he had managed to find paint and had given them faces; eyes, noses and smiles. The paint had run, making them look as if they were dribbling.

Their smiles weren't enough to save them, I thought. I wanted to blow them to pieces. I rummaged through the kitbag and took out two bullets. I cocked the rifle, fitted them in, then snapped the gun back together. I lifted it to my shoulder, trying to remember what he had taught me, steadied it and squinted through the sights, aiming at the scarecrow with the trousers. Its stuffed face and lumpen body became William. I took aim at his heart, breathed out and squeezed the trigger gently.

There was a loud bang and the rifle jerked back against my shoulder, hard enough to make me stagger. When I had got my balance back I stared at the scarecrow's remains. His chest and head were scattered around me, yellow wisps of straw and scraps of trouser. The smell of gunpowder and scorched dust hung in the air. The birds had been stunned into silence.

For a moment I had truly believed that the scarecrows were William and Grace. But now that the moment had passed, I wanted to hide away. I was scared of myself and of what I might have done if the scarecrows hadn't been there. I started to shake.

They came quickly, running through the trees, Grace calling out my name. She rushed over to me.

'Nora! Why did you go running off like that? We thought you'd done something stupid.'

She seemed genuinely puzzled. I wondered if I had invented what had happened at the lake.

'Are you all right, Miss?' said William. He had his cap in his hands and was twisting it nervously. He looked horrified.

'I'm sorry for taking your gun,' I muttered. 'And I'm sorry for shooting your target. I'll help you make another one.'

Together we gathered up the pieces of sacking and straw and stuffed them into William's kitbag. I kept my eyes on the ground as we did it, too ashamed to look at either of them. He left the other scarecrow bound to the tree.

'Reckon I'll come back tomorrow to practise on that one,' he said.

*

Grace and I didn't discuss what had happened. Instead, we went back to the rectory and had tea with Mrs Rivers. But all the time, I was thinking about it, trying to fathom out what was true and what was not.

That evening I looked at myself in the bathroom mirror. A bruise the colour of midnight spread across my chest from where the rifle had been balanced against my shoulder. It was as if all the darkness inside me was seeping out through my skin and marking me as wicked. Grace had sucked out the sting, but by doing so she had added to the poison within me, the desire that seemed to grow and grow, no matter what I did to smother it.

Eleven

HAMPSTEAD HEATH HAS ALWAYS BEEN A REFUGE, A PLACE to lose myself, to wander in the woods until London is out of sight. It is full of life, a place where children play and lovers kiss, but it is also a place of commemoration, where the dead are remembered, their names carved into benches, each inscription marking a connection; spouse or lover, parent, child or friend. The flowers that appear from time to time, tied to the benches with ribbon or a piece of string, remember lost loves. I have never felt alone there, surrounded by other people's memories as well as my own.

It is a hopeful place, where death is not forever. Grass burns, leaves fall and branches wither but there is never any doubt that in a matter of months, life will begin again. No matter what might happen to the city, there will always be the Heath, with its snowdrops in January and daffodils in March, yellow leaves in

October and ice on the ponds at the end of the year.

I wanted to show it to Rose. I wanted her to like it as much as I did. She had hardly left the house since she had moved in. We had done a few things together to pass the time. The garden had kept us busy for a while. We had tidied it up, sanding down the old iron furniture and rearranging the plant pots. We had gathered up the dead leaves and built a bonfire, warming our fingers on the flames as it burned. We had enjoyed ourselves. But I knew that it wasn't enough. I wanted Rose to see new things. The Heath would be a start.

'Can I ask you something?' I said one day.

'What is it?'

'It's a favour. I want to go to Hampstead Heath on Sunday. It's Remembrance Day. I go every year. I wondered if you'd come with me. I'd be glad of the company.'

She frowned. 'Are you going to church?'

'No, no,' I said. 'It's nothing like that. I just want to go for a walk, that's all.'

There was more to it than that, of course. For me, the British Legion poppies have nothing to do with the battlefields of France; they take me back to the hayfields in Kent, golden meadows streaked with drifts of red. They remind me of the tickle of grass against my arms and lying back to look at the summer sky. I never feel the cold on those November Sundays. For me it is August, and I am happy.

'Okay,' she said. 'I'll come.'

I prepared carefully for the outing. Rose was still very thin and I thought it would tire her to carry the baby all that way. I decided to pawn my last piece of jewellery and buy a pushchair with the money.

Like the Heath, the pawnshop never changes. Cheap necklaces glittered in the window like always. The sign was much the same as it had been fifty years before, tall golden letters on a background of black. *Pawnshop and Jewellers.*

When I pushed open the door, heavy from the iron bars that stretched the length of it, I was met by the usual smell of stale tobacco, damp clothes and old possessions. Customers waited on plastic chairs pushed back against the wall, looking resigned and clutching bags that held the residue of unlucky lives.

I am used to the rat-faced men who sit behind the grille playing God, judging the little you have left. I understand the game. But I was still nervous as I laid the earrings out on their velvet bag, two silver loops, each with a single pearl suspended from it. For a moment I hesitated.

'Come on love,' said the man.

I pushed the bag across the counter and braced myself for the negotiations.

They began with him exhaling though his nose as he picked up one of the earrings. Neither of us said anything. He lodged his eyeglass in front of his right eye and looked at it. I waited, knowing there was nothing I could do to hurry him. After a while, he sighed and leaned back in his chair.

'They're fakes,' he said, shaking his head.

'That's impossible.'

He shrugged. 'They're not heavy enough.'

'But they change colour against the skin. Only real pearls do that.'

He laid an earring in the palm of his hand. 'I can't see it changing colour, can you?'

I suddenly realized that my visit was pointless. Pawning is the stuff of fools. To do it you must convince yourself that one day things will be better and you'll be able to buy back what you pawned. I had never been able to bring myself to lose her jewellery forever and so for many years I had been one of those fools, pawning things when times were hard. But now I knew I had no chance of coming back to redeem the earrings. Things weren't going to get any better. I was going to die. The certainty of it made me strangely cheerful. I felt reckless, almost drunk. I snatched the earrings from him, turned around and marched out of the shop, holding my head high.

On my way back up the street I passed a charity shop. In the window was a pushchair, exactly the sort that I wanted. Feeling hopeful, I pushed open the door and went inside.

At first glance, everything was jumbled up together, piled up, crammed onto rails and shelves that sagged under the weight of it all. But there was an underlying order to it, the clothes hanging according to colour and the books arranged by size. There was a shelf for cassette tapes and records and underneath was a collection of glasses and crockery, ornaments and candlesticks. I liked it that nothing matched, that a shop could still hold some surprises. A glass-fronted counter had jewellery in it, laid out on faded silk scarves. Sitting behind it was a girl who looked up from a magazine and smiled at me.

'Hello,' she said. 'Do you need any help?'

'How much is the chair in the window?'

'The pushchair? Twenty pounds.'

It was more expensive than I'd hoped.

'It's a very good make, you see. And it's nearly new.'

Her voice was friendly, and my experience in the pawnshop had made me feel more confident than usual. Bargaining was one of the things I'd learned to do over the years. I decided to try.

'I haven't got quite enough money with me. I wonder if there's any chance of an exchange.'

She shook her head.

'I'm sorry. We're not allowed to do things like that. I'd get into trouble.'

'Oh,' I said. 'Of course.' My little burst of boldness drained away and I turned to leave, but as I reached the door, the girl cleared her throat.

'What did you want to swap?'

I brought out the bag from my coat pocket and passed it to her. As she took out the earrings her eyes widened with pleasure.

'They're lovely!' she said, going over to a mirror and lifting them to her ears. 'Are they very old?'

'They're from the 1940s,' I said. The earrings looked nice on her, I thought, next to her glossy hair and her smile.

She came away from the mirror. 'Here's an idea. What if I bought them from you? I could give you twenty pounds. Would that be enough?'

I liked this girl. I wanted her to have the earrings. It didn't matter how much they were worth. The chair was all I needed out of it.

'I'd like that very much,' I said.

'And then you can pay me for the pushchair with the money. We won't have done anything wrong and I won't get into trouble.'

We smiled at each other as we made our exchanges, pleased with our little conspiracy.

*

Remembrance Day was cold but the sky was clear and the Heath seemed full of possibility. Children were everywhere, running and chasing, throwing sticks for dogs and scattering breadcrumbs for the ducks. They looked like little splashes of paint in their colourful clothes, vivid against the faded winter grass. Joggers puffed along the pathways and people were flying kites from the top of Parliament Hill. It was exactly what I'd hoped for Rose's first visit. She looked better than I had ever seen her, her cheeks pink and her eyes bright.

'I like it here,' she said. 'It'll be lovely in the summer. We can come for picnics. Grace might even be walking by then.'

We had arrived at the ponds. The water was very still, undisturbed by wind. I didn't want to ruin things. I wanted her to enjoy our day out. But I knew I had to tell her. I couldn't put it off any longer.

Two ducks came paddling past us, breaking the surface of the water and sending ripples out in circles.

'I'm a dead duck,' I blurted out. As soon as the words left my mouth I knew I should have put it differently.

'What?'

'I'm a dead duck,' I said, trying to sound calm. 'I mean, I'm dying. I don't think I've got long left.'

Rose stared at me, her face white with horror and I knew that I had to keep talking.

'It's cancer. I've had it for a while. It's spreading, I think. I can feel it.'

I began to fidget, shifting from foot to foot and balling my hands up into fists. For a moment, she looked dazed, as if she hadn't understood what I'd said. Then the questions came.

'What treatment are you taking?' she said. 'Are you in a lot of pain?'

'Sometimes,' I said cautiously.

'What do the doctors say?'

I tried to explain. I told her I didn't have a doctor. I told her about the receptionist with the long nails and the dying carnations in the water that needed changing. I told her about the pills from the chemist's and the books I'd bought about our different predicaments.

'That's how I knew what to do when you went into labour,' I said. 'It was all there in the manual.'

But she wouldn't be distracted. She kept on with her questions. 'Who's looking after you? Who else knows about this?'

I could see that I wasn't going to get away with it. 'There's no-one else to tell.'

'Haven't you got any family?'

I stiffened. 'No.'

'No-one at all? No brothers or sisters?'

'No.'

'No children?'

'No.'

'Nora,' she said. 'You can't always have been on your own. Didn't you ever get married? Did you ever have a husband?'

It was a perfectly reasonable question. I shouldn't have found it so hard to answer.

'Yes,' I said eventually. 'I had a husband. His name was George.'

Dear, kind George, I thought. You took care of me, as much as you could.

'I can't believe you've never said anything about him,' she said, shaking her head.

'You never asked.'

'Tell me about him.'

'What do you want to know?'

'When did you meet him? When did you get married?'

'I met him after the war,' I said, looking out over the pond. 'He ran a bookshop. I went in there by chance.'

Her eyes were shining. 'That's so romantic.'

She didn't need to know all of it, I thought. I would keep some of it to myself, at least for now.

'And what happened?'

'He died,' I said. 'A long time ago. It was sudden. A heart attack.'

He'd been reading Dickens by the fire one cold November evening, a glass of whisky on the table next to him. I had gone to the garden to get more coal and when I came back he was slumped in his chair. I had sat at his feet, holding his hand, crying for the man I had loved, never quite enough, but as much as I could.

'Oh,' she said. 'I'm sorry.'

There was a pause.

'Was there nobody else?' she asked. 'I mean, after him?'

'No.'

'It's just that if there's someone who ought to know, we should tell them.'

'There's nothing to tell,' I said. 'And no-one to tell it to. Please.'

'But you should still see a doctor. They might be able to help you.'

'I don't want to see a doctor,' I said. 'There's no point. I'm tired. I've lived long enough.'

Grace had woken up and was starting to whimper. Rose bent to lift her out of the chair.

'You're the only person I've got,' she said. 'You're my friend. I don't want you to die.'

I hadn't foreseen this when I crossed the street on that August evening. I hadn't wanted any more attachments, any more involvements. But somehow Rose had slipped under my guard and now I was paying the price.

She said something else, so quietly that I couldn't make it out.

'What?'

'That's what he had,' she muttered.

'What?'

'Dad. He had cancer. He found out he was ill just before I did my A-levels and he died just after I got the results. He was so happy when I told him. He said it was the best day of his life.'

Her eyes were brimming with tears.

'That was why I couldn't have an abortion. I couldn't stand the thought of losing someone else. But he would have been so disappointed that I left university. I've gone over it so many times in my head. I've let him down.'

I realized that I had the easier part to play in my death. By inviting her to live with me I had dragged her into it. I'd given her someone else to grieve for. I held her as she wept on my shoulder, trying to pass on what I knew about loving and losing, silently telling her I was sorry.

After a while, she stopped crying and pulled away. 'Shall we keep walking?' she said, sniffing. 'I'm cold.'

I tried to lighten the mood.

'It's me who needs that chair,' I said. 'You should be pushing me!'

Despite herself, she smiled at the thought. I hooked my arm through hers and we made our way along the path, both of us puffing as we climbed to the top of the hill. It was worth the effort. All of London curved below us, vast, like a familiar painting in which I recognized all the features but could still find new things to surprise me. I raised my eyes to the pale sky, thinking of the many years that I had stood on that spot. I had been there on summer days, wanting to run through the long grass but feeling too old and shy to do it, on dark afternoons in winter when the woods were filled with menace, in spring, when the air was thick with the sound of birds. I had shared it all with one person, who I thought of every time I saw green shoots on the trees or the first primroses in the woods, when I heard, just once, a cuckoo call. Now, on this, my last visit, I was with someone new. I had a friend. She had said so herself.

Rose was rummaging in her bag.

'Do you mind if I take some pictures?' she said, pulling out a camera. 'I want a photo of Grace.' She smiled, a small, sad smile. 'I want a photo of you.'

She went up to a couple standing nearby and said something. They took the camera and nodded.

We stood close together.

'Smile!' said the woman.

I heard a click and a flash came that made me blink. Rose passed Grace to me and went over to the man. They looked together at the camera. The woman joined them.

'It's a lovely one,' she said. 'That baby's so sweet.'

'Now let's have one of you and Grace,' said Rose.

There was another click and a flash. Rose came to me and showed me the back of the camera. I saw myself, standing with the baby in my arms, kissing the top of her head. My eyes were closed. I looked at peace.

Twelve

As soon as Reverend Rivers said that lessons were finished for the summer we bolted, leaving behind the silence of the rectory for long days spent drinking wine by the lake and shooting at targets with William. Grace's hair was blonder than ever, bleached by the sun. I was strict with myself, rationing how often I looked at her. I watched her only when she was sleeping or when her attention was distracted. I came to understand what feasting your eyes on something really meant.

We still had to put in an appearance on Sundays, all present and correct, but I didn't find the church as soothing as before. As Reverend Rivers led the service, his words, which I had come to know by heart, seemed to be aimed directly at me.

Almighty God, unto whom all hearts be open, all desires known, and from whom no secrets are hid.

The thought of my desires being known by God made me tremble. Each week as we came closer to the moment of Communion, I started to sweat. I blushed when Reverend Rivers asked us to examine our consciences. My longings weren't mentioned anywhere in the Ten Commandments or in any other part of the Bible that I had read, but I knew that they were sinful and I knew that if I took Communion in a state of sin, bad things would happen. It was written in the prayer book.

For then we are guilty of the Body and Blood of Christ the Saviour; we eat and drink our own damnation, not considering the Lord's Body; we kindle God's wrath against us; we provoke Him to plague us with divers diseases and sundry kinds of death.

Grace and I had mocked the words that Reverend Rivers said when he stood at the altar preparing to give out the bread and wine. When we were sitting in the long grass, listening to the singing of the birds and feeling the sun on our faces, they had no power to frighten us, making us giggle instead. But in the church they meant something serious and I shivered with shame when I heard them.

I sweated and trembled my way through the service each week, knowing that I shouldn't go up to the altar rail but that if I didn't, there would be questions. Living in the rectory had taught me about secrets and so each Sunday I walked up the aisle behind Grace, staring at her hair and praying for salvation. The rest of the week I trod carefully, wishing for the comfort of a priest behind a curtain, someone who could tell me what to do and save me from damnation.

I did my best to find distractions, working in the fields in an effort not to think. Reverend Rivers had read out a notice in church that came from Mr Churchill himself, asking us all to join in with the war effort. *Lend a Hand on the Land*, he had said, and we went every day after that to help bring in the harvest. Almost everyone in the village was there, apart from Reverend Rivers, who stayed shut up in his study, and Mrs Rivers, who kept to the drawing room and her piano. Grace and I were glad to escape the rectory and worked long days turning the grass with pitchforks so it could dry out in the sun. As the cut grass turned from green to gold, my skin turned brown, covered with a fine dust that smelled of the fields. I developed muscles in my stomach and arms from lifting the pitchfork and two rows of calluses spread across my palms from rubbing against the wooden shaft.

The last day of the harvest was the hottest of the summer. Fields the colour of Grace's hair stretched about us as far as we could see in a haze of heat that hovered just above the ground. The forecast had said that the weather was about to break and we arrived early to lift the hay one last time. By the end of the afternoon, when it had all been gathered in, we were thirsty and hot. There was no shelter in the fields. They had been stripped of every blade of grass, and the rough stalks that were left were clipped shorter than a soldier's hair. Small patches of parched earth showed through like scalp. The only noise was the cawing of the crows that circled overhead, looking for field mice. Grace and I sat observing the devastation.

'We should go back,' I said.

Grace had her face lifted up to the sun, her eyes closed. Despite her fairness, she never burned. 'Go back where?' she murmured.

I still couldn't bring myself to call it home. 'To the house.'

'What's the point? Tea will be bread and butter with Mummy looking miserable and wanting to get back to her piano. Father won't come out of his study because all he can think about is his beastly sermon.' She opened her eyes and grinned. 'Have a look in the knapsack. I packed some apples and a bottle of the Bad Blood. That should wake us up.'

Bad Blood was what we called the communion wine. I shivered with excitement.

'Let's go to the lake and have a swim. It would be heaven to get this hay off. I'm itching all over.'

The thought of washing away the gritty dust was appealing. Seeds had gathered in the creases of my elbows and behind my knees. My face was tight from the dust.

'Besides,' said Grace, 'we should take the chance whilst we still can. The weather's going to change. This could be the last swim of the year.'

I looked at the sky. Dark clouds were beginning to gather, casting shadows over the stubble, and the air was heavy with the prospect of rain.

'All right, then,' I said.

We scrambled to our feet, picked up the knapsack and set off across the fields.

*

It had only been a week since we had last been at the lake, but it had shrunk so low that we could see the bleached bones of an animal that had drowned in it. Small insects skated over the surface, sending out tiny ripples as they went. The clouds made the water look dead and grey.

Grace was disappointed. 'Let's wait for the sun to come back out,' she said. 'We can have a drink in the meantime.'

We sat on the bank, so close that our shoulders touched, alternating between bites of apple and mouthfuls of wine. The apples were mealy and soft from being knocked about in the knapsack and the wine was hot from the sun, but it didn't matter. It took effect more quickly than usual, making me giddy and glad. Grace seemed to feel the same way and as we worked our way down the bottle we told each other jokes and larked about, doing impersonations of people from the village whom we had worked with in the fields.

We had been there almost an hour when Grace said, 'Nora, I feel tight.'

'That's all right, isn't it?' I said. 'I'm squiffy too. It's rather wonderful.' I wriggled my toes, noticing how grubby they were and not caring.

'I can say things when I'm tight. Difficult things, I mean. Somehow it's easier.' She sounded grave. I kept quiet, wondering what she was going to say next. I dared not hope but I crossed my fingers just in case.

'Do you remember the first time we were here with the wine?' she said.

Every minute of that afternoon was burned into my memory but I didn't want to talk about it. I wanted to push it away and not let it ruin anything else, so I shook my head.

She knew me better than that. 'You do remember, don't you?' she said, looking at me closely.

I knew that lying was pointless. 'All right,' I said. 'Yes, I do. But I haven't anything to say about it.'

'But I want you to know what happened.'

'I already know,' I said. 'It was quite plain to me what was going on between you and William. I left so that you could be alone together, just the two of you.' I remembered exactly how I had felt that day. I had frightened myself with my reactions. But I knew I mustn't say so. I shrugged and hung my head.

'I knew that was what you thought,' she said. 'But you were quite wrong. It wasn't like that at all.'

'What do you mean?' I said.

'You think I was making love to him, don't you?'

I looked at my feet.

'Don't you?' she said again.

I felt a little surge of anger in my chest, not as strong as the rage

I had felt that day, but strong enough to make me speak.

'What else could I think?' I muttered. 'You were lying there in the flowers, looking up at him as if you wanted him more than anything else in the world. Even William understood it. You did, he did, and so did I.'

Grace looked uncomfortable. 'I don't know what got into me,' she said. 'I didn't want anything to happen, not really. I supposed I just wanted to see if I could make somebody want me like that.'

If only you knew, I thought. If only you knew how you could make somebody want you. It doesn't take communion wine and a sunny afternoon by the lake. I want you on rainy days when we're drinking tea with your mother in the kitchen. I want you in the morning when your eyes are still full of sleep. I want you when you don't know the answers to your father's questions on algebra and you're ashamed of it. But I can't tell you any of that because I know you don't want me.

She was still talking. 'When you went off like that, we just sat there, wondering where you'd gone. And then we heard those gunshots. Nora, I was so frightened. I thought something terrible had happened. We both jumped up and came running to find you. Nothing happened before that, I promise. Please believe me. You're my best friend. You're my sister. I'd never do anything to hurt you.'

I wanted to believe her, to pretend that the afternoon had never happened. I couldn't refuse her, no more than I'd ever been able to. I reached out my hand and laid it on top of hers. She smiled, and turned over her hand so that our palms were touching. We interlinked our fingers like we had when we were little girls and the war was just beginning.

*

137

The rain came in a noisy rush, a thousand fat raindrops slapping the surface of the lake. Thunder rumbled in the distance like a squadron of fighter planes. Rivulets of water ran along the cracked earth and the smell of warm mud filled the air.

My first thought was to run for shelter but Grace had thrown her head back and was lifting her face to meet the rain. For a moment she stayed perfectly still, as if she wanted it to drench her completely, then in one quick movement she stood up and pulled her blouse over her head.

'Come on, Nora!' she shouted over the din.

'What?' I said, but she was already ripping off the rest of her clothes, not caring where they fell; her dress, her petticoat, the brassiere that she had stitched together from an old satin bedspread – and then, to my shock, her navy blue knickers, which she pushed down her legs to the ground. She stepped out of them and stood naked in front me, her hands on her hips.

'Come on!' she said.

I stared at her. She had changed since that first summer when she had stood in her knickers and vest, her body like a boy's. Now her breasts were bigger than mine, and very white, apart from her nipples, which had stiffened against the rain into two dark peaks. Her hips were a perfect balance, curving out from her waist. I drank it all in with silent fascination. I had never seen the whole of my body. I had stood on tiptoe in front of the mirror above the basin in the rectory bathroom but I could never see all of it. My notion of how I was shaped came from timid explorations of myself in bed at night, carried out discreetly in case Grace woke. But I couldn't believe that I looked anything like she did. I wanted to touch her, to run my hands over her curves to prove to myself that they were real. I stood, frozen to the spot, unable to tear my eyes away from her.

'Come on,' she said impatiently. 'I'm getting cold.'

The raindrops were falling harder by the second, drumming on the ground and bouncing off the lake. I felt suddenly reckless and pulled my shirt over my head, slid off my skirt and kicked off my sandals. The sensation of the rain stabbing at my skin was exciting. Not letting myself stop to think, I peeled off my underclothes and stood facing Grace, my hands on my hips like her, breathing hard. The thunder came again, closer now and startling. As I stood there, strangely unashamed of my nakedness, feeling wonderfully awake and alive, I heard another sound, like someone clearing their throat. I looked about but could see nothing.

'Did you hear that?' I shouted.

'What?' said Grace.

'A noise, a sort of cough.'

'I can't hear a thing over this rain. I'm sure it's nothing. Come on, run!'

Catching hold of each other's hands, we ran into the lake, slipping and sliding on the mud, then wading until the water was deep and our stumbles were transformed into sudden elegance as we began to swim. We dived down and as I watched her body, pale as moonlight, slip through the water, brushing against the plants that grew at the bottom of the lake, I felt utterly at peace. In this silent world I was calm, free of the shame that weaselled its way into my heart whenever I thought of her. I wished that I could stay in it forever. I held out until my lungs were about to burst and I was forced to come up for air.

*

The rain soon passed. Grace and I walked back to the rectory through the fields, friends again, letting the evening sun dry out our clothes. We had a makeshift supper with Mrs Rivers, listening to the wireless as we ate. I went to bed happy and my dreams were filled with images of Grace in the water.

I was woken by the wail of the air raid siren, a long, high note that rang in my ears. Grace and I dragged ourselves out of our beds and put on dressing gowns. Mrs Rivers was waiting at the back door, her hair loose, holding a candle and a thermos flask. She looked distraught.

'Your father isn't here,' she said. 'I don't know where he is. He never came to bed. I thought he was still writing his sermon but he's not in the study. He's disappeared.'

A fighter plane passed over the rectory, flying low. The ground shook.

'We'll have to go without him,' shouted Grace.

She ran outside and Mrs Rivers and I followed her, weaving in and out of the raspberry canes. I could see a faint orange glow on the horizon, proof that a bomb had met its target. I ran as fast as I could, making for the shelter in the corner of the vegetable patch. Grace got there first and threw open the door. We followed her inside, and the three of us sat on the bunks, panting, trying to catch our breath.

After a minute, Mrs Rivers unscrewed the lid of the thermos and poured out tea. Her hands were shaking and she spilled some on the ground, which swallowed it up quickly as if it were thirsty too. The thunderstorm had made no difference to the temperature inside the shelter. It was stiflingly hot. We sat in silence, waiting for the next plane. It arrived soon enough, roaring like some hideous creature from a book in search of its prey. At the same moment, the door to the shelter began to rattle. Grace shrieked and grabbed my hand. Mrs Rivers turned pale. I swallowed hard. I could hear shouting, a man's voice, but it was impossible to make out his words over the noise. The next moment, the door burst open to reveal neither the German soldier nor the British airman that I had imagined, but Reverend Rivers, looking exhausted.

The temperature in the shelter seemed suddenly to drop. I felt an icy anger in the air, cold as the church on a winter morning. It was coming from Mrs Rivers.

'Where have you been?' she demanded.

'I was in church,' he said.

'At this time of night?'

Reverend Rivers looked uneasy. 'I was praying,' he muttered.

'Praying!' Mrs Rivers' voice was disbelieving. 'You're taking Matins in the morning. Couldn't you have waited until then?'

The expression on his face was a curious mix of excitement and guilt. I was puzzled, unable to understand why Reverend Rivers might look like that.

'No, I couldn't,' he said in a flat voice. 'I'm here now. There's nothing more to be said about it.'

I fell asleep soon after, curled next to Grace on the bunk. It was a cramped space, too small for the two of us, which made my nights in the shelter a complicated pleasure. The only way to fit was to lie on our sides, one behind the other as close as a deck of cards. It took all my concentration to make sure that I kept my breathing steady and slow but inside my heart banged against my chest and I found it impossible to sleep for long. That night my dreams were full of her. I saw her at the lake again but now her movements were considered and deliberate. She exposed her body slowly, without speaking, challenging me with her eyes, no longer the Grace that I knew, who spoke her thoughts as soon as they came into her head and acted on her desires as soon as she felt them, impulsively, with no thought for the consequences. The Grace of my dreams knew exactly what she meant to do. When she was naked she stood for a moment, looking at me directly, then turned on her heel and waded into the lake, the water rising up her body as she went further in until at last it closed over her head and she was gone. As if I were with her, I began to choke and flail, feeling the pressure of the water push me down into depths from which I would never return.

I woke suddenly, gasping for air and confused by the shadows that danced on the walls, thrown by the flame of the candle. As my eyes slowly focused I saw Reverend Rivers with his back to me, kneeling by the door of the shelter. He was muttering to himself and I listened hard, trying to make out what he was saying. There was a rhythm to his words that I recognized and I listened harder, straining my ears until at last I understood. He was reciting the Lord's Prayer, repeating it over and over, urgently, as if he were asking for God's protection from something dangerous.

Our Father, who art in heaven
Hallowed be thy Name
Thy kingdom come
Thy will be done
On earth as it is in heaven
Give us this day our daily bread
And forgive us our trespasses
As we forgive those who trespass against us –
    And lead us not into temptation
But deliver us from evil
For thine is the kingdom, the power and the glory
For ever and ever
Amen.

I felt a strange sympathy for Reverend Rivers and his loneliness. I had felt it before, at the end of our lessons, when the light in his eyes faded and he became awkward again. But Reverend Rivers was a priest, someone with a position and a place in the world. I was just the evacuee, the girl from the city whom he had taken into his house.

It seemed almost impertinent to pity him. I closed my eyes and willed myself to sleep. When I woke again, he had gone.

After that night, Reverend Rivers kept to himself even more, spending all his time in church or in his study. On the first of September, after breakfast, Grace and I knocked on his door. He seemed surprised to see us.

'We're here, Father,' said Grace, without enthusiasm. 'It's September. That's when you said we'd start again. Lessons, I mean.'

A look of great unease spread across his face.

'I cannot teach you any more,' he said.

I couldn't tell whether he meant there was nothing left for him to teach or that he didn't want to do it.

'What do you mean?' said Grace, unable to believe her luck.

'There won't be any more lessons. I have other things to attend to. More important things.' He looked down at his book, dismissing us.

I was bitterly disappointed but I didn't dare argue. After everything that had happened over the summer, I had been looking forward to the distraction of learning. I was determined not to stop. That winter I chose books at random from Reverend Rivers' study and read them by the fire. The scent of bluebells and the sound of birdsong was replaced by the smell of burning wood and the hammering of the rain against the window. They were dull, drab days that seemed to go on forever. Mrs Rivers continued to play the piano, locking herself away as soon as breakfast was over. Reverend Rivers disappeared for whole afternoons at a time, slipping a Bible into the pocket of his overcoat and turning up his collar against the cold. When he returned, usually well after dark, his shoes were soaked through and spattered with mud. He ate very little, leftovers from our supper, taking a plate into his study and closing the door behind him. It was as if he were sickening for an illness or pining for something that he had lost. Like an animal, furtive and watchful, he scurried from his study to the church and then back again, his head down and his hands in his pockets, hunching up his shoulders against whatever it was he was trying to escape.

Thirteen

THE TRIP TO THE HEATH WAS MY LAST OUTING. I BEGAN TO feel much worse, as if by admitting my illness to Rose I had made it a reality. I was always tired and walking became difficult. My world shrank to the four walls of my bedroom, the bathroom and the corridor between them.

I had never liked to lie about in bed. Mornings had been my favourite time of day. I had kept myself busy, always occupied. Now, as if to make up for my captivity, my mind roamed and roved, flitting to places that would have been better left unvisited. I began to remember things that I hadn't let myself think about for years and my sleep was disturbed by horribly vivid dreams.

Our conversation on the Heath marked the beginning of a new intimacy between Rose and me. When I took to my bed, she assumed charge, looking after the child and myself with gentle competence.

She was no longer the sullen, grieving girl that I had watched at the window. I saw how she must have been before the disappointment of her love affair. She seemed to know when I needed company, bringing Grace to gurgle and kick on the bed. I liked to hold her, hugging her close and inhaling her sweet, powdery smell. Rose knew as well when I'd had enough, seeming to sense the sudden tiredness that came over me like a cloud. Quietly sympathetic, she would close the curtains and take Grace away, leaving me to sleep.

She took to bringing me little surprises, things to tempt my taste buds or make me smile. One morning I woke to find myself in a magical world of stars and twinkling lights. I looked in wonder at them, utterly captivated.

Rose was sitting in the chair next to the bed. 'What do you think of my Christmas decorations?' she said. 'I put them up last night when you were asleep. Aren't they pretty?'

I had lost all sense of time since I had been confined to bed. I was astonished to hear that it was December.

'Here's something else,' she said, pulling a package out of a shopping bag.

I peered at it, trying to guess what it was.

'It's an advent calendar. Look, there's a door for every day and behind each one there's a chocolate. I'll leave it here by the bed so we can count down to Christmas.'

She opened a door each morning as we drank our coffee together. I played along, joining in, exclaiming over the picture behind the little flap of cardboard and sharing the chocolates. On the front of the calendar was a winter scene, people ice-skating on a village pond. Children wove in and out of couples who held hands as they skated, looking into each other's eyes. An old man roasted chestnuts on a brazier. Dogs skidded on the ice and birds observed it all, perched on branches that were heavy with snow. In the background was a church, which held the last door, the twenty-fifth, in one of its stained glass windows.

But when I was alone, I was afraid. It was as if the calendar marked out the time that I had left to live. Every door we opened brought me one day closer to the end. I began to dream of the village in the picture, terrible dreams that left me shaking and drenched in sweat. On Christmas Eve I willed myself to stay awake, staring at the twinkling lights, certain that if I closed my eyes, I would never open them again. When I finally fell into an uneasy sleep, unable to fight it any longer, I dreamed of skating on the ice with Grace, holding hands and gliding fast. We skated as if no-one else were there, faultlessly, laughing as we went, exhilarated by our speed, going faster and faster until the church bells began to chime, bringing us to a standstill. The ice cracked and we fell together, into the freezing water, which closed over our heads like a grave. The weeds wound about our legs, pulling us apart, down into nothingness.

For a long time I stayed perfectly still, feeling what it was like to be dead. Then I heard Rose's voice. 'Happy Christmas, Nora!'

I opened my eyes. Rose was standing next to the bed, holding the baby. She smiled and bent to kiss my cheek, her lips soft against my skin.

It was as if I'd been given a second chance. 'Happy Christmas,' I said.

'It's a lovely day.' She went over to the window and opened the curtains. 'There's a carol service on the radio. Shall we have it on?'

'Yes,' I said. 'That would be nice.'

The sound of children singing filled the room. It was instantly uplifting. We sat, playing with Grace, who yelped with pleasure as she grabbed hold of our fingers, trying to keep herself upright.

When the service was over, Rose stood up.

'I'm going to see to lunch. Can I leave her with you?'

'Of course.'

When Grace noticed that Rose was gone she roared with grief.

Good for you, I thought. Things might have turned out differently if I'd made a bit more noise.

But after a while I couldn't bear to see her so distraught. I pushed back the sheets, swung my legs over the side of the bed and, gathering my strength, stood up. I took her into my arms and held her close, rocking her gently. As I paced about the room, her sobbing was gradually replaced by deep, shuddering breaths. I stood at the window, feeling the heat from her small body. Soft flakes of snow were starting to fall, quietly efficient, making everything clean.

'That's what we need,' I whispered. 'A nice, fresh start.'

She fell asleep, nestling against me. I came away from the window and climbed back into bed, pulling the blankets around us.

When Rose came back she was carrying a tray with bowls, a plate of bread and butter and a piece of cheese. She had tucked sprigs of holly in amongst the crockery and folded the napkins into peaks. She smiled when she saw us.

'Thanks for looking after her. I heard her making all that noise.'

'We were all right,' I said. 'Weren't we, Grace?'

'I'm afraid lunch is only soup. I thought it would be easy to swallow.'

'It's perfect,' I said. 'I wouldn't have expected you to roast a turkey!'

*

After lunch I felt rather jolly.

'Let's have a drink,' I suggested. 'To celebrate.'

Rose looked at me as if I had lost my mind. 'What?'

'Well, we're all still here,' I said. 'All three of us. I think that's worth a toast, don't you? There's a bottle of port in the kitchen cupboard. Can you get it?'

She wasn't convinced. 'You're ill,' she said. 'I'm sure you're not supposed to drink.'

I winked at her. 'Think of it as medicine.'

By the time she brought the bottle the sky was dark. She drew the curtains and pulled her chair close to the bed, then poured an inch of port into two glasses. She passed one of them to me. I cleared my throat.

'To Grace!' I said. 'To her first Christmas.'

And to my last, I thought, suddenly calm at the idea. Not long to go now.

Rose raised her glass. 'To Grace!'

We touched glasses and drank. I held the port in my mouth for a long and lovely moment, enjoying the taste of it. I looked fondly at Rose, who held the baby snuggled against her shoulder.

'Here we are,' I said. 'We've got our own nativity, mother and child. Although I don't know what that makes me.'

Rose giggled. 'You're the midwife. I can't imagine she got any thanks in the Bible but Mary couldn't have done it without her.'

As I sipped at my port, I felt hazy and happy, as if the alcohol was washing the rotten parts of me, making me clean.

'I wonder what she's doing,' Rose said.

'Who?'

'Mum.' She sighed. 'She's probably remembering last Christmas and what a mess it was. She's probably still angry about it all.'

'She's probably missing you,' I said carefully. 'And I'm sure she's wondering about her grandchild. Don't you think she'd like to meet her?'

Rose stiffened, and lifted her chin in her old determined pose.

'She's not going to,' she said, her voice stubborn. 'She didn't want her to be born. She wanted me to get rid of her, remember?'

I remembered. But I also remembered the relief in Rose's voice when she had mistaken me for her mother on that night in her bedsit. I remembered her tears when she saw the rose in her room. I remembered other things too, uncomfortable, unsettling things. I thought of my own mother and of how the small seed of separation that was planted on the day that I left her had grown, winding around my heart like the convolvulus in the garden, choking it until she was gone forever. I thought about Mrs Rivers and Grace, and of how they had been lost to each other.

I tried to persuade her. 'I think your mother was trying to protect you.'

She shook her head, unconvinced. 'Well, it didn't work.'

'It wasn't that she wanted Grace dead,' I said. 'She didn't know her. She wasn't thinking of your child. She was thinking of you.'

The port had loosened my tongue.

'You could telephone her. Just to tell her that you're both all right.'

'I don't want to talk to her.'

There was an awkward silence and my happiness slunk away. I was worried that I had pushed it too far.

You've messed it up again, I thought. You've said too much.

But after a minute, I felt a soft hand on mine. I turned my head to see Rose looking at me with concern.

'I'm sorry,' she said. 'It was the port. I'm not used to it. I haven't had a drink since I found out I was pregnant.'

She reached under the bed and brought out a package wrapped in red paper. 'I've got something for you,' she said. 'Happy Christmas! I hope you like it.'

'For me?' I said.

'Go on,' she said. 'Open it.'

I slid my finger under the strips of sticky tape and drew out a silver frame. In it was the photograph from the Heath; Rose, Grace and me, smiling at the camera with London stretched out behind us. I gasped with pleasure.

'Thank you,' I said, hugging it to my chest. 'It's wonderful.'

'Do you really like it?' Rose said.

'There's nothing I would have liked more,' I said, meaning every word.

Fourteen

By the time the primroses had begun to appear on the riverbanks, a feeling of anticipation had spread through the village. The narrow road that connected us to the rest of the world, empty of traffic for so long, was busy with squat tanks crawling towards the coast. Girls stood and waved at the soldiers who hung out of them and there were dances on Saturday nights at the army base three miles away. Grace and I were forbidden to go. Reverend Rivers was firm.

'Anything could happen,' he said. 'Young girls like you should not be seen in that sort of place.'

Grace tried to argue but I was secretly relieved. It was easy to imagine her at a dance, tight on drink and dancing with servicemen whilst I stood by and watched. It would be a hundred times worse than seeing her with William and I was grateful for Reverend Rivers' strictness.

As spring became summer, people began to be hopeful and excited. The wireless told of successes and when D-Day came at last, the church bells rang out for the first time since the war had begun. Everyone agreed that it was nearly over and that it wouldn't be long before we won it once and for all. Mrs Rivers even played a polka on the piano and Grace and I danced around the room.

It didn't last. The flying bombs came whilst the celebrations were still going on. They flew by themselves, without any escort, clattering across the sky all day and night. They were meant for London, not us, but we got them anyway when they ran out of fuel. The newspapers gave Kent a new name, Hellfire Corner, and like hell itself, there was no way out. When a herd of cows was found lying dead in a field with their tails blown off, Mrs Rivers said it wasn't safe for us to leave the rectory.

She gave us chores to pass the time and we were at work on one of them when the telegram arrived. It was a Saturday and Grace and I were polishing the silver. Reverend Rivers had added to the job by bringing the candlesticks, collection plate and chalice from the church. We spent all morning rubbing on polish, working it in with a cloth, then buffing up each piece to make it shine. The things that Reverend Rivers had brought, which seemed so sacred on the altar, were very ordinary in the rectory kitchen. We sat at the table in our aprons using butter knives to loosen the wax that had dripped down the candlesticks and peeling off the rest of it with our fingernails, trying not to scratch the metal. The collection plate was tarnished from all the copper coins that had been dropped into it and the chalice was covered in smears. This was the part that people didn't see, I thought, as I scraped around the curves of a candlestick; the real bits, like the smelly water at the bottom of the flower vases and the hem of Reverend Rivers' white cassock, which trailed in the mud and had to be scrubbed and starched before the next service.

It was dull work, and so when the knock came we were glad of the interruption. Grace and I threw down our cloths, scrambled to our feet and raced to the door, skidding on the tiles in the hallway. Grace got there first. On the doorstep was Jack, the post-mistress's son. He avoided my eyes as he handed me a piece of paper, then turned and ran down the garden path.

Grace and I looked at each other. I turned the telegram over. The ink had bled into the paper but the message was clear enough.

Regret inform Mrs Kathleen Lynch killed, V1 attack 28 June.

It was as if someone had taken hold of my guts and was twisting them. I doubled over and retched. Ma was dead. She was gone forever. Far away I heard a terrible noise, like the screams made by animals when they were caught in William's traps.

A bitter smell made me shudder and blink.

'They're just smelling salts.' Mrs Rivers' voice was gentle. 'You've had an awful shock.' She put something into my hands; a glass. 'Drink this,' she said. 'It's brandy. It will do you good.'

The smell of the alcohol made me realize something terrible. Ma's death was a punishment for all the wickedness of the past year, for stealing the communion wine, for swimming naked in the lake, for being jealous of William. Most of all, it was a punishment for loving Grace. I remembered the words in the Book of Common Prayer.

For then we are guilty of the Body and Blood of Christ the Saviour; we eat and drink our own damnation, not considering the Lord's Body; we kindle God's wrath against us; we provoke Him to plague us with divers diseases and sundry kinds of death.

I had made God angry. I had provoked him and Ma had paid for it. I had started it all and now I would suffer the consequences. Kent had seemed like Paradise to me, a world that I would never have been able to imagine if I hadn't seen it for myself. I had wanted very badly to be part of it. I thought of Ma's visit, the last time I had seen her alive. I had been ashamed of her and of our shabby London life. She had understood, I knew, from the look in her eyes as she said goodbye and the way she had told me that I'd always be her girl. I imagined her sitting in the corner of the train compartment, watching the fields fold away behind her and knowing that she had lost me to the rectory.

But Kent wasn't Paradise any more. The newspapers were right after all. Hellfire Corner was what it was and I was stuck in it, facing an angry God. If I had been able to confess, I thought, I might have been forgiven and Ma might still be alive. If Reverend Rivers had been a priest and not a rector, it might all have been stopped. If I had prayed to the Virgin Mary instead of God the Father, she might have saved me. But the Virgin Mary didn't live in Kent so I had sinned and Ma had suffered for it.

Mrs Rivers took the glass from my hands and held it to my lips. She tipped it up and the brandy trickled down my throat, burning as it went. The taste of it took me back to lying in the grass by the lake with Grace and I began to panic. I had done enough damage. I had to stop what I had started before anyone else was hurt. If I had no choice but to pray to God the Father rather than the Virgin Mary, then that was what I would do.

'I'm going to pray for Ma,' I said and ran past Mrs Rivers and Grace, through the kitchen and out of the back door.

As I raced through the vegetable patch, past the raspberry canes and cabbage stumps, I thought of Grace and me, two little girls on that first day, hurrying to find out if there would be a war. I remembered us, older, hiding in the hut and running back to the rectory screaming at the racket of the dogfight above us. I thought of us, older still, creeping to the vestry to find the communion wine. I wanted to ask God to help me put it out of my mind, to pretend it had never happened.

When I got to the porch I stood still for a moment, trying to collect my thoughts. They seemed too big to be contained within a building, better suited to the outdoors; to the fields or to the lake. I took hold of the heavy iron ring with both hands and turned it, feeling the weight of the latch as it lifted, then pushed open the door, just wide enough to slip inside.

I had never been in the church by myself. The smallest movement was enough to disturb the musty air. My heart was hammering and I leaned against the font, trying to calm down. I looked around the church. Wild feelings like mine were out of place in it. Everything about it was modest and restrained. Without sunlight shining through them, the stained glass windows were dull. The covers of the hymn-books stacked up on the back pew were faded and the flower arrangements had dropped most of their petals onto the window-ledges. The carpet in the aisle was threadbare and worn. A bird had left white splashes on the lectern, a wooden eagle that held Reverend Rivers' Sunday sermons in its wings. Above it hung a board with the numbers of the hymns for the week before. Ma had been alive when we had sung them. The thought made my eyes fill with tears. I hurried to the front pew and knelt on the cold flag-stones. I put my hands together and bowed my head.

I didn't know what to say, whether to ask God why, or to ask him to stop, or simply to confess.

Almighty God, unto whom all hearts be open, all desires known, and from whom no secrets are hid.

He already knew it all. I began to recite the Lord's Prayer in a panic, stumbling over the words.

Our Father, who art in heaven
Hallowed be thy Name
Thy kingdom come

Thy will be done
On earth as it is in heaven
Give us this day our daily bread
And forgive us our trespasses
As we forgive those who trespass against us –

I faltered when I reached the next line, the one about temptation. I had already given into it. I knew I was supposed to want to be spared but that wasn't what I wanted at all. I wanted Grace. I was frightened of what other punishments might follow if I didn't give her up but I couldn't bear to be without her. I began to cry, tears spilling over my fingers as I thought of Ma and the girl that I had been when I left London. I had lost Ma and I had lost myself. I couldn't stand the thought of losing Grace as well.

'I'll try,' I whispered. 'I'll try to give her up. Just don't do anything else. Don't hurt her.'

*

I was still kneeling when I felt a hand on my head. For a terrible moment I thought it was the hand of God. I stayed perfectly still, too frightened to move. Then I heard a man's voice, quiet and low.

'Nora.'

I twisted around to see Reverend Rivers standing just behind me. Usually he was removed from everyone, kept apart by his black frock and his habit of making himself invisible. It was odd to feel him so close.

'I was so very sorry to hear about your mother,' he said gravely.

Mrs Rivers must have told him, I supposed, and he had come to the church to comfort me like he did with people from the village when news came of a dead husband or a brother. But I didn't want to be comforted. I wanted to be left alone. I pressed my face into my hands, not knowing how to say so without offending him.

He was still for a while, saying nothing, then dropped to his knees next to me. He smelled musty, like the church and tobacco from his pipe. He clasped his hands together and looked towards the altar.

'Nora,' he said. 'We must pray for your mother's soul. And that this terrible war may soon be over.' He bowed his head. 'Let us pray.'

I was used to hearing him say it every Sunday from the pulpit. I felt easier and closed my eyes too.

Reverend Rivers prayed for a long time. He prayed for Ma's soul and for all the other people killed by the bombs in London. He prayed for the Forces. He prayed for the King. But then he began a new prayer, something altogether different.

'Almighty God,' he said. 'We pray for your servant Nora.'

I was suddenly afraid.

'Help her through this difficult time. Cleanse the thoughts of her heart, by the inspiration of thy Holy Spirit.'

Sweat began to trickle down my back as I wondered how much he knew.

'Cleanse the thoughts of her heart. Forgive her trespasses. Let her be guided by what is right.'

I wished that I were anywhere else, even under the rubble with Ma, than next to this strange man, this priest who seemed to know everything about me.

'Let her conscience lead her to the path of righteousness.'

I breathed in sharply. Reverend Rivers lifted his head and looked at me.

'Nora, what's wrong?'

I couldn't look back at him.

'Is it your mother?'

I shook my head.

'I do understand how you are feeling.'

I wrapped my arms around myself, wishing he would leave me alone.

'I know what it means to lose someone very dear to you.'

Suddenly I wasn't scared of answering back to him. 'No you don't,' I said, and it was my old voice, my London voice, not the new one from Kent, cracked with anger. 'You've got Mrs Rivers and you've got Grace. I never had a father and now I haven't even got Ma. I haven't got anyone.'

Reverend Rivers looked agitated. 'Please don't worry about what will happen to you. I know you have no family left. But—'

He paused.

'What?' I demanded.

He was studying my face as closely as if it were a book, something religious, in very small print. 'Nora, you – you are like a daughter to me.'

I blinked in surprise. 'What?'

'A daughter. A very dear daughter.'

I spoke without thinking. 'But you don't even like your daughter.'

Reverend Rivers looked shocked. 'What do you mean?'

'Grace. You never pay her any attention. You wouldn't care if she weren't around. You probably wouldn't even notice.'

He sighed. 'Yes I would,' he said. 'Believe me, I would. Nora, listen to me. I understand.'

I shook my head stubbornly.

'Grace wasn't an only child,' he said.

I stared at him in disbelief. 'What?'

Reverend Rivers had gone very pale.

'Grace had a twin sister called Elizabeth,' he said in a low voice. 'She died when she was less than a year old.'

I couldn't believe what I was hearing. Grace had a sister, a sister whom she had never once mentioned to me.

'What happened?' I whispered.

Reverend Rivers hesitated.

'You have to tell me,' I said. 'If you don't, I'll ask Grace.'

'No!' he said wearily. 'I'll tell you.'

He sighed. 'Evelyn – Mrs Rivers – had come down with influenza. Usually she would let nothing come between her and the girls. She was devoted to them. But she was very ill that night, with a fever. I told her that I would bathe the children and put them to bed whilst she rested. She didn't want to leave them, but I managed to persuade her.

'It was the first time I had bathed them. Evelyn had always taken care of that sort of thing. I was a young curate then, and busy with the parish. When there was a knock at the door, I went to answer it. It was the organist with the numbers of the hymns for the next day's service. We spoke for a minute, said good night, and I went back to the bathroom.

'Grace was sitting in the same position that I had left her in, chuckling to herself. Elizabeth should have been sitting opposite but she wasn't. She was lying face-down in the water at Grace's feet. I ran to the bath and snatched her up. I tried to bring her back to life, but it was no good, she just lay there on the floor, like . . . like a doll.'

He was stammering now, his eyes fixed on the altar.

'Evelyn must have sensed that something was wrong. She came running into the bathroom. When she saw Elizabeth she screamed. It was a terrible sound that I shall never forget. She fell to her knees and picked her up. She began to talk to her, muttering into her ear.

'When the doctor came, I told him all of it. I had to admit that I had left them alone. When Evelyn heard that, she flew at me. Then she started to cry. The doctor gave her morphine to make her sleep but as soon as she woke the next morning she began to cry again. She has cried every morning since.'

He hung his head, as if his memories made it too heavy to hold up.

'I don't know . . . I don't know how things might have been otherwise . . . We buried Elizabeth in the churchyard in a little grave by the wall. Evelyn was inconsolable. I blamed myself and she blamed me too. From that moment on she has despised both me and the rest of the world. I thought that she would pour everything into the child that she had left, but she didn't. For a long time she acted as if she had never had any children at all.

'I distracted myself with my ministry. It took me many years to make my peace with God. I told myself that it was his will, that there was some reason for it. I learned to accept. I had to. He was all I had left. Evelyn could scarcely bear to look at me. I dared not go near Grace for fear that something might happen to her too.'

Reverend Rivers' eyes clouded over. 'I must admit . . .'

He hesitated. When he spoke again, it was almost as if he had forgotten I was there.

'I have to say . . . I developed a dislike for her. For Grace. For my own daughter. It was the way that she chuckled when I went back to the bathroom. I know that she was only a child, a baby, but I felt as if she were mocking me. I can't forget it. It comes back to me every time I look at her.'

I stared at him in horror. So many things made sense to me now; the strained silence at the rectory, Mrs Rivers' unhappiness and Reverend Rivers' coldness towards Grace. But knowing was no relief. It was too much to hear. I wanted to squirm and block my ears with my hands like a child. But there was something else that I needed to know. I made myself ask.

'But why hasn't Grace said anything about it? She never told me.'

He shook his head. 'The doctor assured us that she was too

young to remember. He said that it would be best never to tell her, and so we didn't. We even left Elizabeth's gravestone blank, without an inscription, so she wouldn't come across it.'

His voice was filled with sadness. 'But I know that something has stayed with her. She has always wanted a sister. When she was younger she used to ask us why she had to be alone. That's why your arrival meant so much to her, to all of us. It was as if Elizabeth had come back.'

Whether Grace knew anything about it or not, I would never be able to look at her in the same way as before. Everything had changed. I had chosen to stay with the Rivers. I had chosen them instead of Ma. But now I knew it wasn't me they had wanted. I was someone else, a replacement for a ghost.

'So you see,' Reverend Rivers said desperately, 'I understand. I know how you are feeling. I understand what it is to lose someone whom you love.'

I couldn't think of anything to say.

Reverend Rivers went on speaking, almost pleading with me now.

'But I also know that some good can come of it. We lost Elizabeth. But God sent us you. You were the answer to my prayers. When you first came to us I dared to hope that you would make things better. You were – how can I put it? – a consolation.'

Two small blotches had appeared on his cheekbones as if he were wearing rouge, vivid against his pale skin. He was acting like he did in the study when he talked about books. But in the church his excitement was out of place, somehow wrong.

He swallowed and went on, avoiding my eyes.

'But then . . . I have also been troubled . . . '

There was something about the way he said it that made me nervous. I stayed very still as he carried on.

'By feelings . . . '

He looked up again at the altar and began to speak quickly, his words tumbling over one another.

'I have begged God not to allow me to be led into temptation. I have prayed for strength.'

The church seemed suddenly very cold.

'I thought God had listened. I thought it would be all right.'

My mind was racing, trying to work out what he meant.

'But then I saw you—'

He broke off abruptly and buried his face in his hands, mumbling something to himself. I listened, trying to make out what he was saying, telling myself that it couldn't be what it seemed. But as the words became clearer, I shivered. It was the prayer that I had been reciting just before he had come into the church in my effort to bury my desire for Grace.

. . . And lead us not into temptation

But deliver us from evil . . .

As he went on praying, my horror grew. I had heard him pray like this before, when I had watched him on his knees in the shelter, begging God to save him from something terrible. I remembered how I had heard someone at the lake that day when we were swimming. I suddenly realized who it was and what he must have seen.

Reverend Rivers lifted his head and smiled at me, a peculiar sort of smile.

'Nora,' he said. 'If you knew how I have dreamed—'

He lurched forward and took hold of my shoulders. I felt the scratch of stubble and his breath against my skin as he bent to kiss me, over and over, searching for my lips with his. He slid his hands down my back, then further still, pressing himself hard against me. The smell of old tobacco and sweat filled my nostrils. As his hands began to move over my body I held myself rigid, too shocked to move, but when they reached under my skirt, something inside me snapped.

I wrenched myself away from him and scrambled to my feet. 'No!' I shouted. 'You can't mean that.' I pushed past him and ran down the aisle. When I reached the door I turned to look at him, hunched in the pew.

'You shouldn't have done that. You just shouldn't,' I whispered, then turned and ran.

*

Knowing that Grace and Mrs Rivers would be waiting for me in the kitchen, I went in through the front door instead and ran up the stairs as fast as I could. I threw myself into the bathroom, slammed the door behind me and drew the bolt. I took the towel from its hook, stuffed as much of it into my mouth as I could and began to scream. I screamed until my throat was raw and my head felt as if it would fall apart. When I couldn't scream any more I sunk to the floor, drawing my knees up to my chest and hugging them tight.

From where I was sitting, pressed up against the bath, I could see dirt at the base of the lavatory and balls of dust along the top of the skirting boards. It was like everything else at the rectory, I thought bitterly. Things looked clean enough on the outside, but under the surface, secret dirt had been building up like the hard yellow scum around the bath taps. My skin began to crawl, as if a thousand little creatures were swarming over me. I started to scrape at my arms with my fingernails. I wanted to be clean. I stood up and opened the hot tap as far as I could, until the water was tumbling out fast.

I went over to the door and tried the bolt, checking that it was secure. My blouse became a second curtain, looped over the rail. I rolled up my skirt and blocked the gap under the door. I climbed into the bath, keeping my knickers on until I was hidden, then I inched them down my legs and dropped them over the side.

I lay back, watching the water rise past the Plimsoll Line. I didn't care any more about making do and playing my part. I would break the five-inch rule. He had broken the rules and so would I. The water poured into the bath and I let it keep coming until it had turned cold.

I took the sliver of soap from the dish and rubbed it over my arm but it did no good. The crawling sensation was still there, all over my body. I looked about the room for something stronger. There was a bottle of Vim on the window-ledge. I reached for it, twisted off the lid and shook some of the whitish powder into my hand. It stung, a good sign, I decided. It would be strong enough. I stood up out of the water and brought my hand to my chest, rubbing in the Vim with small, circular movements, then reached down to my thighs and rubbed it in as hard as I could. My skin turned white, then red. I rubbed until I began to bleed, then I sat back down, watching the water turn pink, my mind racing.

I was frightened. I was sitting in the same bath that Elizabeth had died in. I thought about Grace, wondering how much she really knew. Nobody could be trusted, not Reverend Rivers, not Mrs Rivers, not Grace and not me. We all had secrets, all of us. The whole damned war was about secrets, keeping quiet and hiding things from each other.

Reverend Rivers had kept the same secret as I had, hidden it inside until he couldn't stand it any longer. When he had said it, I had been afraid and then I had hated him. If I ever told Grace how I felt about her she would hate me like that too. I would seem as monstrous to her as he was to me. I was just as bad as him.

I remembered what Mrs Rivers had said at that first Sunday lunch. 'Nora will stay with us for as long as it is safer for her to be here than in London.'

The time had come, I thought, when I would be safer in London than in Kent. It would be safer for me and it would be safer for Grace. I had to take myself away from temptation, to protect her.

I didn't want her ever to feel the terrible panic I had felt when Reverend Rivers moved towards me.

Now that Ma was dead, there was nobody left to go to. There was nobody left to look after me and so I would look after myself. I would start by leaving this place that I had thought of as Paradise. I wasn't going to wait to be cast out of it by God or any other sort of father. I would go back to London. If Paradise could turn out to be so rotten, perhaps the city that they said was like Hell would turn out to be all right.

Fifteen

THE NEW YEAR BEGAN WITH A CHILL WIND, AN ILL WIND,
blowing no-one any good. It howled outside my window, sending
freezing draughts down the chimney that made me shiver. I had new
pains that were as persistent as the wind. I tried to ignore them. I had
come to like my room, particularly in the afternoons when Rose
would close the curtains against the dark and build a fire. Whilst the
baby slept she read to me. I chose old favourites, remembering nights
at the rectory when Grace and I had sat close to the hearth, taking
turns with *Rebecca*, desperate to know what would happen next. I
thought of George, reading out loud at the kitchen table as I cooked
dinner. He had spent hours looking through books, searching out
passages about food. When money was short, he read out descrip-
tions of feasts as we ate scrambled eggs. It had never failed to make
me smile.

One day as Rose was reading, I began to feel a dull ache in my stomach. I tried to concentrate on what she was saying but it soon became worse and before long it was impossible to ignore. I started to breathe through my nose very slowly, trying to keep calm, but then a spasm of pain passed through me, so strong that I gasped.

'What's wrong?' said Rose in alarm.

I couldn't answer. An enormous pressure was building up inside me, pushing out my stomach as if I were filling up with air. It grew stronger and stronger until something seemed to snap and I felt a sudden burning between my legs. I leaned forward and was sick, retching again and again until there was nothing left in my stomach.

Rose moved quickly, holding me up until I had finished. She smoothed back my hair and wiped my face with one of the damp cloths that she used when she was changing Grace. She brought a glass of water and held it to my lips.

'Nora,' she whispered. 'What happened?'

With an effort, I pointed to my stomach.

'Don't worry, I'll clean it up,' she said, and drew the blanket back. She put her hand over her mouth. I looked down. A dark stain spread out underneath me. I was lying in a pool of blood.

Our eyes met.

'Oh God,' she said, and the baby began to scream.

*

Rose changed the sheets and washed me gently with a sponge. I closed my eyes in shame as she did it, holding back tears. She pulled the sodden nightdress over my head and brought another that smelled of lavender. She brushed my hair carefully, keeping the bristles of the hairbrush away from my scalp. Then she sat down on the bed and took my hands in hers, cradling them between her palms.

'Please let me call a doctor,' she said. 'I'm scared. I don't know what to do. I'll look after you as well as I can, but I'm not a nurse. I don't think I can do it on my own.'

I stared into the fire, watching the flames leap high as if they were trying to escape up the chimney.

'It's going to get worse,' she said quietly. 'I've seen what happens. We need someone who knows what to do.'

I knew what was going to happen too. The book had explained it all, down to the very last detail. I turned my head towards her and saw the pain in her eyes. I remembered what she had told me about her father. She didn't need to be dragged into it again.

'All right,' I said finally. 'Call a doctor. I don't mind.'

*

She made a telephone call and a doctor came to visit. I felt like a child, tucked up tight by an anxious mother. When I heard the footsteps coming up the stairs and along the corridor the room seemed smaller than before. I lay very still, waiting.

The door opened. 'Dr Armstrong's here to see you,' said Rose.

I turned my head to see a blonde-haired young woman, her cheeks pink from climbing the stairs. She looked like an actress, not a doctor. She wasn't what I had expected at all. She was smiling at me. Perhaps, I thought, it wouldn't be as bad as I had imagined.

'Hello,' she said.

She came to sit down, not on the chair but on the bed.

'Well, Nora, Rose says you've been ill for quite a while. Can you tell me what's wrong?'

What's wrong? I thought. I didn't know where to start.

'She says you think you have cancer.'

I nodded.

'But you haven't seen a doctor. Is that right?'

I tried to think of a suitable answer but my mind was blank. 'No,' I said. 'I haven't.'

She frowned and scribbled something in a notebook. 'But if you haven't seen a doctor,' she said gently, 'how do you know it's cancer?'

I mumbled my answer, knowing it would sound ridiculous. 'A book.'

'I'm sorry?'

'It was a book about cancer. A medical book. It gave a list of symptoms. It told me what to expect.'

'And what were the symptoms?'

They weren't things I wanted to talk about, but the doctor simply waited, saying nothing, and I realized I would have to tell her.

'I couldn't eat but my stomach grew. I felt sick. I started . . . to bleed.' I said the last few words very quietly.

She nodded. Her eyes were kind. I hung my head.

'It's all right,' she said. 'Rose told me. I'm just sorry that you've felt like that for so long. I'd like to do some tests, to be sure of the diagnosis.'

'Why do you need to be sure? I know I'm going to die. That's enough, isn't it?'

She frowned. 'If we know what it is, there's a chance we can do something about it. There are lots of ways to fight cancer.'

I imagined myself in a hospital, being prodded and poked by strangers who would come to know everything about me. I would be there for everyone to see, laid out on a bed as if I were already on the mortuary slab, unable to hide a thing. They would make notes and record every detail. I would be parcelled up all over again, just like the day I was sent to the train with a label around my neck.

I wanted to shout it out for everyone to hear. Don't you see? I surrendered a long time ago. I gave up that day in the church. Ask those stained-glass angels in the windows, they saw it all. I carried on dying all the way through the war, while everyone else was trying so damned hard to stay alive. Now it's time to finish the job.

'I don't want to fight,' I said instead. 'I'm tired.'

'Nora, can't we—?'

'No,' I said firmly.

She sighed. 'I can't force you to have treatment. But I can make you more comfortable. I can help you manage the pain.'

I couldn't tell her that the pain was a punishment, one that was long overdue.

'Please, Nora,' said Rose. 'I can't bear to see you like you were today. I want to look after you but I'm scared.'

'She's right,' said the doctor. 'It's not going to be easy, especially with a baby here as well.'

They were sitting on either side of me, pinning me to the bed with the counterpane. I was trapped.

'Here's a suggestion,' said the doctor. 'I think you're probably right, but I want to be certain. If it *is* cancer, I won't ask you to take any kind of cure, but I'll find a nurse to come to the house and help Rose look after you. That way you can stay at home. You won't have to go to a hospital. Will you agree to that, at least?'

'Must you really examine me?' I said, without much hope.

'I'm afraid so. I want to send a specialist cancer nurse. But first we have to be sure that's what you have.'

*

The examination was another humiliation.

'I'm afraid this might be uncomfortable,' said the doctor. 'Take a deep breath.'

Rose squeezed my hand as something nudged between my legs, something cold and blunt. When it began to push into me I felt a pain worse than anything I'd felt so far. I whimpered.

'You're doing really well. Now I'm going to take some cells. This might hurt a little.'

I felt a wave of nausea as something scratched and scraped deep inside me. I would have screamed out but I knew it wouldn't make any difference. I bit my lip instead and tasted blood.

'Good,' the doctor said, when it was over. 'All finished. Well done.'

I felt my nightdress being brought down over my legs and the blankets tucked back around me. I lay on my back, rigid with humiliation.

'We'll be in touch very soon,' she said. 'Look after yourself, Nora. I mean it.'

I couldn't meet her eyes after what she'd just done.

'Goodbye,' I mumbled.

'Goodbye.'

*

The results came quickly and confirmed what I had known from the start. It was, as the doctor put it, terminal. But when I thought of where I was going, I felt oddly calm. All I had to do was wait.

Sixteen

I had made up my mind. I was going back to London, as soon as I could. The next day was Sunday and I wasn't about to let myself be trapped in the church with Reverend Rivers again. The thought of seeing him pray for our souls from the pulpit made my flesh crawl. There was nothing that I could believe in any more; he had made sure of that. The place I had loved had all been built on lies. The family I had chosen over Ma had its nasty little secrets, secrets that would never stop eating away at it. I had been stupid. I had stayed where I thought I was wanted. I hadn't stopped to think why I was so welcome. I should have gone back to Ma when I had the chance. It was too late for that. She had lost me and now I had lost her, but I would go back to where we came from, back to where I belonged.

After scrubbing myself in the bathroom I got into bed to plan my escape. I wanted to be under the blankets, to shut everything out.

But before long there was a knock at the door. It was Mrs Rivers, as kind and concerned as she had been on my first day at the rectory.

'I came to see if you were all right,' she said quietly. 'You've had an awful shock. Losing someone you love is a terrible thing.'

I knew that she didn't mean just Ma. I flushed, both at the memory of the things that Reverend Rivers had told me and in shame, because I knew that I was about to throw her kindness back at her by running away. When she bent to kiss my forehead, as if I were a little girl again, I wanted her to put her arms around me and hold me so that I could wish her a silent goodbye, but instead she straightened up again and smiled a small, tight smile.

'Grief is exhausting,' she said. 'I'll leave you to rest. Call me if you need anything.'

I watched her go, closing the door gently behind her. Reverend Rivers would know why I had left. My departure would be a relief to him. But Mrs Rivers wouldn't understand and he wouldn't tell her. She would have lost her second Elizabeth. I would hurt her and I would hurt Grace, who would be left alone again without a sister. I curled myself up as small as I could, waiting for the sound of the piano. When the first notes drifted up through the floor, I pushed back the blankets and got out of bed.

Five years ago I had arrived at the rectory with just a few things in a pillowcase. Now I took the same one from the chest of drawers and quickly filled it with clothes, a hairbrush and the copy of *Rebecca*. There wasn't much more to take and I was glad. But then I saw the Shakespeare, the book that had done more than any other to make me feel better. I picked it up, hugging it to my chest. It wasn't a practical thing to take, I knew. It would be awkward to carry. But I would have no friends in London. I was going to be lonely. There were enough characters in there to keep me company forever. I wrapped a cardigan around the heavy book and put it in the pillowcase.

I planned to creep down the old servants' stairs and out through the back door. From there I knew the paths and fields well enough to get to the bus stop at the far end of the village without being seen. But on my way out of the room I couldn't help myself. I fell onto Grace's bed, burying my nose in her pillow. I knew that when I got up again I would be leaving her forever and so I lay there much longer than I meant to. I was still lying there when she walked into the room.

'Nora,' she said. 'Are you all right? Mummy said that you were terribly upset. She sent me to ask if you'd like something to eat.'

Then she caught sight of the pillowcase. 'What are you doing?'

She picked it up and looked inside. 'Are you running away?' she said, sounding hurt.

The game was up but I said nothing.

'You were going to go on your own, weren't you? You were going to leave me here. How could you?'

'I want to go home,' I whispered. 'I have to go on my own. You wouldn't like it.'

'Let me come with you.' She was excited. 'Please say yes. I've never been to London. It'll be an adventure.'

It was all going wrong. She wasn't supposed to come with me. 'You can't!' I blurted out.

'Why not? If you can run away, so can I. There's no point in me staying here without you.'

'It's different,' I said. 'My mother's dead. There's no-one to care where I go. I'm just an evacuee. But your mother and father would mind if you weren't here.'

'They wouldn't care. They'd be more upset about you. They're much more fond of you than they are of me. It's true – you can't pretend it isn't.'

'It's not,' I said uncomfortably, remembering what Reverend

Rivers had said in the church. 'You're their daughter. Don't be silly.'

'Don't you remember what Father said that day when we were reading Shakespeare?' she said in a flat voice. 'He called me a disappointment. He meant it. I know he did. He's always been like that, ever since I was small. That's why they sent me away to boarding school as soon as they could. They couldn't wait to be rid of me. Why shouldn't I go now? At least you're my friend. You like me, don't you?'

'Yes,' I stammered.

'If you don't let me come with you,' said Grace, 'I'll go downstairs and tell them. You won't even get as far as the village green.'

We stared at each other. Of course I wanted her to come with me, just as much as I knew I should leave her behind.

'Please,' she said. 'I couldn't bear to go back to how it was before you came. I was so lonely. Please let me come with you.'

'London's hard,' I said. 'There are people everywhere. It's dirty and it's noisy and there are bombs. It's not like here, you know. It's dangerous.'

She grinned like she had on that first day in the cattle-pens. 'I chose you, didn't I? I'm not going to let you go that easily.'

*

She threw some things into another pillowcase and then we slipped out of the rectory, through the churchyard and across the fields to the bus stop, where we waited nervously for the bus to arrive. When it came, we sat at the back, trying to keep out of sight.

Just as we were getting to Sevenoaks, Grace took out a pair of nail scissors.

'What are those for?' I said.

'Watch.'

I watched as she took her ragdoll from the pillowcase, laid it on her knee and unpicked the seam that ran up its back. Inside the doll were pound notes, folded up into little squares. I had been so anxious to escape from the rectory that I hadn't thought about how I'd pay for anything in London. I'd brought just enough money for the bus ride.

'See,' said Grace. 'You'll be glad that I came. These are my savings. I kept them in case I ever needed to run away from school.'

I was glad that she was with me, and not just because of the money. I couldn't have left her behind. But I was frightened of the journey and of what we would find when we got to London. As we arrived at the station I could see an advertisement for beer, painted on the side of the railway pub. *Take Courage* it said, in tall white letters. It was all very well to say so, I thought. It was odd enough to be surrounded by strangers. I hadn't left the village since the war began.

It was a long time since we had eaten. I was used to being hungry, to the vague feeling of never being satisfied, even at the end of a meal. But now I felt a sharp ache in my stomach. I kept swallowing, trying to put something inside me, even if it were only air. I realized that from now on we would have to find our own food. We would have to find everything for ourselves. The more I thought about it, the gloomier I felt. Grace was the opposite, excited by the novelty of it all. Going to the buffet was her idea.

'Come on!' she said. 'We'll feel better once we've had something to eat.' She said it in the same way that she had suggested swimming in the lake or drinking the communion wine, expecting no resistance, and as usual, I gave none. I followed as she strode along the platform, as confident as if she travelled to London every day.

The buffet was full of servicemen in uniforms and land girls dressed in trousers, smoking and playing cards. I trailed after Grace, feeling awkward in my patterned frock. The waitress ruled the room from her position behind the counter. She snorted when we asked for something to eat and tossed her head in the direction of the shelves behind her. They were all empty.

'There's nothing left,' she said. 'Never is, these days.'

My stomach rumbled with disappointment.

'Might we at least have some tea?' Grace said, her clear voice slicing through the smoky air.

The waitress looked at her with evident dislike. 'Have you brought a cup?'

'A cup?'

'For the tea.' She spoke slowly, as if Grace were being very foolish. 'We haven't cups in here since 1942. The railway doesn't give them out any more. Didn't you know? Where have you been hiding?'

I took hold of Grace's arm and led her away. As we went I heard the waitress talking to one of the land girls.

'Unbelievable! Don't they know there's a war on?'

The land girl said something that I couldn't make out and they laughed. I hurried through the crowded room to the door. A notice was stuck to it.

The Time Has Come for Every Person to Search his Conscience Before Making a Railway Journey, it said, in bold lettering. *It is More Than Ever Vital to Ask Yourself. 'Is My Journey Really Necessary?'*

I thought of all the things that had happened. Our journey was necessary, all right. I would rather starve on the streets than go back to the rectory and its lies. I pushed the door with rather more force than was required, leaving it swinging behind us.

*

Huddled on a bench at the very end of the platform, I felt like one of the rabbits that William hunted in the fields, quivering as they waited to make a dash for it. I wanted to be on the train, in a compartment with the door shut, taking me out of sight and out of Kent, out of the reach of Reverend Rivers. When at last the train drew into the station I ran to it and dashed up the steps as quickly as I could.

It was very full. It seemed we weren't the only ones ready to take our chances in London. People were packed two to a seat, spilling out into the corridors. We went along the train, picking our way between servicemen's legs and their kitbags, looking into compartments to see if any seats were free. I remembered the lurching, pitching sensation from the last time that I had made the journey. I had changed since then. I was different, no longer a little girl. Reverend Rivers had shown me so that morning and now the servicemen confirmed it, calling out as we passed.

'Breathe in and let these pretty ladies through!'

'You can sit on my knee if you can't find a space, darling!'

'I've got two knees. You can have one each!'

Grace giggled. I kept my head down and my hand on her arm, pulling her after me and trying to ignore them. Eventually we came to a compartment that was less crowded than the others. There was space for one of us to sit down.

'Go on, Grace,' I said. 'You have it.'

A soldier stood up. 'Here,' he said. 'Take my seat. I was about to stretch my legs in any case.'

'Thank you,' said Grace. 'That's awfully kind.'

We squeezed past him. I was so concerned with trying not to tread on the other people in the compartment that I almost missed the look that he gave Grace, an admiring look that went from her head to her toes and back again in one swift moment, taking in all of her.

'Don't talk to anyone,' I hissed. 'Don't attract attention. Pretend to be asleep. We've run away, remember?'

Grace giggled again. 'Don't be so stuffy! I've only ever taken the train to school and that was just full of girls. This is much more exciting.'

She sat, looking around the compartment and smiling, wedged between me and a stern-looking woman with a Highland terrier on her knee. Everyone else was asleep, apart from two servicemen by the window who were sharing a cigarette and talking quietly. I looked past them, through the window, watching the fields rush by. Leaving Kent had happened without warning, just like leaving London. I never seemed to say a proper goodbye. I stared at the fields, the woods and the hundred shades of green, remembering how I had marvelled the first time I had seen them.

As the train stopped and started through deserted stations, stripped of their signs, I began to wonder whether anything would be left of London when we arrived. A dreary gloom settled over me and I huddled into my seat. A guard came through the train to punch our tickets, a thin, pale man who looked as if years of squeezing through crowded corridors had crushed the life out of him.

'Pull the blinds,' he shouted as he went. One of the servicemen drew them down and the compartment seemed to become even more cramped than before. I remembered the smell of the potted meat sandwiches from the last time and my stomach turned. I thought of how I had escaped into the lavatory, only to find something much worse.

As if she had read my mind, Grace turned to me. 'I need to use the W.C.,' she said, and stood up.

As soon as she was gone I began to count the minutes, fearful of the servicemen with their winks and smiles and afraid that she would never come back to me. The longer she was gone, the smaller the compartment seemed to become. It was as if I could feel the breath of the other passengers, damp against my skin. I smelled sweat that was much older than the journey. I listened to conversations from the corridor, trying to make out Grace's voice, but the woman with the dog kept trying to talk to me.

'Going to London, are you?' she said. It sounded like an accusation.

I nodded.

'There can't be many girls like you and your friend on this train.'

I shifted about in my seat, feeling uncomfortable. I was sure the servicemen were listening.

'Haven't you heard?' the woman went on. 'People are trying to get out, away from those – what do you call them – those doodlebugs. They're saying that there's going to be lots more of them. You want to be going in the other direction, not this one.'

I had started to feel very hot. I imagined a serviceman, smiling at Grace and stretching his arm across the corridor to block her way. I imagined them looking at each other and laughing, Grace tipping back her head to show her small white teeth. The woman's breath was sour. I dug my nails into my palms, silently begging her to stop talking. I saw the serviceman bending over Grace and her lifting up her face to meet his kiss. I smelled tobacco and sweat and felt Reverend Rivers' body against mine. I screamed.

Grace was with me in an instant.

'Nora! What's wrong?' She put her arm around my shoulders.

'Is she all right?' the woman asked.

'Her mother was killed,' Grace said quietly. 'She was hit by a V1. We only heard today.'

'Oh Lord.' The woman sounded ashamed. 'I probably set her off. I was talking about the bombs. I thought she looked a bit queer.'

She got off at the next station. I kept my eyes closed, resting my head on Grace's shoulder, still shaken. I was starting to feel as if we would be trapped forever in the swaying compartment. Every so often the train would jerk to a standstill, stopping for a few minutes, then the carriage would begin to lurch and rock again, making the heads of the sleeping servicemen fall to the other side. I resisted sleep and I was soon stiff from holding myself up against the motion of the train. The smoke from the men's cigarettes had made my throat tight and I was horribly thirsty. As the train rocked, my thighs rubbed against each other, sore from the scouring that I had given them with the Vim.

When the whistle blew, a long shriek, the servicemen woke. They yawned and stretched, then one of them looked down at his wrist-watch.

'Not long now,' he said to his friend. 'We'll be in the Smoke before we know it.'

'Christ,' the other man said. 'I wonder what sort of mess we're going to be faced with this time.'

I liked the way that he said *Ker-ist*, drawing out the blasphemy. I tried it out for myself, under my breath. I liked it very much.

Ker-ist, I muttered to myself. *Ker-ist.*

As the train came into the station there was a flurry of movement as the other passengers leaped to their feet, packing away leftover sandwiches and books. The servicemen checked their cigarette packets to see how many were left and stowed them away in their pockets. They reached up for their kitbags in the luggage rack and threw them to each other as if they weighed nothing at all. When the train stopped everyone seemed to move very quickly, rushing to get out. Grace and I stayed in our seats, keeping tight hold of our pillow-cases. Now that we had arrived, I didn't want to leave the compartment, which had suddenly become pleasantly familiar. But soon the conductor came striding through the train.

'All change!' he shouted. 'Waterloo station! End of the line! All change!'

We made our way along the corridor, littered with cigarette stubs, dead matches, scraps of paper and crumbs. The train had a desolate air about it and a thick yellow fog was beginning to creep through the windows and doors. When we were almost at the end of the carriage the lights went out and everything was suddenly dark. Grace cried out and we ran to the door, scrambling down the steps as fast as we'd climbed them just a few hours before.

Everything seemed to have changed since then. We stood on the platform, shoulder to shoulder in our flowered dresses, looking at the crowds of people, more than I had ever seen in one place.

'Ker-ist,' I said, rolling the word off my tongue. 'Ker-ist.'

Grace looked shocked. I shrugged. There was no-one around to tell us what to say or do. The rules had changed again, like they had the last time I had stood at this station, looking at a train. This time, I had decided, we would make them ourselves.

*

That night we slept at the station, huddled together on a bench. I dozed fitfully and woke up groggy and stiff. In the morning we set off to find the house that I had lived in with Ma. I was ashamed to show her where I had come from, the small street where I had lived all my life before I met her, but I didn't have a choice. I had to see what was left of it and there was no question of splitting up. It was as if we had traded places. Grace wasn't fearless like she was in Kent. As she hesitated, I became bold, and I led us through the streets from Waterloo to Bethnal Green, asking passers-by for directions as we went.

As we walked through the streets that had been my world, along the pavements that I had played on every day before I had taken the train to the countryside, I became aware of a strange, heavy silence. The women had gone from their front steps. No-one gossiped to neighbours. We walked on a carpet of leaves as if it were October, but the carpet wasn't the colour of autumn, it was green and slippery underfoot. When we turned the corner of my street, it changed again, giving way to bricks and shattered glass.

I gasped when I saw it, stripped back to its bones. If the street before had been autumn, this was midwinter. The trees were bare, flayed of their leaves and bark. Sap dribbled down their trunks like blood, its fresh scent mingling with the choking smell of brick dust. A nightdress flapped in the branches of one of them as if the tree were trying to cover its nakedness, knowing it was out of place. The houses were exposed as well, scalped of their roofs, their fronts ripped away, leaving flights of stairs like vertebrae, just managing to hold up what was left. The only living things on the street were the cats, picking their way through the broken glass and howling with hunger. Their whines echoed around the shells of the houses like something supernatural, as if the ghosts of the people who had died were present and restless.

Like all the others, our house was open to anyone who cared to look. I made my way over to it, tripping up over the rubble. When I saw what was left of the kitchen I understood where the smell of wet and burning wood was coming from. The walls were black with soot and pools of water lapped at the broken furniture. The fire brigade had tried to put out the fire, I supposed. I wondered what they had seen when they had arrived. I imagined Ma when the bomb came, sitting at the kitchen table with only the woodlice for company, or lying alone and afraid in our bed, praying to the Virgin Mary to be spared. Perhaps that was what she had done every night since I had left her, I thought, five long years of being frightened while I was running in the fields and swimming in the lake and forgetting all about her.

I sat down on a pile of bricks and put my head in my hands. I had mourned Ma before, first when I was sent away from her and then after the terrible day of her visit. I had wept both times but now that she was truly gone, all I could do was to try and hold myself together, exhausted at the prospect of starting again in this strange, battered city. It had changed since I had left and so had I. London and I would have to get used to one another again.

'Are you all right?' Grace said.

I nodded. 'I suppose so,' I said. 'I don't know what to do, that's all.'

She sat down beside me. 'Where will we go?'

I didn't have an answer. I had thought there would be enough left of the house to shelter in but I could see now that there was no chance of that. 'I don't know. It's all so different. I hadn't expected it to be quite so bad.'

'Couldn't we tell someone that you were evacuated but you've come back to London and found that your mother's dead? It's true, after all. They'd have to find you somewhere to live, wouldn't they?'

I didn't think it would be so simple. 'I can't do that,' I said. 'They're telling people not to come back at the moment. It would look suspicious. Besides, I'm seventeen. I'm not a child. No-one has to look after me.' I sighed. 'And Grace, we've run away. They'll have reported us missing. If we tell anyone who we are we'll be found out. And I'm not going back to the village. I'm staying here.'

But for all my defiance, I knew that she was right. We needed to find a place to shelter. I tried to think. Grace had followed me to London and it was my duty to look after her, to lead her through the city, just as she had been my guide to the strange world of the rectory.

'Let's walk into town,' I said, trying to sound confident. 'There'll be boarding houses for girls there, I'm sure. We're bound to find somewhere to stay'

*

And so we turned away from what little was left of my street. I decided that I would keep my feelings for a time when I was alone. For the moment I would keep them locked away with my memories of Ma.

We walked for hours through street after deserted street, over mountains of rubble and broken glass. Buildings loomed above us, held up with giant timbers that looked like upside down Victory Vs, as if any thought of victory had been turned on its head. The streets were quiet and the only sound was our footsteps as we stumbled along. It was hard going and by late afternoon we were weary. As we picked our way across Islington, down through Bloomsbury and into Fitzrovia, a fine drizzle began to fall, half-heartedly at first but then harder, until the pavements became slick and wet.

My stomach began to rumble as we trudged on and Grace said that she was hungry too. We came to a café on a corner and peered in through the steamed-up windows. The customers looked tired and ordinary, dressed in drab clothes. I looked down at myself and then at Grace. Our old mackintoshes were beginning to let in the rain and my sandals were already sodden. We didn't look so different to the people in the café. No-one would notice us. I nudged Grace.

'Let's go in,' I said.

She looked doubtful. 'It doesn't look very nice.'

'But we're both hungry. We haven't eaten since yesterday. And I can't think of anywhere else to go.'

A taxi rumbled past, spattering the back of our legs with dirty water. Grace gave a quick nod and I pushed open the door.

Nobody paid any attention to us as we made our way to a booth and sat down. I had never been in a café and I was nervous. Grace said that she had been to a teashop once when her mother came to take her out from school.

'It was lovely,' she said. 'We had great piles of sandwiches and scones with jam and cream. There was seed cake too. I was bursting by the end of it.' She looked wistful at the memory. 'I don't suppose they'll have that here.'

She looked about, as if she might guess what would be on the menu from our surroundings. At first I was too timid to take my eyes off the table but after a while I grew bolder and began to look around for myself. Our booth was towards the back of the room and from where we were sitting I could see the other diners, couples leaning close together, servicemen in twos and threes and groups of girls, drinking tea and smoking cigarettes like they had in the station buffet. They weren't much older than us and I envied them their factory overalls and easy attitude. I wanted to be able to laugh like them, without a trace of self-consciousness, not caring who might hear or see. I suddenly realized that I was still wearing my wet mackintosh and shrugged it off, using it to cover up the pillowcase.

Grace ordered fish and potatoes for both of us from a waitress. When our tea arrived, I began to feel better, as if the small green cup gave me the right to be there. I sipped it gratefully, the hot liquid warming my mouth and getting rid of the chilly damp that had seeped through my clothes.

When the food came we ate quickly, tearing at it with the blunt knives and shovelling it into our mouths. It wasn't anything like the teashop feast that Grace had talked about. The fish tasted mostly of the salt that had been used to preserve it and the potatoes hadn't been boiled for nearly long enough. But it didn't matter. The first bite was enough to make me feel better. It seemed to have the same effect on Grace and we grinned at each other across the table.

The next minute she had put down her knife and fork.

'What's the matter?' I said, feeling anxious again.

'We forgot to say grace! That's bad, isn't it?' But she was smirking as she said it and I smirked back at her. I didn't care about not saying grace. We didn't need things like that in this new world. God hadn't come up with much yet, I thought. I didn't feel inclined to thank him for anything.

Just then a hush fell over the room. The only sound to be heard was the car horns in the street, which all blew together as if they were giving out a warning. The other people in the café seemed to be listening for something, craning their heads towards the windows, frowning with concentration. A distant, humming noise was growing louder, like a giant insect coming close. As I listened, the humming turned into a rattle, like a stick being dragged along a fence, louder and louder until it hurt to hear it. Everyone was still, gripping their knives and forks like good luck charms. I saw mouths moving, noiselessly repeating the same three words.

Please keep going. Please keep going. Please keep going.

The rattle went on and on, seeming as if it would never come to an end, until suddenly, just as quickly as it had begun, it stopped and there was silence. A second passed, we held our breath, and then came a dreadful crunching bang that echoed off the walls. As soon as it had happened, all the tension in the room was gone. People took up their conversations again, drank tea, lit cigarettes, drew on them deeply and exhaled as if they had been holding their breath forever. Grace put down her cutlery and turned over her hands. A row of little red weals marked where she had dug her nails into her palms. I looked down at my own hands, which were trembling. I wanted to fold them around hers and hold on for dear life.

It took me a while to notice the man who was standing next to our table. Out of the corner of my eye I saw five fingers with little tufts of black hair sprouting below the knuckles. I saw a white cuff, then a sleeve, made of heavy grey material. I was immediately on my guard, but when I eventually dared to raise my head and look at him, the man was smiling. He didn't look as if he had been sent from Kent to take us back to the rectory. He belonged to the city. He was aged about forty, I thought, and dressed more smartly than the other customers, in a suit. His dark hair was smoothed flat to his head with something that made it shine. He was heavily built and when he spoke his voice matched the way he looked, as if he were used to people listening to what he said.

'Everything all right, girls?'

I looked at a poster on the wall behind him, a pen and ink drawing of two women talking on the top floor of a bus. A pair of German soldiers sat behind them, eavesdropping on their conversation.

Careless Talk Costs Lives, said the caption.

'We're quite well, thank you,' I said in a prim voice.

'Did the doodlebug scare you?'

I shook my head, but I hadn't bargained on Grace.

'Yes!' she said. 'It gave me a terrible fright. We've seen them before, of course, but it's different when you're in a city with all these big buildings. You feel trapped.'

'Ah,' he said. 'So you're from the countryside.'

'Well, Nora's from London but she was an evacuee. She came to our village at the start of the war.'

I kicked her under the table but it was too late. The man looked pleased with himself.

'I thought you were from the country,' he said. 'You look far too healthy to have been here for very long. There's a glow about you. Just look at the rest of us. See what I mean?'

He was right. Everyone else in the café had a grey pallor, as if they had powdered their faces with the dust from the broken buildings. Even after a night of sleeping in the station and a day spent walking the streets, Grace had pink in her cheeks and her skin was clear. I supposed that I looked the same. But I didn't like him being right.

I found it unnerving. If he could spot that we had just arrived, other people would too.

'We have to go,' I said. 'We've got an appointment to keep.'

He raised his eyebrows. 'Before you've finished your food? That won't make you very popular. There's a war on, you know! I'll leave you to it.' He smiled again, turned on his heel and went back to his seat.

Grace leaned across the table. 'Nora!' she hissed. 'That wasn't very polite.'

'He shouldn't have been so familiar,' I said crossly. 'We're in London. We have to look out for ourselves. Don't you understand? We can't just go about talking to people we don't know. It's not safe.'

She said nothing, but picked up her knife and fork and bent over her plate to eat. The food had gone cold and was even less appetising than before but I didn't know when we would eat again so I forced myself to finish it. The waitress came to take our plates.

'No need to pay,' she said. 'The gentleman over there's taken care of it. Lucky girls.'

There was nothing for it but to gather up our things and leave. Grace stopped at his table to thank the man but I couldn't bring myself to say anything. I nodded in his direction and hurried out of the door.

It was almost seven o'clock and, although it was still perfectly light, there was an eerie, nocturnal feeling in the air. The drizzle had stopped but the sky was dark with the threat of more rain. We stood outside the café, looking up and down the street. I had no idea of where we should go next.

'You see, he was just being nice to us,' said Grace. 'It was very kind of him.'

I didn't want to discuss it. 'Shall we go this way?' I said. 'I think it leads towards the river. We're bound to find somewhere to stay

190

around there. We only need to find a bed for tonight, then we can look again in the morning.'

Grace hesitated and I immediately knew why. She believed in the man more than she did in me. She would have gone anywhere that he suggested. A sudden fury came over me and I bolted, running down the street as fast as I could.

'Nora!' she called out in panic. 'Nora, don't leave me. Come back. Please.'

I ignored her cries. I wanted to get as far away as I could from the café, the man and from her. I had meant to come to the city alone and that was how I wanted to be, looking after only myself and keeping things simple. I ran faster, turning into a narrow passage, racing along it and then through the back streets until I couldn't run any further.

I stopped for a moment, panting, trying to get my breath back. I could smell the smoke and grease from the café on my skin and in my hair and feel the potatoes sitting heavy in my stomach. I set off again, taking in great lungfuls of the damp air, marching along, indifferent to danger, passing through stinking alleyways and crossing the ruins of burnt out buildings. But after I had been walking for a while, I realized I was lost. I had walked blindly, without thinking, and I had no chance of retracing my steps. I set off, turning this way and that, knowing that I was making things worse but not wanting to stop moving. The alleyways and ruins that I had passed through without a thought were sinister now and I stumbled on stray bricks and pieces of wood. After I had tripped up for the third time in a minute, I sat down on a doorstep to think, feeling horribly alone.

I was still sitting there, wondering what to do, when I heard a nervous call, as if whoever made it was not sure that they wanted to be heard. Footsteps followed, then a cough. Too tired to hide, I turned my head to look. Around the corner came Grace, peering anxiously and taking great care of where she stepped. I felt a warm rush of relief.

'I'm sorry,' I said. 'I'm sorry for leaving you like that.'

She smiled at me weakly. 'It doesn't matter,' she said. 'We're here now. We're together again. That's what's important.'

Seventeen

FIGHTER PLANES ROARED ABOVE US, TWISTING AND DIVING, spitting out gunfire. Grace and I were pinned to the ground, chilled by the shadows that they cast. My head was filled with a screaming noise that grew louder with each breath that I took. My heart was lodged in my throat.

I woke with the sound of it still ringing in my ears. Dark shapes swooped in front of me and I blinked, unsure of where I was, until they began to sharpen and I understood that they were only birds, building a nest in the tree outside the window. I closed my eyes again, relieved, recovering from the nightmare.

Before long, I realized there were other people in the room. I could smell the powdery scent of the baby as well as Rose's sandalwood soap, and something else, something almost familiar that reminded me of another time and place. When I opened my eyes I saw a young man sitting in the chair next to the bed. Rose was standing behind him. She stepped forward and took my hand.

'Nora, this is David,' she said. 'He's a nurse. Dr Armstrong sent him.'

He was aged around thirty, I guessed, with tousled sandy hair and grey eyes that met my gaze easily. He was smiling, inviting me to like him. There was nothing about him to dislike but I felt strangely out of sorts. Everything was topsy-turvy, women as doctors and men playing nurse, as if they were deliberately trying to confuse me.

'Hello,' he said. 'I've come to help Rose look after you.'

I slumped back against the pillows and stared out of the window at a sparrow perched on a thin branch, singing to itself. As I watched, another sparrow came to join it. The branch swayed gently under their weight and they twittered happily to each other, their heads cocked to one side, until a large crow swooped down and landed next to them. The branch bent and shook as if it were about to snap. The sparrows scattered.

I knew I was too much for Rose. I had agreed to the doctor's suggestion. And the nurse looked perfectly pleasant. But we had been happy together, Rose and Grace and me. We hadn't needed anyone else. I wanted to hold onto the world that we'd made for ourselves. I wanted to talk to Rose alone, to make her understand. But I knew it was too late. His arrival made my illness official. I was in no position to argue. I'd given myself up.

'I've cleaned the room next door,' Rose said. 'David's going to sleep there so he can hear you if you need him in the night.'

I began to tremble. I'd been so meticulous, taken such care to hide the evidence before she came to the house. I'd forced myself to open the drawer that had been kept locked for so long, picked it up and carried it, still wrapped in an old petticoat, to the room next to mine.

I'd slipped it into the pocket of a winter coat, bulky enough to conceal it. I'd washed my hands afterwards, scrubbing away the evidence. I hadn't expected other visitors.

Careful, I thought. Don't give anything away. Be polite.

'How do you do,' I said. 'I'm sure you'll be a great help.'

'I'm going to show David the rest of the house,' she said. 'Then we can all have a cup of tea before he unpacks.'

'I'm tired,' I said quickly. 'Why don't you two have your tea in the kitchen? I think I'll take a nap.'

She frowned. 'Are you all right?'

I forced myself to smile. 'Just sleepy, that's all.'

'Okay. I'll come back in a bit to see how you are.'

I listened to them tramp around the house, up the stairs and down, my apprehension growing with every footstep.

*

I'd been confined to my room for so long that crossing the threshold was like stepping into a foreign country. My heart thudded as I made my way along the corridor, feeling like a thief.

The door to the next room was ajar and I slipped through it. On the bed was a large black bag; the nurse's, I supposed. I crept towards the wardrobe, trying to swallow back my nerves. I pulled the door open quickly, before I could change my mind, and was met by the smell of mothballs. The wardrobe was half empty, with just a few things hanging in it, coats, a couple of cardigans and an ancient dressing gown. My hands shook as I brushed past them, feeling for the opening to the pocket. When I slid my fingers inside they met silk, then the blunt contrast of metal.

Back in my room I looked about, trying to think of a hiding place, aware that nowhere was private any more. I had no place to call my own. I stood, panicking, knowing that I didn't have much time.

'Think,' I muttered to myself. 'Think.'

And then it came to me. There was a place in the bedroom that was safe. I wondered why I hadn't thought of it before. I went over to the little bookcase, three shelves behind glass doors. It was where I kept my favourite books, the special ones, like the first edition of Tennyson that George had given me as a wedding present. On the bottom shelf was the serious stuff, thick volumes, too heavy to be read without a table to rest them on. No-one would browse through them just for fun.

I pulled out the biggest one. I put the gun to the back of the shelf, then slid the book back in. It stuck out a little, but not so much that anyone would notice.

*

I fell into a troubled sleep that lasted until late afternoon, when I was woken by a rustling noise. The nurse was bending over the chest of drawers with his back to me. He had changed into some kind of uniform, loose fitting and made of thin blue cotton. He was sturdily built, almost stocky, and I watched the muscles in his shoulders move as he shifted things about, making neat piles of boxes and packets. There were an awful lot of them.

The smell that I'd noticed that morning was still there and I suddenly remembered what it was. I began to cough, choking on the recollection.

He was at my side immediately, holding my shoulders with strong hands. 'It's all right, Nora,' he said. 'Easy. Try to breathe. Deep breaths. Slowly now.'

I couldn't speak. He kept hold of me as I gasped for air, cradling my head until I could breathe again, then he lowered me gently back against the pillows.

'I'm sorry about the disinfectant,' he said. 'I know it's strong. I was just making sure that everything was ready. Just in case we need it later on.'

I couldn't bring myself to ask what for, but he seemed to guess what I was thinking.

'Don't worry,' he said, 'They're just syringes. If it all gets too much, I'll give you an injection. It'll make the pain go away.'

I wanted to ask where he and his injections had been for the last fifty years.

*

I started to go downhill from then on, as if my body were justifying the nurse's presence. A stale smell hung in the room, which came, I knew, from me. It was as if I were already dead. Each morning brought more strands of hair on the pillow. I seemed to shrink a little more each day. David and Rose handled me carefully, as if they were worried I might break.

The time came when I had been in bed for so long that I began to develop sores. The skin on my feet hardened and then split like over-ripe fruit, exposing the flesh underneath. My heels stuck to the sheets. The smallest movement made me wince with pain.

'We've got to do something,' said Rose. 'This is horrible.'

David nodded, looking thoughtful. He knelt at my feet and peered at them, cupping his hands under my heels and turning them from side to side, his face so close that I could feel his breath on my soles.

'Right,' he said. 'Have you got any spare quilts or blankets?'

I nodded. 'In the bathroom. The airing cupboard.'

'I'll get them,' said Rose.

David lifted me out of bed as easily as if I were a child and set me down on the chair, wrapping a shawl around my shoulders. When Rose came back, her arms full, they stripped off the sheets and piled layers of blankets on the bed. I remembered the fairy story of the Princess and the Pea. I would have detected it, I thought. By now I felt every last little thing.

I turned my head away as they put a rubber sheet on top, ashamed of what it implied.

Not a fairy story, I thought sadly, a cautionary tale.

The newly made bed was wonderfully soft. But that wasn't the end of it.

'We need to do something about those sores,' David said. 'I'm going to wash your feet and put some bandages on them.'

I stiffened.

'It won't hurt, I promise. And you'll feel much better afterwards.'

I watched as he spread a towel under my feet. They looked like claws, blotched skin stretched tightly over bone. I was becoming something diabolical.

When he'd gone to get the water, Rose patted my shoulder.

'You see,' she said. 'He knows what he's doing. I feel a lot better with him here. We're in good hands.'

I didn't want his hands anywhere near me. I watched warily as David took hold of my right foot, his fingers fitting around my ankle as easily as if it had been my wrist. He rubbed a piece of soap against a sponge, then pushed it between my toes, making little rivulets of water trickle down over my skin. His touch was light and sure, covering every last inch. He did the same to the other one and patted them dry with a towel. Then he brought out the bandages.

'They're padded,' he said. 'To take the pressure off.'

I knew I should be grateful but I wasn't. I couldn't help myself. I felt like the Chinese women whom I had read about in books, trapped in their houses by their bound up feet. Now I had no chance of escape.

Eighteen

By the time we reached Soho we had begun to despair of finding a place to spend the night. The rain had started again, drenching the streets and making them slippery underfoot. As we made our way along, keeping close to the shopfronts, Grace let out a cry.

'What's wrong?' I said.

'There's something in my shoe,' she said. 'Something sharp. It's digging into me.'

She balanced on one leg, holding onto my shoulder, and lifted up her foot. When she pulled off her sandal I saw a piece of glass embedded in her heel. She groaned.

'Pull it out, will you? Please. I don't think I could do it.'

We sat down on the kerb. I cradled her foot in my hands, looking sadly at the patches of raw skin and blisters. I wondered if she were regretting her decision to come with me to London. It had been nothing but trouble so far. I knew I was about to make things worse. Gritting my teeth, I took hold of the glass. It had gone in deep and I had to pull hard to get it out. Blood began to form around the wound, dripping down her foot into the gutter to be washed away by the rain. Grace's lips began to quiver.

'I can't walk any more,' she whispered.

The rain was getting heavier by the minute. I peered up the street. At the far end was another road, with cars and buses passing along it.

'All right,' I said, trying to sound optimistic. 'If I wrap my handkerchief around your foot to stop the bleeding, and you lean on me, do you think you could get to that road? It's busier than this one. I think we'd have a better chance of finding somewhere to stay.'

She nodded. 'I'll try.'

I took my handkerchief from my pocket and wound it around her foot. Grace squeezed into her sandal and we limped to the end of the street.

It was there that I saw the sign, for a picture-house. I squinted at the black letters, spelling out the name of the film; one word, hazy through the rain. It was *Rebecca*! At last we had found something familiar. It seemed like a sign that we would be all right. We would be warm in the cinema, out of the rain, which was getting stronger by the minute. I looked at Grace and she nodded, as excited as I was.

The woman in the ticket booth told us to hurry. 'The programme's started. But you'll have seen it before. It's an old one. We're waiting for *This Happy Breed*. It'll be here this time next week, if we're lucky.'

We hadn't seen it. We hadn't seen any films since the war began. There was no cinema near the village and even if there had been, Reverend Rivers wouldn't have approved. We hurried inside.

When I sank into my seat I felt safe for the first time since I'd left

Kent. No-one would ask us questions in the dark. Next to Lawrence Olivier and Joan Fontaine, Grace and I would be invisible.

I liked the feeling of knowing exactly what the next few hours would bring. Even if the siren went, I decided, I wouldn't move. I wanted to stay there forever, in the dark, away from everything. For as long as the film was playing I could sit next to Grace, as close as the servicemen and their girls, who came to the cinema as two people but, as soon as they sat down, became one shadowy shape. I wanted to be like them, to put my arm around her shoulders and pull her close to me. Instead, I nudged my arm next to hers on the narrow armrest between our seats, making do with that.

I sat through the supporting film, the newsreel and an announcement about salvage, but I wasn't really watching. My senses were quivering, awake like they had been when I had tasted roast beef for the first time at the rectory. I was as excited as I had been then, drawing the smoke from a hundred cigarettes up into my nostrils and looking around, taking in not just the screen, but everything else as well. There were more people in the cinema than there had been in the whole of the village. The newsreel showed soldiers marching in tidy groups, land girls in overalls working in the fields and people sheltering in the Underground to avoid the doodlebugs. I had seen nothing of the war whilst I was in Kent. I felt as if I had been in some other country, a place that was far away from the rest of the world. I hadn't thought about armies and battles. All I had known was that I wasn't with Ma and that I loved Grace. All my thoughts had been about her. Mrs Rivers had only thought about her dead Elizabeth. Reverend Rivers had thought about me. But here in the cinema was a new world, a bigger world, presenting itself to be looked at, not hidden away and kept secret. I opened my eyes wide, looking at every detail, drinking it in.

From the moment *Rebecca* began, I was transfixed. I began to see things in it that I recognized in a way that I hadn't when I was reading the book. As soon as I saw the driveway to Manderley, winding through the woods, I was back in Kent on that first day, in the motor car driven by Mrs Rivers. When the heroine danced with Maxim de Winter I understood her expression, as if she had been transported to somewhere magical. I had felt like that during our afternoons by the lake, so happy that I felt as if my heart was about to burst out of my chest.

If you should find one perfect thing or place or person you should stick to it, said the heroine, and it was as if she were speaking directly to me, telling me to hold onto Grace and that our luck was about to change.

But as the film went on, there were other things that I recognized, other less welcome moments, like Mrs Danvers' expression as she showed the heroine Rebecca's things, laid out untouched in her bedroom as if she were still alive. Her pride at having known her was like the way I felt about Grace, as if knowing her made me somehow better. I didn't want to catch glimpses of myself in Mrs Danvers. I didn't want to be like her. But I could understand her. When she burned down the house I could see why she had done it. It reminded me of the time I had shot down the scarecrows. I decided that from now on I would be careful not to let my temper get the better of me.

It was after eleven when we came out of the cinema. We lingered outside for as long as we could, but the crowd quickly scattered into the night. We stood and watched people disappear into the darkness and it was not until the street was empty that I realized we should have followed them.

'Most of them went that way,' I said, pointing. 'If we hurry we might be able to catch them up.'

We set off, stumbling as we tried to follow the grubby white line that was painted along the kerbside. London at night was not as dark as Kent. Chinks of light crept under doors and the sky was lit up by the beams of the searchlights. Although it was late, there was a strange wakefulness about the streets. As we walked further into Soho I began to feel as if we were being watched. I heard scuffling and low voices. Grace heard them too and took my arm. We made our way along nervously, peering into the darkness and as my eyes became accustomed to it, I began to make out shapes in the doorways, standing still for the most part but sometimes shifting. Red tips of cigarettes glowed brighter as the shapes drew on them.

'Who are they?' whispered Grace. 'What are they doing?'

'I think they're women,' I said uncertainly. There had been women like that on the corner of our street. Ma had always pulled me past them quickly, holding my hand. 'I think they're waiting for men.'

'We shouldn't be here,' she said. 'We're not men. We should be somewhere else. We should be in bed. Oh, Nora, where are we going to sleep?'

We kept walking, more quickly now, hurrying to the end of the street. We had nearly reached it when I heard a hissing sound, like an angry cat. A sudden flash lit up a doorway, then another, and another. I caught sight of women's faces as they switched torches on and off.

As we passed, one of them muttered something that made the others laugh. Grace's hand tightened on my arm. When we finally turned the corner we were out of breath. The moon had come out from behind a cloud and I caught sight of her face. She was very pale.

'I'm scared. I want to go home. I want to be in my own bed. I want Mummy and Father to be sitting downstairs.' Her voice shook and for the first time since I had met her, she looked as if she were about to cry. All her old recklessness, her flirtatiousness on the train, her excitement at being in London were gone. I wanted to go home too, whatever that meant. I felt utterly lost, as if I were twelve years old again, sitting in the cattle-pen at the station. But I knew I mustn't let her know that I was frightened too.

I thought quickly. 'We could always shelter in the Underground, like they were doing in the newsreel. It would be dry, at least, and there would be other people down there. Then we could look for somewhere else tomorrow.'

She had started to cry, great fat tears that rolled down her cheeks and dropped down into the road. I choked back the panic that was beginning to rise up from my stomach.

'Please don't cry,' I said. 'I'll find us somewhere to go, I promise.'

I decided to head back to the big street that we had crossed on our way to Soho. It was the kind of street that would have an Underground station, I was sure. I would lie next to Grace on the platform and hold her until she slept. The next day we would wake early and find a place to stay. Once I had made the decision I felt better. I would make sure that she was all right, whether God wanted to help us or not. Grace followed after me, sniffling. As we turned a corner I saw a man coming quickly towards us, like a flying bomb towards its target, and we froze like we had done earlier in the horrible silence before the explosion.

'You don't suppose he thinks we're like those women, do you?' said Grace.

I wasn't sure. As he approached I saw that he was tall and well built, and that he was wearing a hat and an overcoat. As he came closer still and stood in front of us, I knew that I had seen him before. It was the man from the café.

*

He could give us a place to stay, he said, just around the corner, a flat that he used to store things for his business. I saw Grace's eyes light up at the thought and I knew that I was no longer the one in charge. Compared to this man with his overcoat to keep out the chill, somewhere to sleep and money in his pockets, I was nobody, just a girl, and like a girl, I did as I was told, following him along the street, around the corner, through a door and up two flights of stairs to a flat. I sat on a sagging bed and watched him light a candle. I heard him say that he would be back to see us in the morning and I waited for the door to slam as he left, then peeled back the blankets and slipped between the sheets. I fell asleep immediately, still fully dressed, next to Grace.

I woke early, disturbed by the unfamiliar noises from the street. I climbed out of the bed, wrapped a blanket around my shoulders, and went to sit in an armchair by the fireplace, trying to think. I didn't want to be in debt to this man. I didn't like the way he looked at Grace and I didn't believe that he had just happened to be in the same street as us. I didn't like his flat. Most of it was covered with a thick layer of dust, although the sheets on the bed were clean. Light patches on the walls suggested that pictures had hung on them not long before. There wasn't much furniture; a bed, an armchair and a table pushed against a wall, piled high with boxes and packages, all of them sealed tight, leaving no clue as to what they held inside. I tried to swallow down my curiosity, telling myself that it was better not to know anything more about him. I knew that before long he would be back and when he came I wanted us to leave. I thought hard as I waited for Grace to wake, planning what I would say to get rid of him.

At half past eight there was a knock at the door and before I had answered he came into the room. He was smiling and had a parcel wrapped in newspaper tucked under his arm.

'Good morning, girls,' he said. 'I hope you slept well. I've brought you some food.'

Grace stretched under the blankets and then sat up, looking bewildered. Then she smiled, one of her wide, dazzling smiles.

'Breakfast!' she said, as if it were the most wonderful thing in the world.

The man smiled back at her. 'I'll wait outside while you dress,' he said.

As soon as he had gone, Grace gave me a warning look. 'Nora, at least try to look as if you're grateful. You should be. He gave us somewhere to stay and now he's brought us food. We would have been lost without him. We'd still be walking about the streets with those women. Make an effort, won't you?'

She rummaged in her pillowcase, pulled out a skirt and slipped into the little bathroom that was just off the main room. After a moment I heard the lavatory flush and then the splash of water into the basin. She was tidying herself up for him, I thought dully, making herself look nice. I bit my lip and waited for them to appear through their two doors, either side of the fireplace, like a Christmas play in the village hall.

*

He had brought a packet of tea, sugar and milk, as well as bread, butter and the first jar of marmalade that I'd seen since the start of the war. Grace was impressed.

'You must have used all your coupons up on us,' she said. 'It's very kind of you.'

'I couldn't let you go hungry,' he said, sounding pleased.

She went over to the table with its pile of packages. 'Let's move some of these boxes so we can sit down.'

'There aren't enough chairs,' he said quickly. 'Why not spread that blanket on the floor? We can put the food in the middle and take a corner each.'

'Like a picnic!' she said. 'What a nice idea.'

I took the blanket from around my shoulders but didn't move from the chair.

'Why don't you put the kettle on? Here's some matches,' said the man, throwing me a box. I was forced to stand to catch them, and once I was on my feet I had no option but to do as he said. I snatched up the bag of groceries, pushed through the ragged curtain into the kitchen and stood in front of the stove, scowling at the matchbox in my hand. I was careless with the kettle, banging it against the sink as I filled it with water and crashing it down onto the gas ring. I scraped the match along the side of the box and lit the gas. When the kettle had boiled I made tea in a pot that I had found in the little cupboard that seemed to serve as a pantry. There was no milk jug so I put the bottle next to the teapot on a tray and pushed my way back through the curtain.

It was odd to see a grown man sitting on the floor. His legs were too long for it and stuck out awkwardly in front of him, but he didn't seem to care. He had taken off his jacket, as if he felt perfectly at home, and was cutting slices of bread. I sat as far away from him as I could.

'Oh dear,' said Grace. 'We've only got two plates between us.'

'That was all I could find,' I said. 'You and I can share.'

I looked at him over my teacup while Grace spread butter and marmalade on the bread. He was older than I'd thought when we saw him in the café but the war didn't seem to have touched him like the other people I'd seen in the streets. He didn't seem at all anxious, but rather jovial, with deep lines around his eyes as if he laughed a lot. Nor did he seem to be hungry, eating only half a slice of bread and marmalade and leaving the rest of it on his plate.

He took out a silver case, which sprung open to show a neat row of cigarettes, and held it out towards us. I shook my head and carried on eating but after a moment's hesitation Grace picked one out, holding it awkwardly between her fingers as he took a lighter from his pocket and flicked at it with his thumb.

He took charge of the conversation from the start. His name was Mr Masters, he said, but we must call him Bernard.

'Did you sleep well?' he asked.

Grace nodded eagerly.

'You're welcome to stay for as long as you like.'

'We'll be moving on after breakfast,' I said.

He blew out a ring of smoke, a little 'o' that drifted over my head. 'Why leave? Where will you go? It's hard to find rooms in London, you know.'

'We're going to look for a ladies' hostel.'

'What? And surround yourselves with a pack of factory girls?' He looked Grace up and down. 'Forgive me for jumping to conclusions but they're hardly your sort.'

I didn't like him thinking about the sort of girls we were. 'We might go to the people in charge of housing,' I said, trying to sound as if I knew what I was talking about. 'My mother's house was hit by a V1. They'd have to find us somewhere.'

He chuckled. 'So you're willing to go and stand in a queue for hours and fill in all those forms, then get a talking-to from some busybody who wants to know everything about you? You'll have to prove it all, you know; who you are, when you were bombed and why they should help you rather than any of the other poor souls with nowhere to go.'

Grace looked troubled. 'Nora, we haven't got anything to prove who we are. We won't be able to do anything without that.'

'She's right,' said the man. 'You haven't a hope.'

I knew she was right. I had been in such a hurry to get out of Kent that I hadn't stopped to think about it. I felt stupid and small.

Without identity cards and ration books we were nobody. It was as if we didn't exist.

The man blew another smoke ring. 'You're in luck. I can get my hands on some ration books.' He got to his feet and walked over to the table, taking a bunch of keys from his pocket and using them to slice open one of the boxes. He took out two green books and threw them to us.

'These will see you through until I can get you some new identity cards. Shouldn't take long.'

I stared at him. It was as if he had anticipated everything that we might need. I didn't like it. I didn't trust Mr Masters and his generosity. No-one gave anyone a place to stay for free. I had learned that from Reverend Rivers. There was always a price to pay and I was almost certain I knew what it was this time.

Grace wasn't worried. She was looking up at him as if he had just performed a miracle.

'That's so kind of you. We just didn't think. We left in such a hurry—' I scowled at her and she stopped mid-sentence, blushing.

'But we don't want to trouble you any further,' I said firmly. 'We'll be quite all right.'

He looked amused again. 'It wouldn't be any trouble. Having you to stay would be a great help. I use this flat for storing a few things that I sell on from time to time. You could keep an eye on it all for me.'

'There!' said Grace. 'We could be useful.'

The man went over to a chest of drawers and pulled the top one open. As he turned around I gasped and Grace took hold of my arm. He was holding a gun in his right hand, a stubby black gun that was pointing straight at us.

That's us done for, I thought. We've messed it all up.

But he was smiling. 'You can't be too careful these days, girls.

You never know who's about. There are things in these boxes that people would like to get their hands on. You need to be able to defend yourselves. There's some ammunition in the drawer. Look, I'll show you.'

I felt Grace's fingers pressing into my arm. I was angry with him for scaring us and with myself for showing that I was frightened.

'It's all right,' I said coldly. 'We know how to shoot. We did it all the time in Kent.'

He laughed. 'I should have known. Anyway, it's here if you need it. If you decide to stay, of course.'

I watched Grace take a puff on her cigarette. As she exhaled, she coughed, unused to the smoke. Her awkwardness made me soften. I could see that she was relieved at the thought of not having to tramp the streets looking for a place to stay. I didn't want to make her walk another night past all the women in the doorways. If we were in the flat I could look after her. We would be as close as we had been in Kent, perhaps even closer. Mr Bernard Masters might get us our papers and put a roof over our heads but it would be me who shared the bed with Grace at night.

I sighed. 'All right,' I said. 'We'll stay. For a while, at any rate.'

Nineteen

DAVID BROUGHT ORDER AND ROUTINE TO THE HOUSEHOLD.
Everything had its place. Rose and I had fallen into the habit of
living around the baby, sleeping when she did and eating easy food;
small snacks, soup and boiled eggs. Now mealtimes were fixed and
David spent hours in the kitchen, cooking proper things; meat and
vegetables, sometimes even puddings. I hadn't eaten like that since
George died.

'Just finish as much of it as you can,' he said. 'You need it. So does
Rose, for feeding the baby.'

Rose had been shy about that, the first time. When Grace started
to cry, she had blushed and scrambled to her feet, ready to take her
somewhere else.

'It's all right,' said David. 'I'm a nurse. I don't mind.'

She shot me a look that I understood exactly, then lifted her shirt, exposing as little of herself as she could. He busied himself with my medicines. They came after every meal and I swallowed them down as I was told. As he had promised at the start, he was always there to help. I had his undivided attention whether I wanted it or not.

A comfortable complicity had grown between Rose and me as we hid ourselves away. David brought the world back into the house. When he cooked, the sound of unfamiliar music drifted up the stairs. He read out stories from the newspaper and asked us our opinions. He brought brightly coloured magazines that looked out of place next to my old furniture. He tried to persuade Rose to go out, sending her to the shops for groceries.

'The fresh air's good for the baby,' he said. 'And you've been doing a lot. You should take some time off.'

She didn't like his concern. Each time he made a suggestion I saw traces of her old stubbornness flicker in her eyes.

'He's meant to be here for you,' she muttered. 'I don't need a nurse. I can look after myself.'

But he didn't give up.

'Haven't you got any friends with children?' he asked one day. 'What about your ante-natal classes? Didn't you like anyone there?'

Rose and I exchanged glances. She shook her head.

'There's a group at the library on Fridays,' he said. 'You know, for parents and babies. You should go. You might meet people.'

'Maybe,' she said. 'I might.'

*

One morning soon after, David passed the newspaper to Rose.

'Have a look at that,' he said. 'There, at the bottom of the page, in the box. What do you think?'

She glanced at it. 'Which one?'

'The one for the special screening at the cinema. You can take babies. I think it's a great idea.'

Rose looked wary. 'I think it'd be weird.'

'Why?'

She shrugged. 'I'd feel funny going on my own, just with her.'

There was a pause.

'What if I came with you?' he said.

She shook her head. 'It's on Tuesday. That's your day off.'

'I wouldn't mind,' he said. 'I like going to the cinema.'

'But not with a baby. She'd probably scream all the way through.'

'She wouldn't be the only one.'

I watched her try to think of another excuse. 'What about Nora?' she said. 'We can't leave her on her own.'

'The cinema's not far. We wouldn't be gone long.'

Rose looked at me uncertainly. 'What do you think?'

I looked forward to Tuesdays, when David went out, leaving just the two of us together like before. But I liked the thought of being on my own for a while, to be able to gather my thoughts without fear of interruption.

'I sleep in the afternoons,' I said. 'You should go.'

*

And so the following Tuesday they went. It was odd to see David out of uniform. He seemed a different person in corduroy trousers and a sweater, just like any other young man. Rose was dressed in her usual black, but had added a green scarf and gloves. Grace was wrapped up in layers, her arms and legs sticking out stiffly from her body.

Just before they left, David put a glass of water and a bottle of pills on the table next to the bed.

'I think this should be all you need,' he said. 'Only take the pills if the pain gets really bad. They're very strong. Okay?'

'All right,' I said.

'Will you bring Nora the radio?' said Rose.

When David had gone to get it from the kitchen, she took my hand. 'Are you sure you don't mind?' she said.

I smiled at her. 'Don't worry about me. I'm looking forward to a bit of time on my own.'

David came back with the radio. 'Are you ready?' he asked.

'Yes,' she said. 'I think I've got everything. Perhaps you could sort out Grace's pushchair. It's in the hall.'

'I could carry her,' he said. 'She's not heavy and it isn't far. It'll be quicker to leave after the film without it.'

'Oh,' she said. 'I hadn't thought of that. All right.'

He held out his arms. 'Pass her over.'

The baby looked very small against his chest.

'Goodbye, Nora,' said Rose. 'We'll be back at teatime.'

'See you later,' said David.

'Goodbye,' I said.

*

For a moment, the sounds of their departure seemed to hover in the air and then silence settled over the house. For a while I lay very still, savouring my solitude. Then I switched on the radio. I was just in time.

'This is our classic serial,' a woman said. '*Great Expectations*, by Charles Dickens.'

I settled back to listen to words that I knew almost by heart. It was so soothing that I fell into a deep and dreamless sleep.

*

When I woke again it was dark. As I groped for the switch to the bedside lamp, my fingers brushed against the radio dial and music blared, a sudden shock. As I scrabbled to turn it off, I knocked over the glass of water. It spilled over the table and dripped down onto the carpet. I swore out loud, cursing my clumsiness.

The silence that I had relished earlier roared in my ears like the sea. The house seemed very empty and I remembered what it was like to be lonely. My head was beginning to throb and I was thirsty for the water that I'd spilled. I suddenly understood how much I depended on David and Rose. I had come to rely on them for everything. It was a horrible thought. I had always made sure that I could manage. I had always looked after myself. This helplessness was a new humiliation. I couldn't stand the prospect of any more of it.

I was getting thirstier by the minute. I wondered when they would be back. I turned my head to check the time on the little alarm clock that stood on the bedside table. As I caught sight of the bottle next to it, I realized that I wasn't entirely powerless. There was something I could do. David had warned me that the pills were strong. My body wouldn't put up much resistance, I was sure. I reached for the bottle and brought it close so I could read the label.

Strictly for use under medical supervision.

David had twisted open the lid, knowing that I wouldn't have the strength to break the lock. I would be able to do it if I wanted.

I tried to think. I wanted to put an end to the memories. I wanted to feel nothing. There were things I wanted to say to Rose, important things, but I knew that this was probably the only chance I would get to end it myself. I remembered what she had said about her father shrinking away into nothing, about things getting worse. Perhaps it was kinder to spare her from having to see that again.

Don't make excuses, I thought. You want to finish it for your own good, not hers.

I tipped up the bottle. Three white pills fell into my hand. I stared at them. He hadn't left enough. I groaned and let them drop to the floor.

I thought of the gun, still loaded, on the other side of the room, hidden in the bookshelf. But I knew I wouldn't be able to do it. I wouldn't have the strength to pull the trigger. I hadn't even been able to pin the remembrance poppy onto my coat in November, months before, my swollen fingers fumbling until I had dropped it.

There was nothing I could do. I had no choice but to lie still and wait for them to return.

*

When at last they came, they smelled of fresh air and cold. Rose's cheeks were pink and she was bubbling with excitement.

'Nora!' she said. 'I'm so sorry we're late. We had something to eat after the film. We were starving. Are you all right? Have you been okay?'

'Of course,' I said.

She came to sit on the bed. 'I'm so glad. I wish you could have come with us. We had such a great time.'

'Did you take any of those pills?' asked David, moving over to the bedside table.

'I'm sorry,' I muttered. 'They're on the floor. I knocked them over by mistake, with the water.'

'Never mind. It's good that you didn't need to take them. I'll get a cloth.'

When he had gone, Rose took off her coat and threw it over the chair.

'Oh Nora,' she said. 'It was so nice to be out of the house.'

I forced a smile.

'It made me think that it might be okay. I could do those things that David talked about, like those groups at the library. He might be right. Maybe I should try to get out a bit.'

I felt as lonely as I had that afternoon.

'Oh, I nearly forgot,' she said. 'We bought you a present.' She reached into a plastic bag and drew out a plant pot.

'Look,' she said. 'Crocuses. They're just about to come up.'

I looked, and saw three green shoots, peeping above the earth. I knew I would never see them flower.

'Aren't they pretty?' she said. 'It'll be spring soon. You can feel it in the air.'

She began to tell me about the film they'd seen. I'd never heard of it. When David came back her description became a conversation between the two of them. I lay there, silent, unable to join in, feeling as if I'd lost something very dear to me.

Twenty

At first it was as if we were back in the hut behind the church, playing house. I took the old rag-rug out to the street and beat it against the wall, adding to the dirt on the pavement. Grace ran a damp cloth along the tops of the skirting boards and the doors, which came away black. We swept out the rooms and got on our knees to scrub the floors, then we scoured every inch of the bathroom. It was odd to see Grace with a bucket, her hair wrapped up in a scarf. I remembered how Mrs Rivers' hands had always seemed wrong in the dirty dishwater.

I wondered if Grace ever thought about her parents. She hadn't mentioned them since her moment of panic when we were lost. I remembered our conversation when she was persuading me to let her come to London and how hurt she had been about their indifference towards her. Perhaps that was why she said nothing now, I thought, and so I didn't ask. I tried not to think about the rectory. I tried not to think about separating Grace from Mrs Rivers. I concentrated on trying to puzzle out this strange man who seemed to have taken us under his wing.

He came to visit most days, bringing us presents; stockings, bacon, bottles of beer. He brought other things too that weren't for us, in cardboard boxes that he stacked on the table. They were to stay in the flat for safekeeping, he said, and we shouldn't worry about what was inside them. One night I looked anyway and what I found made me gasp; ration books and clothing coupons, silver cutlery tangled up together, bars of soap and bags of sugar. I unwound sacking to find bottles of gin and packs of cigarettes. In one of the boxes there was even an electric radiator and an iron, all packed up in newspaper.

From time to time a man would come and take some of the boxes away. A few days later someone else would bring others to replace them. I asked no questions and I said nothing, keeping my own little inventory of goods in my head as they came and went.

One night Bernard brought us another armchair, puffing as he carried it up the stairs. I minded that more than any of the other things. It wasn't to be kept in the corner until someone came to claim it. It was there to stay. He put it by the fire and whenever he came to the flat, he sat in it. It was as if he lived there too, and there was nothing I could do about it.

'He looks after us ever so well,' said Grace. 'Don't you think?'

I began to make excuses, bolting down scraps before he arrived, so I wouldn't be tempted to eat the things he brought. As Grace grew new curves from the unaccustomed pieces of meat and lumps of sugar in her tea, I became scrawny and thin.

I was determined not to rely on him. I found a job in a munitions factory. It was dull work in a stuffy room without windows, but I didn't mind. I left Grace each morning, still drowsy in the warmth of our bed. When I came back in the evening, we drank tea by the fire. This was what it might be like to be married, I thought, and I liked it.

When I was given my first wages, I felt as if I would burst with happiness. For the first time in my life I was dependent on no-one but myself. I could spend the money however I liked. I hugged it to my chest. I knew what I was going to buy. Each morning I passed an old woman on the corner of our street. She sat on a small stool, selling whatever she had managed to find that day; bundles of firewood, old screws, cotton reels or biscuit tins, a little heap of potatoes or carrots with the soil still sticking to them. She had a gentle smile and misty eyes and whenever someone approached her a look of surprise and delight would spread over her face, as if she had quite forgotten that she had anything to sell.

That morning she had a bucket in front of her, crammed with pink flowers. They reminded me of Kent, of our afternoons by the lake, lazy, happy afternoons with just the two of us. They seemed an age away. I would buy a bunch for Grace, I thought, to remind her of them too.

It was evening when I went back with my money and from the other side of the street the bucket looked as if it were empty. My heart sank. The flowers meant something special, something different to a bunch of violets picked from a hedgerow or a daisy chain strung together by the lake. I raced across the road. The woman had her eyes closed and was humming to herself, an old-fashioned tune that I didn't recognize. I looked down into the bucket. There was a single bunch of flowers left, six stems tied together with a piece of string. I cleared my throat, quietly at first and then louder. The woman blinked, as if she were coming back from a place that she was reluctant to leave.

'Hello, dearie,' she said. 'What can I do for you?'

Her voice suited the way that she looked, soft and faraway.

'Please, I'd like to buy the flowers.'

'You're in luck,' she said, picking them out of the bucket and handing them to me. 'This is the last bunch. I've done well today.'

'What are they?' I asked.

She smiled. 'They're sweet williams. I grew them to remember my son. That was his name, William. He was killed in the last war, at Passchendaele.' Her right eye fluttered. 'He was about the same age as you are. He would have liked you.'

I felt myself blush.

'Off you go,' she said. 'Hurry home to your sweetheart. He'll enjoy that bit of colour.'

I reached into my pocket but she shook her head. 'I don't want money for them. You're my last customer. Take them for luck.'

But I insisted, pressing the coins into her hand. I wanted to pay so that the flowers meant what they were supposed to, even if I were the only one who knew what that was.

'Good luck!' she called as I left her. 'God bless!'

I was so excited when I got back to the flat that I could hardly get my keys in the lock.

'Grace!' I called, 'Where are you? I'm back. I've got you something.'

There was no reply. I called again. 'Grace!'

'Wait a minute.' Her voice came from the kitchen. 'I'm coming. I've got something to show you too.'

I perched on one of the armchairs, hiding the flowers behind my back. We didn't have a vase but we could use a milk bottle, I thought, and put it on the mantelpiece. I wanted Grace to see them, to hold them to her nose and run her fingers along the pink frills of the petals. I wanted her to like them and to be pleased with me.

'Come on!' I shouted. 'What's keeping you?'

A hand pushed aside the curtain between the main room and the kitchen and she appeared, holding a vase made of cut glass. In it were red roses, blowsy heads on long stalks. I counted them quickly: a dozen.

'Aren't they beautiful?' she said. 'They're from Bernard. I can't think where he got them. They must have cost the earth.'

My hands tightened around the sweet williams behind my back. I didn't trust myself to speak.

'Aren't they beautiful?' she said again, her eyes shining.

I made myself nod.

'He's awfully generous,' she said. 'I'll put them on the mantelpiece so he can see them when he comes.'

As she carried the vase to the fireplace I stuffed my flowers down the side of the armchair, feeling the stems bend and then snap. Later that night, after Grace had gone to sleep, I pulled out what was left of them. They drooped, as if they were hanging their heads in shame, the dark pink petals crushed and limp. I crept downstairs and threw them in the gutter.

*

Grace had always liked Bernard, right from that first day in the café. She took to him as she had taken to me when I had arrived in Kent. He had saved us from the streets, she said. He had been kind to us. But after he gave her the roses, her liking for him started to become something else. Grace had always been frank about her feelings but now she tried to hide them. She was no good at it. As soon as she mentioned his name, which she did clumsily and often, two red spots would appear, high up on her cheekbones. Whenever it happened, a sour, dull fury crept over me, making my stomach twist and clench. She didn't seem to notice. I had to listen to what Bernard thought of

Mr Churchill, the war effort and everything else, right down to the price of fish in Billingsgate market. I knew when he had been to the barber and what he had eaten for his lunch. I knew what he thought of the latest film at the cinema around the corner and I knew the price of a matinee seat. I knew far more than I ever wanted to know, and she kept on telling me.

As her liking for him grew, she changed in other ways, including her appearance. Bernard started to take her out at night to restaurants and dancehalls. I would come home to find her sitting at the table, peering into a mirror propped up against the cardboard boxes. He had given her a red lipstick and she would run it over her mouth, pursing her lips at her reflection as if she wanted to kiss herself. She would take a piece of cork and hold it in the flame of a candle, then rub it over her eyelids and lashes to darken them. When she heard his key in the lock she pinched her cheeks to bring colour to them. I thought she looked like a doll, stiff and artificial. I hated to see her like that. I took to running to the bathroom when I heard him climb the stairs, locking myself inside until I heard her call goodbye. While I was waiting for them to leave I would hunch myself up on the seat of the lavatory, looking at the mess that Grace had left behind her, the fine yellow hairs in a ring around the bath, and in the plughole the pumice stone that she had used to scrape them from her legs. I pressed my fingers into the white dust on the floor, bicarbonate of soda, which she used under her armpits to stop her from sweating, spelling out her name.

I wondered where she had learned these tricks, to paint her face like the women who stood in the doorways on our street. During the long evenings when she was out with Bernard, I turned out the lights and pushed aside the blackout to watch them, calling out, shifting this way and that to show themselves off, welcoming the cat-calls and whistles from the passing servicemen and the glances from the other men who hurried past. I saw quick bargains being struck on doorsteps. A bit of paint and a smile was all it seemed to take. They did it, Grace did it and so did the girls in the factory. At the end of each shift they crowded about the cracked mirror in the lavatory to comb their hair and put on lipstick. They all seemed to share the same secret, one that was somehow off-limits to me. I didn't understand it and it made me feel stupid and unworldly.

The worst of it was her hair. One night when I came back to the flat, it smelled of something different to the usual stale tobacco. She had taken up smoking as wholeheartedly as everything else in our new life. She smoked when she was happy and when she wasn't, when she was waiting for Bernard to arrive at the flat and late at night when they came back from the dancehall. When she couldn't think of something to say she would light a cigarette instead and when she did speak she would gesture with the little white stick balanced between her fingers. Crumpled stubs were all over the flat, pushed into plant pots, ground out in saucers and thrown into the fireplace. But that night the usual fug was gone and the flat smelled of something sharp and clean. I sniffed at the air, wondering what it was.

'Grace? I'm back,' I called.

There was a clattering in the bathroom. 'I'll be out in a minute.'

'What's that smell?'

'You'll see,' she shouted. 'Don't come in! Wait there.'

I stayed where I was, wondering what it would be this time. A minute later the door to the bathroom opened.

'You've changed your hair,' I stammered.

She twirled about, showing herself off to me.

'I've gone blonde!' she said. 'All the actresses in the pictures are doing it. Platinum blonde, it's called. Isn't it lovely?'

All I could think of was the prostitutes in the street below, twisting and turning like her, to be seen. Her hair was too bright, its colour harsh.

'But your hair was already blonde,' I said.

'I know, but Bernard was storing some hair-dye here and he said that I could have some if I liked. I thought it was a good idea. You know, whenever he takes me to those places, I can't help but look at the girls there. They've got a sort of glow about them. I thought that if I dyed my hair I might feel more as if I belonged.'

I stared at her, searching for the old Grace. Her new hair stood for everything that had gone wrong since we had come to London, I thought sadly. It was deceitful and false and made her look older and hard-faced. Together with the lipstick and the cork on her lashes, it turned her into someone I didn't recognize, an altogether different sort of person, someone who, I realized, was not a girl but a woman. I was skinny and plain, my face bare and my cheeks scrubbed. I wore my hair pulled back for neatness at the factory. I felt like a school-girl still, stuck in the past while she was moving on, pulling away from me to somewhere I couldn't go, a place where I wouldn't be able to reach her.

She said he wanted to take her out for her birthday, somewhere special for turning eighteen. My own had passed unremarkably a few days before. I hadn't wanted to do anything to celebrate. I had begun to take a sour sort of pleasure in keeping things to myself. It was easier, I thought, to keep people at a distance. As Grace changed herself to suit new places and new people, I stuck stubbornly to the clothes that I had brought with me from Kent, trying to hold onto the happiness I had known there before it all went wrong.

Despite my efforts to stay out of it, she made me get involved in her birthday preparations. I was reading, trying to distract myself from the sight of her in her petticoat as she flitted about the flat, getting ready for him. When she came to me with a reel of cotton and a needle I was surprised. I had never been much good at sewing, despite Mrs Rivers' attempts to teach me.

'What do you want me to do?'

She handed me the cotton reel. 'I want you to pierce my ears,' she said.

I was startled. 'What?'

'I need you to pierce my ears with this needle.'

'But why?'

'So I can wear earrings.' She sat down on the arm of my chair and smiled. 'Bernard and I went past a shop yesterday, on Bond Street. It was ever so smart. We looked in the window at lots of things. He asked me if I'd like some jewellery for my birthday. He said that he could picture me in pearl earrings. He thought they'd look nice next to my hair. I think he might give me them tonight.'

'It'll hurt, you know,' I said.

'But it'll be worth it.'

This was the old Grace, reckless and sure, determined to do as she pleased, regardless of the consequences. I glanced up at her earlobe, a soft sliver of skin peeping out from under her hair and I shivered. I didn't think I could push a needle through it, just so she could wear some jewellery that he'd given her. I didn't want to be part of it.

She stood up. 'I managed to get some ice from the fishmonger,' she said, walking over to the kitchen. 'It was a big piece. There should be enough of it left.'

When she came back she was carrying an inch of candle in one hand and the ice in the other.

'I'll hold it against my ear,' she said. 'You light the candle and put the needle in the flame to burn off the germs. Then when my ear's gone numb you push the needle through.'

'I can't,' I said.

Her face fell. 'Nora, please.'

I folded my arms and shook my head.

'But I need them to be pierced,' she said.

'No,' I said. 'I don't want to hurt you.'

'Please,' she said. 'I'll do anything.'

I was beginning to feel a nasty sense of satisfaction at making it difficult for her. I was curious to see how far she would go, what she would promise and how much she would beg, simply in order to please him. I shook my head.

'I'm sorry,' I said. 'I can't.'

For a moment we were both silent, staring at each other and I wondered what was going through her mind. Then she smiled, a sly, not altogether pleasant smile, as if I had infected her with my nastiness.

'I may as well get used to pain,' she said. 'I've heard that it hurts the first time.'

It took me a moment to understand what she meant, but then it was horribly clear.

She shrugged. 'I thought that if he was going to give me something so expensive I should give him something in return.'

I felt a queer, wrenching sensation in my chest.

Damn you, I thought. And damn me as well for loving you.

I hated her then, and I wanted to hurt her in any way that I could. I scrambled to my feet and grabbed a matchbox from the mantelpiece. I struck a match, which flared briefly, then went out. I threw it down onto the table, not caring if it burned the wood, and struck another. I put it to the wick of the candle, then I took the needle and held it in the flame, feeling the heat against my fingers.

'You'd better be ready for this,' I muttered under my breath.

I pulled her skin taut. Holding the needle in my other hand I chose a spot and then without any hesitation, drove the needle through her earlobe and then out again.

I stepped back, breathing hard. My desire to hurt her had gone as soon as I pushed the needle into her. She was very pale but she hadn't made a sound. I understood that she had known that I wanted to hurt her. She had provoked me into it deliberately and I was suddenly ashamed at having risen to the bait. For one brief moment I had wanted her to know what it was like to feel pain. Now I was left with a terrible emptiness. I pierced her other ear as quickly as I could and neither of us seemed to feel a thing.

*

After she had left I lay on the bed, staring at the ceiling, fixing my eyes on a stain from a leak in the flat above. It was no good. I couldn't help but picture them, laughing in a dim booth in a restaurant, somewhere in the centre of town, eating hunks of meat and drinking dark red wine. They would have all the things that were difficult for ordinary people to get. He would insist on the best. After the meat, before their puddings came, he would bring out a box and push it across the table. When she opened it and saw the earrings she would pretend to be surprised. She would take one of them and push it into the hole in her ear, taking care not to wince at the pain, then do the same with the other. She would smile at him and he would think her lovely.

I hated how he had made her into somebody different. I had loved her as she was. I had loved every part of her. I had cut her fingernails when they grew too long, careful not to catch her with the scissors. I had combed out her hair when the winter wind had whipped it into a tangle of knots. I had counted her eyelashes as she lay sleeping. But she had chosen him over me, leaving me good for nothing.

I was still lying there when the clock on the mantelpiece struck midnight. She had been gone too long for just dinner. One thought led to another, each one worse than the one before it, like rot spreading through apples in a loft. In my mind's eye they took a taxi to a hotel, hidden away down a back street, shabbier than she had hoped. He told the woman at the reception desk that they were man and wife; that Grace belonged to him. She would be nervous as she climbed the stairs; he would not. Once they were in the room he would take off her coat, her dress and the stockings that he had paid for and she would be happy for him to do it.

My imagination faltered then. All I could think of was Reverend Rivers lurching towards me, the stubble against my cheek and the smell of tobacco on his breath. The thought of it made me sick to my stomach.

I took the blanket from the bed, wrapped it around myself and went to the armchair to wait for her, counting the chimes of the clock that came every quarter of an hour. It was cold in the chair but the idea of being in bed alone was worse and so I drew my feet up underneath me and tucked in the blanket. We would be sleeping apart for the first time since the war had begun.

I waited all night for her. At three o'clock the sirens went off but I ignored them. When I heard the crunch, followed by the rumble of a falling building, I felt something close to disappointment. I was tired, not just from having stayed awake that night, but from the effort of pretending for so long, of keeping my feelings hidden inside me, where they smouldered like the embers of a fire, ready to burst back into flame with just one word from her. My head ached and my face was tight and sore from crying. A rocket would have finished it all for me, neatly and with no fuss.

At six o'clock the All-Clear sounded. Half an hour later a key turned in the lock. The door opened and Grace came into the room.

As soon as I saw her I knew that she had done it. Two pearl

earrings swung from her ears and she smelled of cigarettes. She was singing quietly to herself, an old song that they played sometimes on the wireless.

I've got you, under my skin,
I've got you, deep in the heart of me.
So deep in my heart that darling, you're really a part of me,
I've got you, under my skin.

She jumped when she saw me in the armchair.

'Nora! What are you doing there? Why aren't you in bed?'

'I was waiting for you,' I said, too tired to lie.

Her cheeks were flushed and her eyes glittered with excitement. She sat in the chair opposite and leaned towards me.

'Oh Nora,' she said. 'It was so romantic. It was just as I'd dreamed it would be. And it didn't hurt, not a bit.'

She began to tell me all about it, starting from the moment they left the flat, then the dinner, the earrings and the rest of it; the whole sordid story. By the end of it I knew that she had let him do to her what Reverend Rivers had wanted to do to me and that she had liked it. I began to feel lost.

Grace carried on talking. 'He told me that he liked me as soon as he saw me.'

I looked at her blankly.

'When we met in that café on our first day here. Don't you remember? It was raining outside and there was that bomb. He paid for our lunch. He said that he followed us to the cinema and waited in a pub until we came out. That's how much he wanted to see me again. He didn't meet us by chance at all. Isn't that wonderful?'

I didn't think it was wonderful at all. It made me feel stupid, as if we had walked into a trap.

'It's like something out of a book,' she said. 'Or a film. He reminds me of Maxim de Winter in *Rebecca*. He always knows what to do. He seems to know what I'm thinking before I know it myself.'

She had always liked Maxim de Winter, from the moment we had picked up the book. I didn't like the way he kept calling the heroine a silly little fool.

'Maxim de Winter killed his wife – remember that,' I muttered.

There was a short, unpleasant pause.

'Why are you being so horrid?' she said. 'He's a very nice man.'

'He's a bloody nuisance,' I snapped.

She flinched, as if I had struck her.

'Well he is,' I said. 'He's always here, pretending to want to look after us, but really he just wants to get his hands on you.'

Grace was staring at me. I stared back defiantly, meeting her gaze. When she spoke, there was pity in her voice, but it was mixed with anger.

'Nora, are you jealous? I think you are. I think you're jealous because he picked me. You want someone like him for yourself. That's what it is, you're jealous.' She nodded slowly as if she had discovered something extraordinary.

She knew me well enough. I *was* jealous. But she hadn't guessed quite right. I started to laugh bitterly. All the anger that I had swallowed back since we had met Bernard came spilling out.

'Jealous over *him*?' I said. 'I wouldn't want *him*. He's a crook.' I went over to the table and pulled out a handful of ration books from one of the boxes. 'They're stolen. They sell them in pubs for five pounds each. It's the same with those bottles of whisky and gin. It's the same with all the presents he gives you. They're stolen, or black market at least. He keeps it all here until it's worth something and then he sells it on for as much as he can get. He's getting rich on this war.'

She was trembling. My heart was beating fast. I knew that I shouldn't go on but I was feeling reckless and cruel. I wanted to hurt her.

'You're the same to him. You're something extra, like those glasses of whisky he likes to have after dinner. When you're not worth it any more he'll drop you. You know he will.'

She was very pale.

'No he won't. He loves me,' she said coldly. 'You just don't understand. But why should you? Your mother gave you away easily enough.'

We were both shaking. Before she could say any more, I turned and ran from the room, slamming the door behind me. I hurried down the stairs, out of the front door, along the street and around the corner to the little square. I sat on a bench and cried until I could no longer see.

Twenty-One

RESENTMENT BEGAN TO SMOULDER INSIDE ME, FEEDING A suspicion that took root and quickly grew. I watched them as they went about their business, lighting the fire, plumping up pillows and changing sheets. Rose was as kind as ever and David was always polite. But I noticed the looks that passed between them. Since their trip to the cinema, something was different. Rose's stubbornness had disappeared. Their conversation was quicker, more intimate, hinting at other discussions that took place out of my earshot. They used words that I'd never heard before and talked about things that I didn't understand.

I decided that he was making a play for Rose. He had planned it all, paying her attention, encouraging her to leave the house and taking her to the cinema. My illness was providing him with an opportunity.

Over my dead body, I thought grimly.

I was unnerved by the strength of my feelings, but they were impossible to control. It was bad enough when the two of them were with me but even worse when I was left alone with my imagination, guessing at what was going on elsewhere. Rose began to take more care over the way she looked, putting away her black vest and wearing colourful clothes. She had never seemed to care much about her hair, leaving it to hang loose about her shoulders, but now it was neatly combed and coiled at the nape of her neck. For the first time, I noticed her wearing make-up, a dash of mascara on her eyelashes. She looked pretty but I couldn't bring myself to tell her so. I said less and less. My mouth had filled with a nasty, sour taste, leaving me with nothing good to say.

I took to keeping my eyes closed so that I didn't have to see them. They talked more freely when they thought I was asleep. One day I overheard them discussing me.

'I don't know what's wrong,' Rose said. She sounded almost tearful.

'What do you mean?' said David.

'It's Nora. She's different. Something's changed. She doesn't want to speak to me. I think I've upset her.'

I missed Rose terribly. I longed to talk to her, to explain myself. After keeping quiet for so long, I wanted someone to know what had happened. I wanted someone to understand. But David was always there. When he wasn't looking after me, he was playing with the baby. He handled her easily, with no trace of awkwardness, and she seemed to like him as much as her mother did, gurgling and smiling, letting out little squeaks of pleasure. He looked after her now when Rose was busy. They thought I wasn't up to it, I could tell. I missed playing with her on the bed. I missed holding her close.

'She's never given much away,' Rose went on. 'She didn't even want to tell me she was ill. I thought we were friends, but now it's as if I've offended her. She just lies there, watching what's going on, but she won't say anything. I don't know what to do.'

'Look,' said David. 'It's like this sometimes, with cancer. It messes up people's brains. I've had patients who've said awful things to the people that they're closest to. They don't mean it. They can't help it. It's the disease.'

'But I don't want Nora to hate me.'

'There's nothing we can do. And, you know, it might get worse. You need to be ready for that.'

She said something that I couldn't make out.

He's right, I thought. I'm not like this. It comes from this thing that's inside me. It's turning me into something hateful.

But I knew that it wasn't quite true. The Menace and I were inextricably linked. We came from the same bad place.

*

A few days later, I heard laughter coming from the garden, two young voices combined. I wanted to know what was so funny. With difficulty, I hauled myself to the edge of the bed and then stood up on my bound feet, holding onto the armchair. The laughter came again, louder. I let go of the armchair and inched my way to the window, where I stood, out of breath, looking down.

The garden had grown back since our efforts to tidy it. I peered at the dark tangle of ivy and the wintry mass of rotting plants and leaves. The flowers were long gone, everything a dull, dead brown apart from a plastic bag caught in a shrub. I looked for the Graces, trying to make them out amongst the vegetation, and as my eyes adjusted to the dim winter light I saw David and Rose, standing close together. She was leaning against one of the statues, looking up at him and smiling. As I watched, he reached out and touched her shoulder. I felt a sudden stab of pain.

My bitterness grew. I wanted to remind Rose of my existence, to show her I was still alive.

'Would you do something for me?' I said to her one morning.

She was as eager to help as always, keen to be useful. 'Of course, Nora. What is it?'

For a moment I was sorry but I swallowed back my regret.

'Would you look in my bottom drawer for a nightdress? It's a white one with embroidery around the collar.'

She rummaged through the chest of drawers.

'This one?'

The nightdress looked smaller than I'd remembered but we had always been the same size. I knew it would fit.

'Yes,' I said. 'That's it.'

She came over to the bed and gave it to me. I pressed the worn cotton against my cheek. I wanted to lose myself in it, just once more.

'Rose,' I said. 'Would you help me put it on?'

She looked puzzled. 'It looks very old,' she said uncertainly. 'It's lovely embroidery. What if—?'

I knew what she meant. She was worried that the nightdress would be ruined, like so many others before it.

'It's all right,' I said shortly. 'It doesn't matter.'

I made her close the door before she undressed me. Although she had done it often enough, I was as ashamed of my nakedness as I had been the first time. I sat with my jaw clenched as she undid the button of the nightdress I was wearing, pulled it up over my head and replaced it with the new one, threading my arms through its sleeves.

I felt better but I couldn't stop myself.

'There's something else,' I said.

She nodded.

'We should pack up my clothes. I won't be needing them again. We can give them to one of those charity shops on the Holloway Road.' I paused. 'Because it's going to be soon, you see. I can feel it.'

I found the sight of tears in her eyes oddly satisfying.

'It won't take long,' I said. 'I haven't got many things. Perhaps you could get some rubbish sacks to put them in.'

She stared at me for a second, then nodded briefly and left the room.

*

Like all the things I had done out of envy, my bid for attention backfired. When Rose came back she wouldn't look at me and she said nothing as she pulled clothes from the chest of drawers and the wardrobe and held them up, one at a time, waiting for me to nod or shake my head. The rubbish sacks grew shiny and taut as they were filled, first with the dresses that George had bought me, little slips of bright material, and then the ones I had bought myself after he died, made of serviceable cloth in drab colours, a testament to trying to go unnoticed. The pile of things to keep was small; some nightdresses, a cardigan or two, old knickers and some bed socks. They would have fitted into the pillowcase that I took with me to Kent at the start of it all, or the one that I ran back with at the end. The thought of those two journeys made me blink back tears of my own.

In the days that followed, I felt a terrible loneliness. I was ashamed of how I'd treated Rose. I thought before I spoke, careful not to cause any more harm. But my suspicions wouldn't go away. I fretted and fumed over every look that passed between them, each smile or exchange of words. I wanted to go back to how we'd been when it was just the three of us. Rose had made me feel useful again. She had given me a purpose. I had cared for her and she had looked after me. We had brought Grace into the world together. But now I had been replaced in her affections. Our little family was breaking apart. I felt a sudden sympathy for Rose's mother, left behind and shut out. I was beginning to understand, I thought, how it was to lose a child.

I knew I wasn't being fair to Rose. It was I who was going to leave her. But I still couldn't bear to think of David taking my place, of having the pleasure of a future with Rose and the baby.

I wanted him to go away, to leave us in peace, but my body let me down by needing him. Each time I lost control of my bladder he was there to change the sodden sheets. He rubbed oil into my sores and washed away the sweat that oozed out of me at night. He smiled as he did it, speaking soft, soothing words.

David and Rose had their kindness in common. I repaid it with a sullenness that kept me apart and alone.

With each day that passed my body crumbled further. I was turning into something between a living being and a corpse, neither dead nor alive. When I began to feel the cold air against my scalp in the mornings I asked Rose to bring me a mirror. My reflection made me shrink away in horror. My eyes stared out from hollow sockets, their faded blue the only colour in a face in which skin stretched over bone in a ghastly premonition of a skeleton. My lips were cracked. They collapsed inwards, pressed together, the lips of someone with secrets. A few strands of hair straggled over my scalp like grasses left after a harvest. The disease had made me into something inhuman. My wickedness was on display to whoever cared to look.

Twenty-Two

Our quarrel made me realize that I needed to be careful. If not, I would lose her altogether. I went back to the flat and apologized. I ate my words. I lied.

I went on lying all through the winter. It was a miserable time. The freezing fog crept into my lungs, making me wheeze and cough. A cold I had picked up at the factory lingered on for weeks and my nose ran constantly, making my skin tight and raw. Everything seemed to matter a great deal. I was always tired, exhausted from the effort of examining the things Grace said or did whilst trying to keep my own feelings hidden. I forced myself to stay awake at night until her breathing was deep, then I would fall into a shallow sleep at the edge of the bed, waking early, shivering and tense.

I came to dread the hour between six and seven at night, when I knew Bernard would arrive at any moment. I would have nothing to say, my mind occupied with black thoughts that left no space for other things. As the minute hand on the clock jerked forward I would shuffle and shift about, chewing at my nails. As soon as I heard his key in the lock, a flat gloom would come over me, reducing me to sullen silence, my only weapon against him.

I tried to ignore them, hiding behind books, but one night I couldn't stand any more of it. Grace was fluttering about him like a bird, bringing him drinks and fussing as he sat in his armchair. I went to the bathroom to calm down. I was sitting on the edge of the bathtub, trying to compose myself, when I heard Bernard's voice.

'She's such a misery. I'd much rather see you on your own. Can't you get rid of her?'

I strained to hear Grace's reply but she spoke too quietly, and I suddenly felt very alone, wondering if she felt the same as he did. When I came out of the bathroom she wouldn't meet my eyes and I felt even worse.

After that I couldn't stand to be there at night. I would make excuses that neither of them cared about and leave the flat, clenching my hands into fists and shoving them deep into the pockets of my overcoat. I would trudge down the stairs and let myself out of the front door, wondering how to fill the hours of darkness that stretched ahead. There was little to do except walk the streets, turning left or right at random, willing myself to be lost. It suited my mood. I crossed roads without looking out for traffic and went down alleyways that smelled of danger, not caring what I found. I ignored the sirens when they came and allowed the winter nights to seep into me in the hope that they might freeze out my bitterness.

When the snow came I went on walking, letting it cover me like a disguise. It seemed to soften the damaged streets, hiding the dirt and muffling the sounds of the city. A strange calm would settle over

Soho on those nights. The only others in its empty passages were the prostitutes, who stayed out like me whatever the weather. As time passed we became friendly and the nights were made more tolerable. They introduced me to dark coffee in small cups from the café on the corner. It had been run by Italians before the war, they said, and that was why it was good. It was more of a comfort than the cups of tea that were supposed to make everything better but never did. When I was with them, drinking the good hot coffee that tasted of faraway places, I could leave myself behind. But as soon as I stepped back into the night, the thoughts returned and I was bleak again, waiting at the corner of the street for Bernard to leave. When I saw him come out of the front door, I forced myself to walk around the block one last time so that when I got back to the flat she would be asleep. I would tiptoe upstairs, take off my clothes as quietly as I could and slide into bed, trying to ignore the warmth that his body had left on the sheets.

*

As winter came to an end and spring arrived, London was filled with hope. Things would be better soon, they said on the wireless and in the newspapers that I read in the café. The nights were less of a trial without the wind and the snow and I began to explore new parts of the city, feeling my legs grow stronger as I walked further and further away from the flat.

But sometimes the thought of dragging myself about the streets was exhausting. One night I came back to the flat from the factory, hungry and tired. I slammed the door behind me and flung myself into Bernard's chair staring at the flames of the fire as if they might hold the answer to all my worries.

After a minute or two, I heard a sob. I turned my head to look across at Grace, who was sitting in the other chair with her legs curled underneath her. Her eyes were red and her skin blotched, as if she had been crying for a while.

I was in no mood to be sympathetic. It was worse for me, I thought, about to be kicked out onto the streets when Bernard came to take my place. I wondered if for once I could persuade her to tell him not to come.

'I feel rotten,' I said.

She said nothing.

I tried again. 'I want to go to bed. Can't you ask your boyfriend not to come tonight? You don't look in much of a state to see him, anyway.'

She sniffed.

'Why are you making such a meal of it?' I snapped. 'I bet I feel as bad as you, but I'm not crying.'

She made a strange noise, a cross between a whimper and a sob. I began to wonder what was wrong.

'He's not coming,' she whispered.

'What?'

'He isn't coming.'

I was curious. 'Why not?'

'I said he shouldn't.' Grace pressed her face into her hands.

I had never seen her like this. I leaped out of my chair and went to her.

'What's wrong?' I said. 'Why are you crying? Tell me, whatever it is, you can tell me.'

She lifted her head away from her hands. 'I told him that I'm not well.'

'What is it?'

She turned her face to me and I saw shame in her eyes. 'I'm in trouble,' she said.

I didn't understand. 'What?'

'I'm expecting.'

I knew what they did whilst I was walking the streets but I had never imagined that it would lead to this. I was silent with shock.

'Please, Nora,' said Grace. 'Please, say something. Don't be angry. I can't bear it.'

I wasn't angry. I was picturing Grace and me, bringing up a child, a little girl, holding her, feeding her, bathing her in front of the fire and sleeping with her between us. It was wonderful. But when Grace touched my shoulder, anxious for me to talk to her, I realized that it wouldn't be like that at all. It would be Grace and Bernard, Grace, Bernard and the baby: a family with no room in it for me. I would be left to fend for myself.

'Does he know?' I said.

She shook her head. 'No. I just said that I wasn't well. I don't want to tell him. I'm frightened.'

'Why? Won't he be pleased?'

She hesitated.

'What? What is it?'

'He's married,' she said quietly. 'Yesterday we had an argument. I said that I wanted to see him more often, in the day, not just at night. He said he didn't have time. I kept asking him questions. I wouldn't stop, and in the end he told me he had a wife.' She hung her head. 'He's got children too, a boy and a girl. He wouldn't say anything more about them. That's all I know.'

I stared at her.

'I've been thinking about it all day.' She was blushing now, and trembling. 'I've been picturing him, going back home after he's been here. His wife is probably happy to see him, like I always am. I hate her for having him. I feel as if I could kill her, just to keep him to myself. I'd do anything, no matter how bad it was.'

I understood, far better than she knew.

'I love him, Nora. But he won't want a baby, I know he won't.'

'I'll help you,' I said. 'I mean, I'll help you look after it. I've got a job. We'll manage.'

She shook her head.

'No,' she said sadly. 'I can't bear to lose him. I know it's wrong, but I don't care that he's got a wife. I won't give him up.'

I looked at her, puzzled. Then I remembered the hushed conversations at the factory, girls covering shifts for one another, whispering, swapping tips like recipes. I saw the determination in her eyes. I shivered.

'You don't mean it,' I said, already knowing that she did.

She nodded, and I knew then that I had lost her. She would do anything to keep him, even get rid of her child. And like all the times before, I did as she wanted. I have regretted what I said next ever since.

'I'll help you. Bernard need never know.'

'But how?'

'Gin,' I said.

'What?'

'Gin. It's what the girls at the factory say. You sit in a hot bath and you drink as much gin as you can. I don't know how it works but it does something to the baby and it comes out.'

Grace looked doubtful. 'Are you sure?'

I wasn't, but I didn't want her to know it. I was frightened, but I had promised to help. Somehow I would make it all right. I wanted her to know that she could rely on me.

I cleared my throat. 'Yes,' I said. 'Tell Bernard not to come tomorrow. Say you're still not well. We'll do it then.'

*

The next day we waited until it was dark outside. It seemed somehow wrong to do it in daylight. I pushed away my worries, passing the time by cleaning the flat. I scrubbed the bathroom, scouring the bath until my arms ached, mopping the floor and rubbing the taps with vinegar to make them shine. I poured bleach down the lavatory, standing next to it with my eyes closed, inhaling the sharp smell as if it might cleanse my thoughts at the same time.

When the clock struck seven, I almost wanted to hear Bernard's key in the lock so that we could pretend that nothing was wrong and I could escape to the streets. Instead, we shut ourselves in the bathroom, locking the door behind us. For once we were pleased there was no window.

'It's all right,' I said. 'We're safe. No-one can see us. No-one will ever know.'

Grace was hunched on the lavatory seat. I had taken a bottle of gin from one of Bernard's boxes. It had a picture of a galleon on the label and its name spelled out in green letters.

'Look!' I said. 'Victory Gin. That's a good sign, isn't it? The name, I mean. It's bound to work. We're going to be all right, you'll see.'

'Where did you get it?' she said.

'From one of the boxes, of course.'

'Do you think we ought to use it? We're not supposed to touch any of those things.'

'Where else would we find a bottle of gin?' I said impatiently. 'Anyway, he owes you something, don't you think?'

Her lips trembled and I was sorry for being sharp. I put my arm around her shoulders. 'Don't worry. There are dozens more bottles. He won't miss it, I promise.'

I turned the tap, hoping that for once there would be hot water. It spat some out, then spluttered and stopped. It was barely enough to cover her heels. We stared down at the bathtub sadly.

245

'What shall we do?' Grace said.

'I'll boil some water on the stove. We'll fill it that way. You stay here. You may as well start drinking. You're supposed to get as much down as you can manage.'

I poured an inch of gin into a teacup and passed it to her. 'Drink up!' I said, trying to sound cheerful.

Grace drank as I boiled kettle after kettle of water, pouring it into the bath, filling it as deep as I could.

The five-inch rule be damned, I thought, remembering the last time I had broken it.

Between kettles, while we waited for the water to boil, I perched on the end of the bath, watching the steam rise, mixing with the smoke from the cigarettes that Grace was lighting one after another so that she was never without one between her fingers.

She insisted that I drank with her.

'I feel funny doing it on my own,' she said. 'Please, Nora, let's pretend we're somewhere else, somewhere nice.'

I brought a cup from the kitchen and poured in a measure of gin. It was strong enough to make me shiver and I wished I had thought of getting something to mix it with.

'It makes me think of those afternoons with the communion wine,' she said. 'By the lake, do you remember? You and me, in the sun. Those were the best days, weren't they?'

I remembered. But I also remembered the trouble they had caused. I hoped we would get away with it this time.

'I think the bath's ready,' I said, changing the subject.

For a moment we looked at each other, frightened. Then Grace held out her glass. She had been drinking quickly and had got through almost a third of the bottle.

'I suppose we'd better get on with it,' she said. 'But will you give me some more? I think I'm going to need it.'

'I'll wait outside while you get undressed,' I said quickly.

'Please stay,' she said. 'I don't want to be alone. Don't leave me.'

I took her place on the lavatory while she took off her clothes and hung them on the hook on the back of the door. It was the first time I'd seen her naked body since we'd left Kent. It was different, fuller, with new curves from the extra rations that Bernard had fed her and, I supposed, from the child. Her breasts were heavy, and her thighs, always lean, now met each other in the middle, plump and soft. I longed to reach out and trace her body with my hands. Instead, with an effort, I looked away and took a long swig of gin. Grace stepped into the bath and let out a cry.

'Lord, that's hot!'

'I'm sorry.' I was apologising for more than the water. 'They said it has to be as hot as you can bear, otherwise it won't work. Do you think you can sit in it?'

She took another mouthful of gin and sat down, breathing hard through her nose. I watched colour rise in her cheeks and spread through the rest of her body. As she lay back, the water came almost to her collarbone.

'What do we do now?' she said.

I wasn't sure. 'I think you just stay in the bath for as long as you can and keep drinking. Can you feel anything yet?'

She took a while to respond. 'No,' she said eventually. 'I feel a bit woozy, but I think that's the gin. It's nice. I feel like nothing matters any more.'

And oddly, she was right. The bathroom was like a private club with just the two of us for members. I felt properly warm for the first time in months. The gin, combined with the steam and the smoke from the cigarettes, made everything easy and vague. Grace and I were together again, partners in crime in a way we hadn't been since we had come to London. We drank more gin and were giddy, laughing at our own silly jokes. I smoked part of a cigarette and liked the way it made my heart beat faster. We held hands and talked about good times in Kent. I was so happy to be close to her again that I almost forgot why we were there. But it came back to me when she started to sing the song that she had sung when she came back to the flat, the morning after her first time with him.

I've got you, under my skin,
I've got you, deep in the heart of me.
So deep in my heart that darling, you're really a part of me,
I've got you, under my skin.

The gin made her sing off-key. I was suddenly sober, nastily aware of what was under her skin; the child that we were trying to kill. I thought of her sister, Elizabeth, the other bath-time death. I still wasn't sure how much Grace knew and I had drunk almost enough gin to ask. But I knew that I couldn't, not now.

'Grace,' I said.

She was still humming.

'Grace,' I said again, more loudly. 'You should get out. The water's cold. It's not going to do any good. We've messed it up.'

*

The only thing to come of it was the pain in our heads the next morning. The thing was still inside her and the drink had made us miserable. We sat by the fire sipping tea. Even lifting my cup was an effort.

'What will we do?' Grace said. She was very pale and her eyelids were swollen from lack of sleep and gin. She kept shifting about in her chair, unable to settle.

'I don't know. There's no-one to ask.'

'There must be somebody. You know more people than me. Please, Nora. I'll do anything.'

I thought of the people I knew. They were not many. My world was the factory by day and the flat by night. The girls in the factory were easy with each other in a way that I could never be. I marvelled at how much they told each other about their lives. I listened to what they said, hovering at the edges of their conversations. But this would mean taking them into my confidence. It would mean gossip, the latest thing to be chewed over in tea breaks and passed from person to person. It was a horrible thought. Apart from those girls we knew no-one. We were as alone as we had been on our first day in London.

We sat by the fire for the rest of the day, trying to come up with an answer. We couldn't think of a way to put off Bernard and so he came to the flat at the usual time. Grace had managed to tidy herself up for him but he commented on my appearance as soon as he came in.

'You're looking worse for wear,' he said, grinning at me.

I shot him a dirty look. 'It was a hard night,' I said, pushing past him to the door.

Once again I found myself trudging through the streets. As I walked past the shut-up shops and dark houses, finding a way out began to seem impossible. Everything was closed, as if London was turning its back on our predicament. The only signs of life were the prostitutes, standing in their doorways, flashing their torches on and off.

'All right, Nora?' one of them called out. It was Mary, one of the girls from the café. She was a big woman, somehow comforting in her bulkiness, and always kind. I waved, pleased to be recognized on a night when I felt so small and so alone.

It was not until I was halfway down the street that I realized that perhaps she was the answer. She would know what to do, I was sure of it. I turned around and went back to her.

'Back already?' she said.

'Can I ask you something?'

'Ask away, but make it quick. I'm working.'

I swallowed. 'It's a friend of mine. She's in trouble—' I trailed off, not knowing what else to say. Mary looked me up and down.

'Oh, lovey,' she said.

'It's not me,' I stammered. 'Really it isn't. It's a friend.'

She glanced at my stomach. 'How far gone is she, this friend of yours?'

I didn't understand what she meant. 'Gone? What do you mean?'

'Lord, you're an innocent! When did she fall pregnant? Can she remember when she last had her monthlies?'

'Yes,' I said eagerly. Grace had told me the night before. 'It was two and a half, almost three months ago.'

She whistled. 'She'll need to do something about it sharpish then. Has she tried anything already?'

'She drank gin in the bath. But it didn't work.'

Mary shook her head. 'It never does. It's an old wives' tale, that one. She needs to see someone who knows what they're doing. Have you got a pencil?'

I scrabbled in my bag and found one. Mary wrote a telephone number on a scrap of paper.

'Tell this girl I sent you. She'll sort it out. She always uses the same woman, Mrs Pitts. She's good. She'll come to your flat and she'll be quick and clean. But do it soon. You haven't got much time.'

Twenty-Three

I KEPT REMEMBERING A SCENE FROM THE FILM OF *REBECCA*, near the beginning, just after Maxim and the heroine have met. They are driving through the south of France in an open-topped car.

'I wish there were an invention that could bottle up memory like a perfume,' she says, 'so it would never go stale and then whenever I wanted to, I could uncork the memory and live it all over again.'

He says quietly, 'Sometimes, you know, those little bottles contain demons that pop out at you, just when you're trying most desperately to forget.'

My demons were well and truly with me now. I spent days floating on a cloud of medication, anchored to the world only by the tightly tucked bedclothes. Other days were blunted and blurred by a dull pain that took over the whole of my body, making the weight of the sheets unbearable and the feathers in the pillows feel like needles against my face. I tried to ignore the pain, concentrating on David and Rose, working out what was happening between them.

David went about his business as calmly as ever but Rose seemed troubled and tense. She was never still, pacing about, twitching at the blankets, changing the water in my glass or wiping away non-existent dust from furniture that already shone from her constant polishing. Her conversation was vague and distracted. She watched David constantly, following every move he made. He seemed oblivious, even to the way that she blushed when he was near.

As the pain worsened, I grew tired of it all. Suddenly I didn't care for secrets. I didn't know what to believe. I had seen them in the garden. I had noticed the looks that they exchanged. I didn't want to be the odd one out again, the one left in the dark. I decided to ask Rose directly.

'What is it?' I said.

She looked startled. 'What do you mean?'

'Between you and that young man.'

'Which young man?'

'How many young men are there in this house?'

She hesitated. 'You mean David?'

I nodded.

'Nothing,' she said, but her eyes darted in every direction except mine, suggesting otherwise. She kept piling up little folds of the sheet and then pulling it through her fingers, pleating and unpleating it, over and over again.

'What do you mean?' I said. 'You like him, don't you?'

There was a pause.

'I can see it in the way you look at him.'

She sighed. 'You're right,' she said. 'I like him. I like how he is with Grace and with you. And how he is with me, as well. When he came here I thought he was taking over. I didn't want anyone to tell

252

me what to do. Do you remember how I tried to get out of that trip to the cinema? But we had such a good time. He made me laugh. That's when I started to like him. But I can't tell whether he likes me in the same way. I thought he did, but now I'm not sure.'

She shook her head. 'I made such a mess of things with Grace's father. I don't want to make a fool of myself again.'

It was no surprise to hear that she liked him, but it was oddly painful, much more than I might have anticipated.

'What do you think, Nora?' she asked.

I played for time. 'About what?'

'About David. Do you think he likes me?'

I looked at her, waiting for my verdict, and I could have made it easy, could have told her what she wanted. The hope in her eyes almost persuaded me. But I couldn't bring myself to say it.

I shrugged. 'I haven't noticed anything in particular,' I said, keeping my voice even. 'He's a very nice young man. But I suppose he's paid to be nice to us, isn't he? That's his job.'

I saw the hope flicker and die and felt a nasty satisfaction.

*

My meddling didn't end there. A few days later, when David was leaning over me to change a dressing, I smelled something that puzzled me.

'What's the matter?' he asked, catching sight of my expression.

'Nothing. It's just that I can smell cigarettes. Have you been smoking?'

'I'm sorry,' he said, sounding embarrassed. 'I try not to, but sometimes I can't help it.'

'I don't mind,' I said, and it was true. I had missed my nightly ritual since I'd been confined to bed. 'I like the smell,' I went on. 'I'd love it if you lit one now.'

'What?'

'A cigarette. It would make me very happy.'

'I can't.'

'Why not?'

He looked appalled. 'Nora, you're my patient. It'd be against everything I've ever been taught about nursing.'

'Do you always follow the rules?' I asked. 'I wouldn't smoke it. I just want to remember what it smells like. What harm could it do? I'm in a bad enough state as it is.'

'What about Rose?' he said. 'She'd smell it. Then we'd both be in trouble.'

'Why do you care what she thinks?'

He didn't rise to my challenge. 'You know, she's very fond of you. She'd be furious if she thought I wasn't looking after you properly.'

'I'm very fond of her too,' I said stiffly. 'I don't know what I'd have done without her.'

There was a pause.

'I've seen you watching her,' I said. 'You look as if you care.'

He was silent.

'Don't you?' I persisted.

'Look,' he said. 'I know what happened to Rose. She told me about Grace's father and coming to London and how you took her in. You're right. I like her. But I don't think she wants a new boyfriend.'

I could have told him he was wrong but I didn't. I said nothing, waiting to hear what he had to say next.

He hesitated. 'Do you know if they're still in touch?'

His eyes were hopeful, just as hers had been, and once again I nearly faltered. But there was something inside me that wouldn't let me stop.

'I'm not sure,' I said carefully. 'Perhaps.'

He pulled a packet of cigarettes from his pocket. 'I'm going out for a bit,' he said in a quiet voice. 'I won't be long.'

Twenty-Four

The date was set. It would all be over soon, they said. Every day the voices on the wireless gave another piece of news; Hitler was dead, Berlin had fallen, German troops had surrendered in Italy. Every day was another day closer to the end of the war, the thing that everyone had wanted for so long. We had wanted it too but now it didn't seem important. We could only think of what was in Grace's belly and how to get rid of it. We wanted our own ending and Mrs Pitts would make it happen.

The night before, we went to bed early and lay close to one another, whispering. Somehow it was easier to talk in the dark.

'I'm scared,' said Grace.

So was I. I felt for her hand and held it tight.

'I wish I knew what she was going to do to me. Do you think it'll hurt a lot?'

I wished I had something reassuring to say. 'I'll hold your hand like this,' I said. 'All the time. I won't leave you, not for a minute.'

She knew I was avoiding the question. 'It *will* hurt, won't it?' she said.

'Mary said Mrs Pitts has done it lots of times. She'll be careful, I'm sure. She won't let you come to any harm.'

I hoped I was right. Ever since I had made the telephone call, sweating and stumbling over my words, I had been worried about what would happen. Our efforts with the gin seemed like a game compared to this. The involvement of a stranger made it horribly real.

'I can't stop thinking about it. Do you think the thing will look like a baby? I couldn't bear it if it looked like Bernard or me.'

The idea of a baby staring at us with Grace's wide blue eyes made me shudder. 'I don't think it's big enough to be like a person,' I said quickly. 'I mean, it takes a long time for a baby to grow. It's not going to look like much of one yet.'

'I hope not,' she said quietly.

I suddenly thought of Mrs Rivers. If we asked for her help she was certain to give it, for the child she had lost and for the daughter she had left. But the next minute I pushed the thought away. I didn't want her to be part of it. I wanted to be the one to help. I wanted Grace to myself.

'You don't have to do it, you know,' I said. 'If you want to keep it we'll find a way to manage. I mean, the war's changed things. And people here aren't the same as in Kent. They don't all know each other and they don't know us. There wouldn't be any gossip. You could say the baby's father was killed in service. We'd be able to pull it off, I'm sure we would.'

I didn't know if I sounded convincing. But it made no difference. She was certain.

'It's the only way I'll keep him,' she muttered. 'I can't have a baby on my own and he can't marry me. There's nothing else for it.'

Neither of us said anything for a while, then she shuffled closer. 'Nora, will you hold me?'

I put my arms around her. We slept curled around each other as if we really had been twins.

*

Mrs Pitts came the next night, late, after dark. She was a perfectly ordinary looking woman, not at all what I'd expected. She could have been anybody's mother, small and round, her hair kept neat under a headscarf. She wore a gold wedding band that had worn thin and when she spoke it was like listening to Ma, soft Irish sounds. I found them a comfort.

'So, girls,' she said. 'Which of you two am I here to see?'

Grace's expression told her all she needed to know. She put a hand on her shoulder. 'Don't be frightened, lovey. It'll be over soon enough, and then you can put it all behind you. Tomorrow's a new start for everyone. You'll be right as rain by then. Just you wait and see. You'll be dancing in the street with your sweetheart.'

Grace nodded but said nothing. We knew all about VE Day, Victory in Europe. Bernard had told us earlier that evening. He had been full of it. He would come again tomorrow afternoon, he had said, to listen to Mr Churchill's announcement on the wireless, and then he would take us out to celebrate, me as well as Grace. We had tried hard to look enthusiastic.

Mrs Pitts rummaged in the bag she had brought with her and took out an old enamel saucepan, slightly chipped. 'Let's get this over with, shall we?' she said.

I nodded.

'What's your name, dear?'

'Nora.'

'Well then, Nora, would you boil me up some water in this? About half a pan.'

When I got to the kitchen I ran the tap and set the pan of water on the stove, then I leaned against the sink, trying to make myself calm. We were going through with it. We were about to kill the baby. We were about to break the law. I wondered how we had come to this. It didn't seem so very long ago that we had been playing with dolls in Kent.

'Nora!' Mrs Pitts called from the other room.

I hurried through the curtain. She was laying things from her bag onto the table next to Bernard's boxes.

'Yes?' I said.

'Have you got a towel, an old one, to spread over the bed, in case there's any mess?'

I didn't like to think of what she meant by mess, but I went to the bathroom and took my towel from the hook on the back of the door. Mrs Pitts grunted approvingly. 'That's the ticket. Good and big.'

She took it over to the bed and laid it on top of the counterpane, smoothing it down. I watched her closely, feeling sick. It seemed wrong to be getting rid of the baby in the very place it had been conceived. I turned to look at Grace, still sitting in the armchair, shivering despite the fire, which was burning high in the grate. She looked wretched but determined. I had seen that look before, and I knew she would go through with it, however painful it was.

Mrs Pitts beckoned me over. 'If you've a drop of brandy, or anything like that, it wouldn't hurt, to steady her nerves.'

I pulled a bottle from one of the boxes, fetched a glass from the kitchen and splashed some of the strong-smelling liquid into it. I took it over to Grace. 'Drink this,' I said. 'She says it'll help.'

She drank it down without saying a word. In the meantime, Mrs

259

Pitts had gone into the kitchen. A strange smell stole under the curtain, a combination of carbolic soap and disinfectant, like the smell that had always hung about Ma when she came home from her cleaning jobs.

I crouched down at Grace's feet. 'Are you all right?' I whispered.

She nodded. 'I'm scared,' she said in a low voice. 'How long do you think it'll take?'

'She seems to know what she's doing. I'm sure she'll be as quick as she can.'

'Don't leave me, will you?' She took my hand. 'No matter what happens. Please. Do you promise?'

I nodded, not trusting myself to speak. Mrs Pitts came through the curtain. 'Nearly ready,' she said. 'Now dear, you go and empty your bladder before we start.'

*

When Grace came back from the bathroom, Mrs Pitts patted the bed.

'Take your knickers off and hop up here.'

Grace looked at me doubtfully. I nodded, feeling as if I were betraying her. She reached under her skirt, pulled down her knickers, stepped out of them, picked them up and put them on a chair. She walked over to the bed and lay down, holding herself stiff. Mrs Pitts smiled at her.

'Lie back,' she said, 'and put your feet together so that the bottoms of them are touching. That's right. Now let your knees drop apart, as far as you can. That way I'll be able to see what I'm doing.'

I moved to the head of the bed so I wouldn't have to see Grace like that. She caught hold of my hand, gripping it tightly. I squeezed it back in a silent pledge that I would stay.

Mrs Pitts went to the table and picked up something the size and shape of a candle that looked as if it were made out of black rubber.

She fitted a piece of hose onto one end of it and then a funnel to the end of the hose, then went to the kitchen and brought back the pan. She dipped her finger into the greyish liquid.

'Just right,' she said. 'Nice and warm, but not too hot.'

She came over to the bed, put her hands on Grace's knees and pushed them apart. None of us said anything. The only sound was the ticking of the clock on the mantelpiece. I felt a pulse hammer hard in Grace's wrist. I held my breath. Mrs Pitts took the black thing and put it between Grace's legs. She seemed to be looking for something, pushing gently. Grace looked at me with wide eyes. I looked back at her, willing her to see it through. At last Mrs Pitts seemed to find what she was looking for.

'Take a deep breath, lovey,' she said, and I saw the tube slither across the towel as she pushed it into Grace, whose eyes grew wider still. She began to breathe hard through her nose, her lips pressed tightly together.

Mrs Pitts nodded, as if she were pleased. She picked up the pan and held up the funnel so that it was level with her chest. She poured the liquid into it slowly, keeping her eyes on Grace as she did it. Grace's breathing quickened and her grip tightened on my hand. The strange soapy smell filled the room again. I tried to tell myself that we were just washing out the baby, but I knew she wasn't feeling clean and neither was I.

Mrs Pitts kept on pouring the liquid into the funnel, tipping up the pan to get the last drops out. After a minute, she carefully pulled away the hose and carried it off into the kitchen. A new smell came into the room; boiling rubber, noxious and thick. I knelt by the side of the bed, my face level with Grace.

'Are you all right?' I said, knowing that my words weren't enough.

She nodded. 'Well, at least it's done,' she said. 'We've taken care of it. That's the important thing, I suppose.'

Mrs Pitts had come back and was standing at the end of the bed, winding the tube around the funnel. It seemed somehow indecent to see her touch the thing that had been inside Grace just minutes before and I looked away.

'How are we?' she asked.

'What happens next?' I said.

'You just wait. Keep her quiet and make her rest. In a few hours she'll start to feel things move down below and then a little while afterwards it'll start to come out. There'll be some blood but it's nothing to worry about. After it's all out she'll be weak at first but she's a good strong girl. Give her some meat, if you can get hold of it, and some greens to build her strength back up. She'll be right as rain again in no time.'

'But what if something goes wrong?' I said. 'How shall I find you? Shall I telephone the girl from before? Or have you got your own telephone? Can you give me the number?'

Mrs Pitts's easy manner slipped and her eyes became hard. Her voice was hard too. 'Nothing will go wrong. If it does, it'll be because you haven't done as I've told you. Don't try to find me. I wasn't here and you've never met me, remember that. I could get into a lot of trouble for helping girls like you and so could you, for asking me to do it. You wouldn't like that, would you?'

I stared at her in horror. She stared back, unblinking.

'Look,' she said, 'if anything goes wrong, which believe me, it won't, call an ambulance. For God's sake, don't tell them what's happened. Say she fell down the stairs and you think she's having a miscarriage. That should do.'

She left quickly, putting my savings into a small leather purse and pushing it to the bottom of her bag. When I came to clear up the table later on I found she had taken the bottle of brandy as well.

There was nothing to do but wait. We said very little, sitting in front of the fire and watching the flames dance until there was nothing left to burn. Grace seemed stunned and her eyes were troubled. When the fire went out, we went to bed and lay looking up at the ceiling, still waiting. Neither of us slept.

It was almost morning when it began. The birds were starting to sing and traces of light showed around the edges of the curtains we had put up the week before when the blackout had ended. Grace let out a little gasp, as if she were surprised.

'Are you all right?' I said quickly.

'I feel as if something's slipping,' she said. 'Slipping out of me, I mean, sort of slithering.'

I switched on the light, got out of bed and drew back the counterpane. Something very bad was happening. Grace was lying in a pool of blood, dark gobbets of it all around her.

I spoke without thinking. 'Christ!'

Grace looked down and went pale. I picked up the towel that Mrs Pitts had used, then realized that I didn't know what to do with it.

'Pass it to me,' Grace said. 'Quick!' She was sitting up now, staring at the mess that surrounded her. I passed her the towel and she pressed it between her legs, her knuckles clenched, very white against the blood. We looked at each other.

'Perhaps I should go to the bathroom,' she said, and started to get up from the bed, but then she let out a terrible wail and collapsed back onto it.

'What is it?' I stammered. 'What can I do? Let me help you. Tell me, please tell me.'

Her body was rigid and her face tight with pain. I grabbed her hand.

'Grace, what's wrong?'

She had begun to pant. 'It's like I'm being stretched inside. I feel as if I'm going to burst.'

I watched a mark the size of a sixpence darken and spread as the blood began to soak through the towel. Grace closed her eyes and for a moment her face lost its strained look, but the next minute she screamed again. The pain kept coming in waves. Each time her face would turn red and then the colour would drain away and great shudders pass through her body. With them came blood. It soaked through towel after towel and I started to fold sheets up into wads, pressing them between her legs until they were heavy and sodden. I held a pillow over her mouth to muffle her screams each time the pain came. When it went we were silent, preparing ourselves for the next bout of it, breathing together in unison as if we had become part of the same body. We went on like that throughout the night, fighting it with all our strength. She wouldn't let me call an ambulance. The old Grace was still there, as headstrong and determined as ever.

'It'll be over soon,' she said, gripping the pillow hard. 'We have to see it through, that's all. I'm not going to give up. You heard what Mrs Pitts said. We could go to prison, both of us. I won't let it happen.'

'But you're losing so much blood,' I said. 'What if—?' I stopped myself.

'She said I would. It's what she expected. That's how the thing comes out.'

I was sure that she shouldn't be in so much pain and I opened my mouth to say so, but before I could speak she went on. 'Besides, we're runaways, remember? If we went to hospital they'd probably make us tell Mummy and Father. Can you imagine what they'd do? They'd be furious.'

I could imagine it all right. Mrs Rivers would rush to Grace as quickly as she could, determined not to lose the only child she had left. I pictured her face, frantic with worry and concern. But then I pictured Reverend Rivers standing, thin lipped and silent, and the looks that would pass between him and me. I couldn't stand the thought of it.

'And there's all the other things. The things in Bernard's boxes. If an ambulance came here there'd be so much fuss. We'd be in terrible trouble and so would he. Let's just stick it out. I can stand it, I know I can.'

I decided to believe her. I bit my lip and held her hand as the contractions came, breathing with her, raising the glass of water to her lips so she could drink. But the blood showed no sign of stopping and as the hours passed, she kept her eyes closed, too tired to hold them open.

Later that morning, as the traffic began to rumble in the street, I went to the kitchen to fetch more water. When I came back, Grace's head had fallen to one side. A fleck of white spittle sat at the corner of her mouth. I ran to the bed and held her face in my hands.

'Grace! Wake up!' I said, shaking her but she was heavy and limp.

For the first time since Kent I began to pray, the only way that I could think of to save her. I bargained with God, falling over my words.

'God, save her, please save her. I'll do anything you want. Just keep her alive.'

I remembered the Book of Common Prayer.

We kindle God's wrath against us; we provoke Him to plague us with divers diseases and sundry kinds of death.

I had started it and now she was paying the price of my wickedness. I fell to my knees, put my hands together and bowed my head. I began to beg.

'Please, God. I know I've sinned. I know I was wrong to love her. But let it be me who suffers, not her. I can stand it. If you save her I'll do anything. I'll stop loving her. This time I won't pretend. I'll make myself stop doing it. I'll go away. I'll leave, I promise.'

When I looked up, I saw a miracle. Grace's eyes were open. He had listened. God had answered my prayers.

Thank you, I thought. Thank you.

She stretched her hand out to me and I took it, squeezing it gently. She had a strange, sad look in her eyes.

'Don't let go, will you?' she said.

'Of course I won't. I'll never let you go.' I took a deep breath. I had to tell her, just once, before I took up my side of the bargain. 'I love you. I can't tell you how much I love you. I always have.' I swallowed. 'Grace, have you ever loved me?'

She smiled her old wicked smile.

'Of course I have. I always have. I chose you, didn't I? Right at the start.'

Then she closed her eyes and was gone.

Twenty-Five

ONE AFTERNOON, ROSE TOOK GRACE FOR A WALK, LEAVING David and me together. He sat in the chair next to my bed, reading, his legs stretched out in front of him. I looked at him surreptitiously, noticing the fine lines that were starting to show around his eyes and mouth. He read quickly, turning the pages with his long fingers, absorbed in his book. As the hours passed, I grew tired of simply watching. I decided to start a conversation.

'Is it any good?' I said.

It was the first time I'd ever addressed him, but he didn't seem surprised. He smiled. 'Yes,' he said. 'It is. I bought it the other day from that little bookshop just off the Holloway Road.'

I stiffened at the thought of my two worlds colliding.

'I got talking to the owner. He suggested some others as well. I'd love to know what you think of them.'

I hadn't been asked my opinion on a book for a very long time. I had missed it.

'You've got a lot of books,' he said. 'Have you read them all?'

'Yes.'

'Have you always liked reading?'

I thought of those lessons in the schoolroom with Reverend Rivers and the tremendous excitement I had felt.

'Yes,' I said quietly. 'I've always loved it.'

'I like short books,' he said. 'Ones about ideas.'

'I like a beginning, a middle and an end,' I said. 'You know where you are with those.'

'Who's your favourite writer?' he asked.

I thought hard. 'It depends on how I'm feeling,' I said eventually. 'It's like friends.'

It was the closest I'd ever come to admitting that books had taken the place of people in my life.

'What if you really had to choose? Just one book, if that was all you were allowed to keep.'

I knew immediately.

'Shakespeare,' I said. '*The Collected Works.*'

'That's cheating!' he said.

Despite myself, I was enjoying the conversation. Books were as good a remedy as always.

'Were you a teacher?' he asked.

I shook my head.

'Did you study English at university?'

'No,' I said. 'I never went. There was the war, you see.'

'So how come you've read so much?'

He was leaning forward, listening intently, his hair falling into his eyes. I decided to tell him some of it, the safer parts.

'It was difficult after the war. There wasn't much I could

do to make a living. I wasn't qualified for anything.'

I wasn't going to tell him about those long, painful days when the rest of the country was celebrating, days that I spent waiting for night to fall so I could forage for food along with the rats. I had picked up scraps, not caring about the dirt, pushing them into my mouth and scurrying back to my hiding place. When I had become too hungry to stand it any longer, I'd forced myself to go out in daylight, stumbling along the unfamiliar streets, sticking to the smaller ones, walking in the shadows, keeping close to the walls. I had come across the shop by chance, drawn by the display in the window, feeling as if I were looking into another world. Then I'd noticed the card in the corner.

Assistant sought. Enquire within.

David didn't need to know how long I'd stood there, gathering the courage to push open the door and step inside. I thought of how I'd hovered in the silent shop, awed by the books that surrounded me, ten times as many as there'd been in Reverend Rivers' study. I had jumped at the sound of the cough from the corner.

'Don't panic,' a voice had said, sounding amused. 'I won't bite.'

It was a voice like Reverend Rivers', expensive and low. A wheel-chair had come forward out of the shadows.

'Hello,' said the man who was sitting in it. 'I'm George.'

He gave me coffee that he brewed on a ring in the little kitchen at the back of the shop. He brought out a plate of stale biscuits that I bolted down gratefully. He didn't ask me where I had come from and I was thankful for that as well. But he did ask if I liked books. I was shy at first, but he nodded as I gave him my nervous opinions and listened carefully to what I said. Slowly I began to feel better. By the end of the afternoon I had managed to screw up enough courage to ask about the job.

He nodded thoughtfully. 'I need help,' he said. 'I had polio as a child. I can't manage all that fetching and carrying.'

'I could,' I said eagerly. 'I mean, I could try. I'm pretty strong.'

He gave me the job and the little flat above the shop; two rooms to call my own and a key to turn in the lock at night. On the wall I stuck up the illustrations from a copy of *Paradise Lost* that had fallen apart too badly to be mended. I put the copies of *Rebecca* and Shakespeare on the nightstand and hung my few clothes in the wardrobe. I kept the other things in the pillowcase under the bed, out of sight.

Each morning I went downstairs early so the coffee would be ready by the time he arrived. I took pleasure in making it as he had shown me, filling the bottom half of the pot with water, patting down the coffee grounds and screwing on the top, then waiting for the bubbling noise, inhaling the aroma that drifted through the shop.

He taught me the trade, every last little detail, from doing the accounts to wrapping up the books. Before long I could guess what a customer would like as soon as they came through the door. And all the while, George and I talked, not about the past, or the war, or what would happen next, but about the books that were stacked on the shelves around us. I tried to put my own story out of my mind, like a second-rate novel forgotten after the last page had been turned.

He taught me other things, too. When I had been at the bookshop for a while, he asked me if one evening I would like to come to his house.

I was wary and it must have shown in my expression. He hastened to reassure me.

'It's not far,' he said. 'Ten minutes away, that's all. There's something I want to show you, something I think you'll like. And we can have something to eat. I'll cook for you.'

'All right,' I said, not knowing what else to say.

I had never seen a man cook before. He made an omelette from powdered egg and forgot to add salt.

'Oh,' he said, after his first mouthful. 'Not one of my best efforts. I apologize.'

I smiled at him. I rather liked that he was bad at something. It made me less afraid. After we had eaten he took me through to the sitting room at the front of the house.

'This is what I wanted you to see,' he said, pointing to a gramophone on a table in the corner. He wheeled himself over to it and opened the box, then turned a little handle at the side. I watched as a black disc began to spin, slowly at first and then faster. Carefully, he lowered the needle onto the disc. There was a crackling noise, then music filled the room, wonderful music, notes from a piano rippling over violins that sang out with joy. I stood very still, lifted up by the sound, marvelling at how the instruments wound themselves about each other, swirling and dipping, on and on, with no hesitation, very sure and very light.

It took me a while to recover myself when it finished. When I came to my senses, I noticed George looking at me, a fond expression on his face.

'I thought you'd like it,' he said. 'I hoped you would.'

We spent many evenings listening to music after that. He introduced me to all of his favourite composers, talking about them as familiarly as if they were old friends. After that first flabby omelette, I suggested that I might take over the cooking. I wasn't sure I'd be much good at it but I had helped Mrs Rivers often enough to try. I experimented, trying new recipes out on George. He was willing to eat whatever I produced, never minding strange combinations of flavours or cakes that failed to rise. I tried to remember the way that

Mrs Rivers had done things. I aimed for something like that first Sunday lunch in Kent. Slowly I became sure of myself, and one day I made an attempt at it, queuing for hours to get the meat and going to three different grocers to find the right vegetables. It was worth it. I arranged our plates carefully, piling the carrots up next to the spinach, three golden roast potatoes each, two slices of pink meat. I knew that the vegetables wouldn't taste of sunshine like the ones from the rectory garden, but he ate up every last scrap and came back for second helpings.

'You're very capable, aren't you?' he said.

I blushed with pleasure. It was a long time since I'd felt good at anything. Over the long winter that followed, as we listened to music by the fire, I began to feel better, as if somehow I was being put back together again. As spring arrived, I felt myself begin to thaw around the edges like the ice on the Forgotten Lake.

One day in April he asked me to go with him to Hampstead Heath.

'I won't be able to walk that far,' he said. 'We'll need to take the chair.'

I insisted on pushing him, although he said he could get along himself. When we arrived at the Heath I was astounded. It was like being back in the countryside. I wanted to take off my shoes and feel the new grass tickle my feet, to wander along the little paths that led off into the woods, to pick the primroses that hid in the hedgerows. I turned to him, exhilarated.

'I never knew London was like this,' I said.

He smiled, looking pleased. 'There's something else I want to show you. Do you think you can push me up that hill?'

I gasped with pleasure when we got to the top. The city spread out beneath us for as far as I could see. George had shown me maps of London in the bookshop. Now it was as if the maps had sprung into life. I had a sudden sense of knowing exactly where I was. It was a good feeling. I was still here, I thought, still alive, whilst London lived around me.

As I stood, looking at it all, I felt a hand touch my arm. I smiled down at George.

'Thank you for this,' I said. 'It's beautiful.'

'Nora,' he said. 'I want to ask you something.'

'What is it?'

There was a long pause. I had never known him lost for words before. Then he gave himself a little shake. 'I wanted to know if you would marry me.'

Six months before his question would have made me want to run away. Now I was oddly unsurprised.

'I know I'm not much of a catch,' he said. 'I mean, I'm older than you. And there wouldn't be any children. I can't—'

I stopped him, as embarrassed as he was. I knew I didn't love him, not like I'd loved Grace. I didn't ever feel very much any more, as if I'd used up all my feelings at the rectory and in the little Soho flat. But I liked him. I liked him very much. I knew he would be kind to me. I liked the bookshop too. When I was in it I felt protected from the world outside. A life in the bookshop with George would be a better life than any other I could think of.

'All right,' I said. 'I will.'

*

I learned about a different kind of love from George. We spent forty years together, never tiring of each other's company. We had other worlds at our disposal, a thousand dinner guests that could be invited just by opening a book. At night we lay in bed, comfortably close. At first I had been anxious, lying rigid and afraid, mindful of Reverend Rivers. I had never said anything to George but he seemed to sense some of it at least, reaching out very gently and holding me as if I were something precious. I slept in his arms from that night on.

*

David was looking at me closely, waiting to hear what I had to say. I would keep it simple, I thought.

'I worked in a bookshop,' I said. 'The one that you went to.'

'Really?' he said. 'No kidding?'

'Really. For a very long time.'

'How long?'

'All my life. I was married to the owner. We worked there together until he died and after that I ran it by myself.'

I had worked harder than ever after he died. The shop was the only thing I had left.

David looked intrigued. 'What about the man I talked to? He's not your son, is he?'

'That's Stephen,' I said. 'I've known him for years. I'm very fond of him. I sold him the shop. I knew I could trust him to run it in the right way.'

'Well, I don't know what it was like when you had it,' he said, 'but it's how bookshops used to be. It's how they should be.'

I nodded. 'It hasn't changed much. Stephen's taken care of it.'

'Nora,' he said gently, 'would you like me to give him a message? Shall I tell him you're not well?'

I didn't want any fuss. I didn't want an awkward visit. I didn't want to explain myself.

'No,' I said. 'Just tell him when, you know, when it's over.'

He didn't try to persuade me, but just nodded, looking thoughtful.

*

When Rose came back from her walk, she was clutching a bunch of snowdrops.

'Look, Nora,' she said softly. 'I picked these on the Heath.'

The white flowers drooped like the heads of shy children.

'I always think they must be tougher than they look to push up through all that frozen earth. I bet it's so disappointing to get here and find that it's still winter.' She said it quietly, her eyes darting over to David and I knew that her words were meant for him, not me, but I minded less than I might have before.

'I'd better put them in water.' She went over to a vase of shrivelled holly left over from Christmas. 'This'll do.'

She fumbled as she tried to take the holly out, still holding Grace and the snowdrops, so determined not to drop anything that she didn't notice David getting to his feet.

'Let me help,' he said.

She let out a little cry and dropped the vase. At once the room was filled with the dank smell of stagnant water. Grace began to scream.

'Oh God, I'm sorry.' Rose's face was blotched with embarrassment.

'It's only water,' he said gently. 'I'll clear it up.'

She flushed darker. 'I spilled it. I'll do it.'

'You keep hold of Grace. I'll get a cloth. I'll be back in a minute.'

He left the room. Rose came over to the bed and sat down.

'I can't stand this,' she muttered.

She was trembling. I felt a sudden affection for this girl who had brought me back into the world. I put my hand on her arm.

'He's so nice. But I know it's just like you said. He's paid to do it. There's no point me saying anything. It would just make things awkward. We need him here to look after you. That's what important, not my stupid crush.'

I was lost for words. My demons had joined forces with my

illness to bring back the past, blinding me with old suspicions and preoccupations. I was suddenly ashamed of my jealousy.

That night I drifted in and out of a restless sleep. Ghosts slid before my eyes, taunting me with the things I'd done. I saw myself as a girl, reciting the catechism on my knees.

My duty towards my neighbour is to love him as myself and to do to all men as I would they should do unto me:
To love, honour and succour my father and mother:
To honour and obey the King, and all that are put in authority under him:
To submit myself to all my governors, teachers, spiritual pastors and masters:
To order myself lowly and reverently to all my betters:
To hurt no body by word nor deed:
To be true and just in all my dealing:
To bear no malice nor hatred in my heart:
To keep my hands from picking and stealing, and my tongue from evil-speaking, lying and slandering:
To keep my body in temperance, soberness and chastity:
Not to covet nor desire other men's goods: but to learn and labour truly to get mine own living, and to do my duty in that state of life, unto which it shall please God to call me.

I had broken every promise of the catechism. I had coveted and I had desired and it had led to terrible things. I had caused damage that could never be undone.

My shame grew worse as I realized the truth of it. I had meddled with Rose as I had meddled years before. I had wanted the same things as I had wanted then. All my life I had tried to be part of a family, but now I could see that I had broken them up all along. I had refused to go back to my mother, I had taken Grace from Mrs Rivers, I had helped Grace to kill her child.

I had told myself that I was helping Rose, that I was making up for the past. But it hadn't been quite true. I suddenly felt exhausted. My demons had governed me for long enough. I wanted the damage to stop. I wasn't so foolish as to be sure that a romance between David and Rose would work out. I'd read too many books to believe in happy endings. But I knew that they liked each other. It was a start.

I didn't have much time left, I knew. The pain was constant now, the disease clawing at me, gobbling me up. I resolved to talk to Rose.

*

My chance came a week later, when David had gone to the pharmacy to pick up some medicine. Rose was building a fire. She had brought up a bucket of coal and some sticks, which she was piling on top of one another, balancing them over more paper, crumpled up into balls.

That morning I'd felt something new in my chest. It was as if my lungs were beginning to silt up with something that I knew would choke me in the end. I wanted to sleep, but instead I raised myself up slightly on my pillow.

'Rose?' I said.

She went on scrabbling about in the fireplace.

I tried again. 'Rose?'

She jumped as if I'd startled her. 'Sorry, Nora, I was miles away. Do you need something?'

'I'm all right,' I said. 'But I want to talk to you.' I patted the bed. 'Come and sit with me.'

She came over, wiping her hands on her trousers, new ones, I noticed. She had put on weight since David had taken over the cooking. It suited her.

'What is it?'

'It's about David.'

She shook her head. 'It's no good, Nora. It wouldn't work. And I've got other things to think about. You and Grace, for a start.'

I tried to reassure her. 'Grace is all right. She's a happy little thing. And I won't be here for much longer; we both know that. Don't think about me. There's no point to it.' I paused, trying to judge how much to say. 'Think of the future. You could have one together.'

'He doesn't want me,' she said. 'I'm making a fool of myself. You saw me drop that vase last week. Whenever he's near, I get so nervous, I feel as if I'm going to be sick.'

'But if you feel like that,' I said, 'then you won't be able to give him up. Feelings like that don't just go away because you want them to. They just don't.'

'How would you know?' she said, and then looked embarrassed. I was silent.

She looked at me closely. 'Nora?'

A terrible, choking panic rose in my throat.

'Nora, what is it? Do you know what it's like? Were you in love with someone you couldn't tell? What happened?'

I should have known she would ask. I began to sweat.

'Was it when you were married? Did you have an affair?'

I wondered if it counted. I had loved the memory of her. I had been unfaithful in my thoughts every night. But I had touched no-one and no-one had touched me.

'No,' I said, slowly. 'I never did that.'

She shook her head.

'Then you don't understand,' she said. 'He's not interested in me and I'm not going to say something stupid.'

'But if you don't say something he'll leave as soon as I die,' I said.

'He'll go to his next job and you'll never know.' My voice had risen and I sounded desperate, even to myself, but I had to go on. 'He likes you,' I told her. 'I can tell.'

She was stubborn. 'I'm sorry, Nora. I won't do it,' she said, going back over to the fireplace. 'There's no point.'

Twenty-Six

My ears were filled with a terrible howling. I was drowning in noise but I couldn't stop. I howled on and on for everything that had happened since the day I left Ma. I didn't care who heard me. I howled until my throat was tight and sore and blood was hammering in my temples. Then I slumped back on the bed. As I lay there next to Grace, the horror of what I had done started to dawn on me and I began to cry fat, painful tears.

'Thou shalt not kill,' I whispered, stroking her hand. I had broken the first rule, the most important one of all. I closed my eyes and began to recite the words I hadn't said since I had left Ma.

'Bless me Father, for I have sinned.'

But it was no good. I didn't believe in it. I had no faith left. I had made a bargain with God and he hadn't kept his side of it. I didn't want his forgiveness. It wouldn't make any difference. I had no-one left to lose, not Grace, not Ma, not the baby, not God. They were all gone.

I took Grace's hand and kissed it, pressing my lips to her skin. I stroked her arm with my fingertips and traced the line of her collarbone. I unhooked the pearl earrings and rubbed her earlobes gently. Then I wound my fingers in her hair and held her close to me, rocking her like a child.

By the time I laid her back against the pillow her body was starting to stiffen. I looked down at the sheets, soaked with blood. It glistened in places, still wet. I didn't want anyone to see her like that. It would be our secret, the last one we shared.

I boiled water and brought it to the bed in a bucket. I found a bar of soap that smelled of roses, one that I had given her for Christmas. I took a pair of scissors and put them to the hem of her nightdress. I watched my hand as if it belonged to somebody else, working the scissors, slicing the material from the hem to the collar, then across the shoulders and down each sleeve to the cuff.

Grace lay exposed, as frank and unconcerned as when she was alive. The thought of her body had occupied my mind and filled my dreams since that first day by the lake. Now the memory of it would stay with me forever. Her breasts were full and her belly slightly curved from the pregnancy. I had to force myself to look at the rest of her. The blonde hair between her legs was matted and stained with congealed blood. Her thighs were streaked with red and her knees were marked with bruises where she had banged them together in frustration at the pain.

I used the scissors to cut strips off the end of the sheet. I dipped one into the water and wiped her forehead with it, then passed the damp linen over her cheeks and across her cracked lips, kissing each part of her as I washed it, fixing her taste in my memory. I washed every inch of her body very carefully, rinsing out the strips of sheet in the bucket and changing the water as it thickened with blood. When I was finished and the evidence washed away, I took away the sheets and brought new ones, smoothing them out underneath her. I took my own nightdress and brought it over her head, pulling her arms through the sleeves. I brushed out her tangled hair and then laid her back down against the pillows. She looked like a bride in the white gown, all dressed up for her wedding day.

'I would have married you,' I whispered. 'He wouldn't but I would, if you'd let me. I would have promised you everything. For better or for worse, for richer for poorer, in sickness and in health. Until death us do part.'

I leaned forward, kissed her and drew the sheet over her face.

*

It was very hot in the flat, and very quiet. I switched on the wireless in the corner to distract myself from my thoughts. I remembered sitting in the pew next to Grace, six years before, listening to the crackle and hiss of the airwaves, then hearing grave words from a careful man.

I am speaking to you from the Cabinet Room at Number Ten, Downing Street.

Just as there had been a moment when the war had begun, there would be a moment when it ended. Mr Churchill would announce it soon, at three o'clock. I didn't know when our story had begun. If there had been no war then this might not have happened. If I hadn't been sent to the village then she might have been all right. If I hadn't loved her so much that I couldn't bear to leave her behind, she might still be alive.

An organ was playing a hymn that I recognized.

Now thank we all our God, with heart and hands and voices,
Who wondrous things has done, in Whom this world rejoices;

Who, from our mothers' arms has blessed us on our way
With countless gifts of love, and still is ours today.

I didn't feel like thanking God. He hadn't blessed me with countless gifts of love. He had taken them all away. He had taken me from Ma, I had taken Grace from Mrs Rivers and now he had taken Grace away from me. I switched off the wireless and stood looking at the clock, watching its hands inch forward. I didn't know what the time had been when she died. I hadn't thought to look. I would never be able to say for sure when her life had come to an end.

Despite the stuffiness in the room, I shivered. I sank into one of the armchairs, drawing up my knees and resting my chin on them. I wrapped my arms around my legs as if I might be able to hold myself together.

As midday approached and the room grew even hotter, I tried to pretend that I was somewhere else. I thought of the fields in Kent; the most space that I had ever known. I remembered the thrill of running as fast as we could through the grass, with no limit to how far we could go. I remembered swimming in the lake, my body slicing easily through the water. But then the fields and the lake became the church, with its door closed tight against the world outside. I remembered crying for Ma and praying to resist temptation. I remembered making my bargain with God. I remembered Reverend Rivers' hand on my head and his arm against mine as he led us in prayer for our souls. I remembered the things that he said next, the secret that had festered inside him, the one he had passed on to me.

I heard him call me a consolation. I saw that small, peculiar smile. I felt the scratch of stubble and smelled tobacco, I felt grass brushing against my legs as I ran through the graveyard. I saw myself, sitting on the floor next to the lavatory and feeling my skin crawl.

I got to my feet and went to the bathroom. My reflection in the mirror was startling. My face was streaked with blood, great smears of it, clotted in my eyebrows and crusted about my nostrils. I looked wild, like something not quite human.

I was suddenly possessed by a strange, furious energy. I tore off my clothes and ran into the kitchen, filling all the pans that I could find with water and lighting the stove. When each pan had boiled I poured the water into the bath like I had done for Grace when we were trying to get rid of the baby. I stepped into it, ignoring the scalding heat that shot up my legs. After a moment, I made myself sit, forcing myself to bear it.

This time I didn't scrub my thighs until they bled. The water turned red from her blood, not mine. As I washed it off, I began to realize what I had done. I thought of Mrs Rivers, smiling down at me as I crouched in the cattle-pen at the station. I had taken her daughter, the only one she had left. I was the one who had found out the telephone number from Mary, who had arranged for Mrs Pitts to come. I had pushed away the thought of asking Mrs Rivers to help us because I'd wanted Grace to myself. Now she was gone forever and there was no way back.

As I moved my hands over my body I felt anger quicken inside me. Reverend Rivers had started it all. He had made it impossible for me to stay. Grace had followed me because she had thought he didn't care. Now she was dead and I was alone again. My head began to pound.

'You made me into this,' I said. 'You killed her. Your own daughter, the only one you had left.'

I knew that there was nothing I could do to make him pay. I held onto my knees and let out a long scream that echoed off the walls and rang in my ears.

*

I went to the chest of drawers and took out the gun. I slid the bullets into it. Then I sat in the armchair, thinking of William's shy smile. I remembered how he had stood behind me, showing me how to fix the target in the middle of the sights and squeeze the trigger gently. William shot scarecrows and small animals. He would have been upset to see me like this. But William was from the past and from a kinder place, from the days when Grace and I were together, when Ma was still alive.

All that had been taken away from me. Now I wanted someone to suffer.

There was someone who deserved it. He had blood on his hands like Reverend Rivers. She wouldn't have been dead if he hadn't wanted her. She had got rid of the child for him and she had died for it. She had wanted to be with him more than anything. It was what she had wished for. I'd always given her what she wanted. I would make her wish come true.

He would be coming in time to listen to the announcement on the wireless. He had told her to expect him. I watched the clock. I waited. I took long, deep breaths to steady my nerves. I heard steps. I took aim. The key turned in the lock. The door opened. Bernard came into the room. I shot him.

*

It was as if the bullet carried everything, all the important things, about Grace, Reverend Rivers and Ma. As soon as I had squeezed the trigger they were gone, leaving only emptiness. I felt nothing as I looked at him, just a body now, lying on the floor. I walked over to the door and closed it, switched on the wireless and went back to my chair. Big Ben's chimes struck three. A man began to speak, Mr Churchill, I supposed.

Yesterday, at 2.41 a.m., at Headquarters, General Jodl, the representative of the German High Command, and Grand Admiral Doenitz, the designated head of the German State, signed the unconditional surrender of all German land, sea and air forces in Europe to the Allied Expeditionary Force, and simultaneously to the Soviet High Command . . . Hostilities will end officially at one minute after midnight tonight but in the interest of saving lives the Cease Fire began yesterday to be sounded all along the front and our dear Channel islands are also to be freed today . . . The German war is therefore at an end . . . Long live the cause of freedom. God save the King!

The war was over. We had so nearly got away with it, right up to the end.

But not quite, I thought.

My hostilities had ended a minute before but not in time to save lives. The country was officially at peace but I couldn't feel any of it. All I wanted was to get as far away as I could from the flat and from everything that had happened. I wanted to forget, to hide away and give in to the heaviness that weighed down my body. I wanted to sleep.

I got to my feet and went over to the wireless, which had started to broadcast a church service. I silenced a bishop halfway through a prayer. Then I took out the pillowcase from the chest of drawers. This time I put in Grace's things, as if I were packing for her, not me; her ration book, her hairbrush with a few strands of hair still caught in it, a lipstick engraved with her initials and a matching powder compact, a bottle of scent, a silver case for cigarettes. I pulled a nightdress from the pile of dirty laundry in the corner and wrapped a tangle of jewellery in it. The only things of my own to go in were the tattered copy of *Rebecca* and Shakespeare, the only friends I had left.

The gun was on top of the chest of drawers. It made me sick to look at it but I knew I didn't dare leave it behind. I picked it up and pushed it into the pillowcase next to the books. I looked around the room to make sure there was nothing that could be traced to us, nothing to show who we had been.

Now that I was about to go, all I wanted was to lie down next to her and wait to be found. I drew the sheet back from her face and stroked her forehead.

'I love you,' I whispered. 'I always will.' My tears fell onto her face and ran down her cheeks as if she were crying too. I bent down and pressed my lips onto hers, then pulled the sheet back over her. I looked down at Bernard, lying crumpled on the floor.

'I'm sorry,' I said quietly, and left.

*

The streets were sticky with heat and full of people acting strangely, as if they were all drunk. Men in uniforms grabbed women, swinging them around by their waists and kissing them. The women didn't seem to mind, laughing and kissing them back. Someone had wheeled a piano into the square around the corner and a man thumped out dancehall tunes on it while a girl in a red dress sang and people danced on the grass in couples. The prostitutes were there, smiling real smiles that nobody had paid for and the air was thick with the sound of car horns and laughter.

I stumbled past the celebrations with my pillowcase over my shoulder, up through Soho, past the crowds in Oxford Street and across to Euston station. Soon I was sweating and my shoes had begun to rub. No matter how often I swallowed, my mouth was parched, as if I were all dried up from too much crying. The only thing to do was to keep walking. I passed groups of girls with flowers in their hair, laughing and calling out to soldiers. I stared for a moment at a blonde girl winding herself around an older man. Tears welled up in my eyes and I turned away, sickened.

As the sun beat down, my skin became tight and sore. I didn't care. I wanted it to burn, to blister and scar, so that what had happened that day would be etched into it forever. I walked on, not knowing where I was going, only that I must get as far away from the flat as I could. At the end of a long street, I came to a fork in the road. I looked at a sign on the building at the corner and when I saw what it said, I knew it was where I must go. *Kentish Town*. In the middle of the dirty city on this, the worst of days, it offered some hope of going back to the very beginning, to the countryside, to green fields, deep water and happiness.

I limped up the road. My legs were heavy, as if I were dragging behind me the bodies of everyone who had died. When I reached a street that was almost entirely destroyed, I stopped. It was deserted, with no party, no flags, no bottles of beer and no dancing. Even the birds were quiet. A few houses were still standing. I chose one at random and pushed at the garden gate. It came off its hinges and fell to the ground. I walked over it and up the path to where the front door had been. I stepped into the hallway and climbed the stairs. In a bedroom I found what I was looking for, a wardrobe in a corner with the key still in its lock. I squeezed in and closed the door behind me. I curled myself up into a ball and, at last, fell asleep.

Twenty-Seven

THE CHILD WAS ALWAYS WITH ME NOW, THE ONE WHO NEVER lived, the one I left smeared on the sheets in the little flat in Soho. The sound of children laughing and shouting in the schoolyard behind the house became unbearable, setting off a refrain in my mind that I couldn't silence.

The child you murdered would have done that. It would have run about. It never got the chance.

Whenever I woke the ghost was there, staring at me with pale eyes that never blinked. Its face was dreadfully blank, without a nose or a mouth. Its translucent skin showed bones and a tangle of veins, the shadow of a liver and a heart that beat in horrible time with my own.

After Rose and I talked about David, the thing wouldn't leave me alone. That night it began to twist and squirm, great shudders of pain passing through its hideous body. I watched in sickened fascination, unable to tear my eyes away from it. It whined at me, pestering me to confess.

Tell her. Tell her what happens when you hide it away. Tell her how it rots and sours inside you, how it infects your very soul. Tell her what you did to me. Tell her what you did to Grace.

I fought the little beast with all the strength I had left.

'I wouldn't know how to say it,' I muttered, but I knew it wasn't true. I'd been telling myself the same story all my life.

The creature's taunts rang in my mind all through the night. For once I could put something right. I could make amends. But it would mean sacrificing my secrets, telling her the whole shameful mess of it. I imagined Rose's face as she heard what I had to say. I would disgust her like I disgusted myself.

But I didn't want Rose to be like me, shutting off possibilities, avoiding the worst and with it the chance of anything better, not daring to speak and being left in silence, fearing a refusal and ending up alone. She needed a family, a family of her own to make her happy after I was gone. By the morning I had decided to tell her, all of it, from the beginning to the end, leaving nothing out.

*

I waited until evening. It was a long day. I knew that once I'd told the truth to Rose, the secret that had shaped my life would be gone. There would be nothing left. I felt a dreadful, hollow loneliness. As the hours passed, I began to ache all over, until all I could do was lie still with my eyes closed, bracing myself against the pain. My mouth was parched and my lips had begun to blister. Each breath was like swallowing fire. A knot of heat in my throat grew quickly. My tongue swelled, crowding my mouth.

It was going to happen, I thought. I wouldn't even have time to say goodbye.

Just then a cool spray of water touched my skin, running over my lips like rain on scorched earth. I heard Rose's voice, tender with concern.

'Nora, can you hear me? Open your mouth.'

The water was a wonderful mist, bringing me back to life. She sprayed again and I stretched my mouth open wider. I knew that it was time to speak, time for the evidence against me. I didn't want absolution. I had given up on God when he took Grace away from me. My last confession was for earthly reasons only.

*

She sat straight and still as I spoke, her eyes never leaving my face. At first, I stumbled and slipped over the story, struggling with the unfamiliar experience of revelation. But soon my words began to tumble out, spilling into the silence of the bedroom. I told her everything, saying it all for the first and last time. With each word I felt lighter, as if I were releasing myself, inch by inch, from the sticky web of memory that had trapped me for so long, washing myself clean with the stream of secrets that poured out. I talked and talked and at last, in the early hours of the morning, it was done. I was free of it. My story had come to an end.

Rose's face was wet with tears.

'You understand, don't you?' I said. 'Try to be happy. Talk to David. Tell him what you feel.'

She nodded.

I risked a final question. 'And your mother?'

Her brow furrowed.

'Will you promise?'

She bent and pressed her lips to my cheek.

'I promise,' she said, and I knew I had done what I could to make things right. I knew that I could leave her.

I am weightless, rid of the secrets that tied me to the past. The Menace has become a mercy, the thing that will set me free.

Nothing matters any more. This room is my world, my refuge, my sanctuary. Someone is tucking in soft sheets. Someone is stroking my forehead, smoothing back my hair.

I am a child again and Ma is here. I feel her warmth as she curls around me, her arms holding me safe. I see her eyelashes, long and dark against her cheeks. I smell carbolic soap and sweat. I taste her tears as she kisses me goodbye in the schoolyard.

Now I am floating in the lake and the water is lapping over me, caressing my skin. A soft breeze tickles the hairs on my arms, making them rise to salute the sun. I feel velvet ferns brush my legs, and a minnow wriggle past. Grace's fingers slip into mine and we laugh, our voices entwining as the wind carries them up to the sky.

Acknowledgements

Thanks to my family and to my grandmother, without whom this book would not have been possible.

Thanks also to Alberto Masetti-Zannini for always knowing when it's time to leave the country; Sam Brookes for being there from the start; Ceri Smith and Jessica Lovell for the weekly supervisions; Flavia Krause-Jackson for her *tenerezza infinita;* Lucy Rix and Justine Cottle for their honesty and insight; Beth Crosland and Graham Broadbent for the oak tree chats; Diana Klein, Paul Lawrence, Heidi Ober, Annalisa Picciolo and Molly Webb for reading and listening; Stena Paternò del Toscano for never being surprised to find me in her house; Sheyam Ghieth for hosting on two continents; Ali Jay for keeping me cheerful, Rod Heyes for keeping me fed and watered, Sandra Lovell for keeping me sane, and Barbara Keating for keeping me solvent; Diana King and

Marie Sansom for their staying power and Bernard Lovell for his memories.

I am very grateful to my agent, Caroline Wood, for her endless encouragement and tenacity.